For the ones who swore they'd never fall, who built walls too high to climb. May you find someone reckless enough to scale them anyway.

And if you're lucky, they'll be a sarcastic bastard who's impossible to resist.

Samantha Todd

> I cannot fix on the hour, or the spot, or the look, or the words, which laid the foundation.
> It is too long ago.
> I was in the middle before I knew that I had begun.
>
> *Pride and Prejudice*
> - *Jane Austen*

# Chapter 1

Aiden

I wake up to the sound of a rooster that I swear to God has a personal vendetta against me.
It's not even dawn yet, and the bastard is already announcing the start of another day like it's got stock in my misery. I roll onto my back, scrubbing a hand over my face, cursing the life choices that have kept me here, on the family farm, single as ever, still answering to my old man and watching my older brother live out his fairy-tale ending.
Blissful. That's what they call it.
Ethan and Brynne, so disgustingly in love it makes my teeth ache. The man who used to be the grumpiest son of a bitch in the county now walks around town like he's been personally blessed by Cupid himself. It would be hilarious if it wasn't so tragic for the rest of us.
I sit up, stretch, and take a glance around my room. It's the same as it's always been, boots kicked off in the corner, half-buttoned shirts draped over the armchair I never actually sit in, a mess of sheets on my unmade bed. A stark contrast to the neat and pristine house my brother now shares with Brynne. Their little domestic paradise in town.

Samantha Todd

She's changed him. Or maybe she just gave him permission to be the man he always could've been. The thought irks me more than it should.
Not because I'm jealous of Ethan. But because I don't have that.
The thing is, I'm not opposed to love. I'm not some heartless bastard who scoffs at the idea. I love 'love'. I love the chase, the flirtation, the way a woman's lips curve when she's holding back a smile meant just for me.
But no one ever holds on.
And honestly? I've never asked them to.
I sigh, rolling out of bed and pulling on a shirt, shoving my feet into boots as I make my way downstairs. Dad's already up, predictably, sitting at the kitchen table with his coffee. He lifts an eyebrow at me over the rim of his mug.
"Late night?" he asks.
I stretch my arms over my head, wincing at the stiffness in my shoulders. "Long one."
"What was her name this time?"
I smirk, but there's no real pride behind it. I used to love these conversations, used to love winding Dad up with stories of my latest conquest, the easy laughs, the harmless fun. But something about it feels hollow now.
"Didn't ask," I lie.
Dad snorts. "One day, Aiden, you're gonna meet a woman who won't fall for your charm. And I'm gonna enjoy watching you suffer."
The words are meant to be teasing, but they stick.

Because I have met a woman who didn't fall for my charm.
Alex.
The woman who walked into the pub a year ago, turned my world upside down with a single unimpressed glance, and then walked right back out like she hadn't just set my whole damn body on fire. A new girl in town, supposedly here to help out at the estate agents, living with her aunt for a while. I haven't seen much of her since, but the memory of that first meeting still pisses me off.
Because she should've wanted me.
And I should've been able to forget her.
Instead, I've spent the last year trying to pretend I don't scan every room I walk into, just in case she's there. That I don't hear her voice in my head sometimes, throwing my own words back at me like they meant nothing. That I don't wonder what it would feel like to have someone like her look at me the way Brynne looks at Ethan.
I shake the thought away, moving to grab a coffee.
"You working today?" Dad asks.
I roll my shoulders. "Always."
Truth is, I don't mind the work. I like the farm. The sweat, the effort, the tangible results. I like fixing things. But there's a restlessness in me that won't settle, a feeling I can't shake, that I'm meant for more than this.
That something is missing.
Ethan found his purpose in Brynne.
Ben found his purpose in this farm.
And me?

Samantha Todd

I don't know what the hell I'm still doing here.
All I know is that something needs to change.
And if that change happens to come in the form of one formidable, sharp-tongued, undeniably beautiful woman who sees right through my bullshit?
Well...
That wouldn't be the worst thing in the world.

# Chapter 2

Alex

If there's one thing I've learned about working with my Aunt Edith, it's that no two days are ever the same.

One minute, we're discussing mortgage rates and property values, the next she's passionately explaining how the position of Saturn in relation to Mars might make our clients "impulsively buy a cottage they can't afford."

I love her. Truly, I do. But some mornings, it takes everything in me not to lose my mind.

Like now.

It's barely 9am, and Edith is twirling in the office, her long, flowing skirt swishing around her ankles as she gestures wildly to the ceiling.

"The moons of Jupiter are in alignment today, darling!" she exclaims, shoving a mug of tea into my hands. "I wouldn't be surprised if someone walks through that door ready to buy the most expensive house on our books."

I stare at her, then at the very large, very unnecessary collection of crystals she's placed around the office overnight.

Samantha Todd

A ruby-red one perches next to the office phone.
A smoky quartz sits by the property brochures.
A massive chunk of amethyst is, somehow, balanced on top of the printer.
I sigh, placing my hands on my hips.
"Aunt Edith," I say slowly, "please tell me you haven't put that enormous rock on the HP DeskJet again?"
She gasps dramatically. "Alexis Whitehorn, this is not a rock. That, my dear, is a vibration amplifier. It enhances our surroundings, clears negative energy, and ensures smooth transactions."
"Right." I rub my temples. "And does it also process colour copies at forty pages per minute? Because that's what the printer is supposed to be doing."
Edith waves a hand, dismissing my logic entirely.
"That machine is always in a bad mood. I'm simply helping it find balance."
Before I can argue about inanimate objects having moods, the door chimes and our first client of the day walks in, a harassed-looking woman clutching a coffee cup and what appears to be a leash with no dog attached.
"Hello!" Edith greets her warmly. "Lovely day, isn't it? Well, actually, no, it's rather chaotic, but that's because the moon is currently void-of-course. What can we do for you?"
The woman blinks slowly at my aunt, clearly reconsidering her life choices.
I step in before we lose the sale entirely.
"You must be Mrs. Fenton," I say with a smile, offering my hand. "You wanted to view the cottage in Harefield Hollow this morning?"

"Yes," she says, shooting a wary glance at Edith, "the one with the big garden."

"Of course! Let me grab the keys."

As I pull the cottage details from my neatly organized drawer (not a single crystal inside, thank you very much), Edith sighs wistfully.

"Harefield Hollow," she murmurs. "That's a Scorpio house, you know."

I freeze, mid-motion.

I don't want to ask. I really, really don't.

But I do.

"What's a... Scorpio house?"

She pats my arm like I'm a child who's just learned to tie their shoes.

"Oh, darling. It means the house has mystery. Passion. Depth. The walls absorb the energy of their past owners."

I glance at Mrs. Fenton, who is looking at us both like she's about to run out the door.

"For the record," I tell her, "it's also four bedrooms, two bathrooms, and south-facing with a double garage."

The woman relaxes slightly.

Edith, however, looks disappointed.

"Such uninspired marketing," she mutters, shaking her head. "You really must learn to sell the story, darling."

I choose to ignore her, because one of us needs to be professional.

Grabbing my bag and the keys, I gesture for Mrs. Fenton to follow me.

Samantha Todd

"Come on," I say, shooting Edith a warning glance before she says anything else alarming. "Let's go see if the house has good 'vibrations', or just a really great en-suite."
Edith gives me a knowing smile,
whispering conspiratorially as I pass.
"You're so closed off, Alex. One day, the universe is going to shake things up for you."
I roll my eyes, pushing open the door.
"Not likely."

Showing houses in the local area has become rather enjoyable. A far cry from my previous life and a fuck of a lot better than the shit show I left behind. Here, the silence, the peace, the people, everything is so blissfully... normal. So unaware of its own simplicity and so delightfully humdrum. Everything is predictable, a slow easy movement in every day. A certainty that today will be the same as yesterday and the day before that. Some might find that boring, painfully so. But I relish in it. I don't need the complications; I don't need the politics. I just need to breathe.
It's been a year since I came here, and they still haven't bothered me. Although I know that it's only a matter of time. But for now, showing houses, dealing with the eccentricities of my late-mother's sister and searching for a good quality cup of coffee is enough. For now, actually, it's everything.

I round the corner, coffee cup in hand when I walk straight into a wall. A 6 foot 2, blonde, floppy haired,

infuriating wall. Aiden-fucking-Gage. The coffee goes everywhere, all over me, all over him.
*For fucks sake.*
"You know this wouldn't have happened if we were in my kitchen like I said." He beams at me with that lopsided grin that I know makes other girls swoon. To me, it just makes me want to punch him.
"You really need to come up with some new material." I say flicking the burning hot coffee off my hands and attempting to wipe myself down with my scarf.
"And you really need to learn how to apologise!"
*Infuriating.*
"Apologise for what? You walked into me!"
"And aren't you glad I did?" he leans forward and takes the scarf from me, wiping himself down with it. 'Where did you get this thing from?" he says holding up the material. I know what he's getting at, it's vile. Paisley and clashing colours, a gift from Aunt Edith. Apparently, the colours mean something. God knows what, she did tell me. I wasn't listening.
'It was a gift" I say pointedly, snatching it back and shoving it into my bag.
"It doesn't suit you." He says flatly.
"And how would you know what suits me?" I retort, staring him down. His moss-green eyes glint with that annoying mischievousness that radiates from him all the damn time. Is this guy ever serious?
"I don't, I just know that that monstrosity doesn't" he says raking his hands through his hair.
*Oh, for fuck's sake.*

"Well, that's just rude, what if this was really sentimental to me?"
*It's not.*
"Is it?" he says, mock concern on his face.
"Well… no… But that's beside the point."
"You're right. I'm sorry" he leans in again, the smell of pine and aftershave filling my nostrils. "See how easy that was to say."
My pulse jumps involuntarily.
"I'm leaving." I say pushing past him.
"Nice to see you Alex" he says laughing under this breath.
The eye roll I give him is audible.
Does this guy ever give up?

"Oh my," Edith gasps from the doorway, clutching her chest. "You two are positively magnetic!"
I brush past her into the shop, scowling. Typical Aunt Edith, sticking her nose where it doesn't belong and watching me through me the windows of the shop. She beams at me, completely undeterred. The many rings on her fingers click-clacking together as she waves her hands around.
"Alex, darling," she says, wafting the air around her, "I felt the energy shift from all the way inside the office. The heat, the tension!"
"Edith," I say slowly, "it's coffee. Not cosmic interference."
She waves a hand. "Nonsense! You two are like two celestial bodies, caught in each other's orbit."

I can just hear Aiden's smug response to that... *"See, Alex? Even the universe wants us together."*
"Oh, fuck off." I mutter under my breath and busy myself in some paperwork.
Edith just smiles at me knowingly.

# Chapter 3

Alex

A glass of whiskey and coke.
I stare down at it. It's become something of a celebratory drink for me. And today I have a reason to celebrate because the house I showed this morning received an offer.
A big one.
Which means a big commission.
Which also means, much to my dismay, that Edith, in all her cosmic wisdom, was in fact right.
And that's the real tragedy of the evening. The moons of Jupiter were indeed in alignment. I'd rolled my eyes, muttered something about capitalism and astrology not exactly being compatible, and moved on with my day.
Yet, here I am.
One house sold. Drinking whiskey.
Because apparently, cosmic alignments can be bang on the money. Quite literally. It doesn't help that that bloody HP Printer has been behaving itself all day as well. Two days ago, I was ready to throw it out the window, today with its crystal perched on top, it practically purred like a kitten. Aunt Edith

might be on to something. Or then again, it's all bullshit and she just got lucky.

It's become something of a tradition for me. Sell a house, whiskey and coke down the pub while I read my book in relative silence. As I take another sip, I flick my eyes down to the book in front of me and force myself to relax.

It's smutty, of course. Contemporary mafia romance. A delightfully over-the-top tale of morally grey men, deadly feuds, and one very unrealistic possessive hero.

Absolutely ridiculous.

Absolutely perfect.

Harlow West has long been my favourite author. There's something so satisfying in the way that she writes about unconventional love. It's not all sunshine and fairytales, it's dark and difficult. It's more realistic in my opinion.

I open to the next chapter, sinking further into my seat.

And that's when I feel it.

A presence.

The weight of someone watching me.

I don't need to look up. I already know who it is.

"Stalking is, in fact, illegal," I state, turning a page.

There's a low chuckle. The sound of a chair scraping against the floor.

And then, Aiden-fucking-Gage is right in front of me. Again. Twice in one day. Must be some kind of record.

Samantha Todd

"Good thing I'm not stalking then," he says easily, leaning back in his chair. "Just casually invading your space."
I exhale slowly, shutting my book with a deliberate snap.
"Don't you have anyone else to bother?"
"Sure," he shrugs, grinning, "but you're my favourite."
I roll my eyes. "God, you're exhausting."
"You say that now, sweetheart, but give it time..."
"Aiden," I cut in, deadpan, "if you finish that sentence, I will end you."
He grins wider, tilting his head as he reaches for my drink.
Whiskey and coke.
He eyes it, amused.
"Whiskey, huh?"
I snatch the glass before he can take a sip, which was undoubtably his next move. "Celebratory drink."
His eyebrow arches clearly interested. "What are we celebrating?"
I hesitate. I don't want to give him the satisfaction, but I also know he won't drop it until I answer.
"...I sold a house today," I admit with absolute indifference, not bothering to look up from my book.
He smiles, rising from his seat, "I'll be right back."
Two seconds later he returns with his pint, raising it in a toast.
"Well," he says, "cheers to you, city girl. Looks like you're finally making something of yourself in this charming little village."
"I will throw this drink at you."

His smug grin grows. "You've already done that today and please don't waste good whiskey."
I huff, but there's no real heat behind it.
I take a slow sip, eyeing him over the rim of my glass. For all his infuriating, cocky bullshit, he's not wrong.
I am making something of myself here.
And I like it.
But I'm not about to admit that to him.
"Didn't peg you as a smut reader," Aiden comments, nodding towards my book.
I don't look up.
"Didn't peg you as a reader at all," I shoot back, flipping a page.
His mock-offended gasp is dramatic as hell. "You wound me, Alexandra."
I sip my drink. "I'll live with it. And my name's Alexis. Not Alexandra."
He tilts his head, squinting slightly. "Alexis? Huh. I prefer that." *As if I fucking care.* "What's it about?"
I *know* he's just trying to annoy me. I know he's hoping I'll get all flustered about the spice level and hilariously avoid answering.
But I refuse to play into his little game.
I keep my face calm, my voice steady.
"It's a mafia romance," I say coolly. "The heroine is kidnapped by a brooding, possessive mob boss with questionable morals and a violent streak."
Aiden leans forward, intrigued. "And she falls for him?"
"Of course."
He grins. "Naturally."
I take another measured sip of whiskey.

"Hot, dominant, knife-wielding men with commitment issues are my weakness," I say flatly, flipping another page.
Aiden laughs, full-bodied, bright.
"Noted."
I expect him to leave. But instead, he stays put, stretching his arms behind his head like he has all the time in the world. "So, tell me," he drawls, "this mob boss, what's he got that I don't?"
I sigh, closing my book with an exaggerated slowness. I rest my elbow on the table, chin in my palm, and look at him.
"Wit."
His brows lift. "I've got wit."
"Untouchable wealth."
He smirks. "I've got a tab open at the bar. That count?"
I roll my eyes. "Cold, ruthless, devastatingly sexy…"
He holds up a finger. "Ah, finally, a category I can compete in."
I scoff, leaning back in my chair, closing the book slowly. "Oh, don't worry, Gage," I say, leaning forward to pat his hand condescendingly. "You're not completely without your charms."
His hand covers mine for a second, trapping it there. The warmth of his palm seeps into my skin.
His smirk deepens. "Is that a compliment?"
"Absolutely not," I say smoothly, slipping my hand free and reopening my book.
Aiden watches me for a moment, still grinning. His eyes boring into me even though I refuse to meet his gaze.

"Try not to fall in love with your fictional mobster too hard, sweetheart," he calls after me. "Would *hate* for it to make things awkward between us."
I don't react. Don't bite.
I just lift my whiskey glass in a mock toast, then flip the page on my book.
Aiden lingers for half a second longer.
Then, finally, he leaves.
*About fucking time*.

The hours pass and two more Whiskey and cokes find their way towards me, bought by Aiden, I'm sure. I don't say thank you. The book is heating up and just about to get to the spicy scene, when like a moth to a flame,
"I'm leaving now."
"This isn't an airport Aiden; you don't need to announce your departure." I say, not looking up.
"Cute. Did you get that from TikTok or something?" he says, hands in his pockets.
"I did actually."
"Original"
I look up, putting on my best fake smile, "You were leaving?"
He runs his hand through his hair "Yeah, I was just thinking, same time tomorrow?"
I furrow my brow in disbelief.
*Is this guy for real?*
"What?"
"Same time tomorrow," he repeats, shrugging. "You can buy me some drinks. You know, return the favour."

I stare at him. "The favour?"

"Yeah. I bought you two drinks. The polite thing would be to reciprocate." He smirks. "You do know how to be polite, don't you?"

I press my lips together, debating whether it's worth launching my beer mat at his stupid, cocky face. Aiden Gage is infuriating. Smug. Completely insufferable.

But I turn it over in my mind. It would be nice to have more friends in this town but is Aiden Gage really a friend I want. I spend most of the time wanting to punch him square in the face.

"I'll make you a deal Aiden, if I sell another house tomorrow then I'll be back tomorrow."

"I like those odds" he says.

I roll my eyes, lifting my glass to my lips, trying to ignore the fact that I do too.

"Enjoy your morally grey men!"

With that he leaves, finally.

# Chapter 4

Alex

Edith is practically glowing when I step into the estate agents the next morning. It's the kind of glow that usually precedes some inane comment about the planetary alignments, and frankly, I'm not in the mood.
"Oh, darling, I just knew you'd sell that house today!" she declares, clapping her hands together like a delighted child. Her bangles clink in unison, and I swear even they sound smug.
I set my bag on the desk and sigh. "I suppose I should start listening to you more often."
She gasps. "Don't toy with me, Alexis. My heart is too delicate for such promises."
I snort, shaking my head, but I can't deny that I'm pleased with myself. The property was a tough sell, far too expensive for most buyers in NorthWood Dale, but an out-of-town couple fell in love with the exposed beams and the 'rustic charm.' Whatever. Commission is commission. Only issue is that it means I have to come through on my deal with Aiden. It's not like he would know if I've sold a house or not, but a Whitehorn never reneges on deal.

Edith leans on the desk, tilting her head at me. "So, where are you celebrating this fine evening? I sense whiskey in your future."

I roll my eyes. "It's not celebrating. It's honouring a deal."

"Ohhh," she purrs, eyes twinkling. "A deal, you say?"

"Not like that," I deadpan. "Aiden said if I sold another house, I'd buy him a drink. That's all."

Edith makes a humming sound that suggests she very much does not believe that's all.

I ignore her and busy myself with paperwork, but the truth is, a niggling part of me isn't completely opposed to seeing Aiden again.

Not that I want to.

I mean, he's insufferable. Overconfident. Too damn charming for his own good.

But he's also... consistent.

Predictable in the way that he always turns up, always has something to say, always makes me roll my eyes so hard I practically sprain something.

And now I know that he expects me to be at the pub tonight. Which is fine. Because I don't care if he's there or not.

But a deal's a deal.

### The White Hart, 7:35 PM

I sip my whiskey and coke, scanning the room.

No sign of him.

Good.

Fine.

Doesn't matter.

I flick my gaze back to my drink, swirling the ice idly. Aiden is the kind of guy who strolls in when he pleases, all easy grins and casual charm, knowing full well he's the most irritatingly charismatic presence in the room.

It's a gift, really.

One that I refuse to be impressed by.

But the minutes tick by. And tick by. And tick by.

And he still doesn't show.

A deal's a deal, right? So, where the hell is he?

I grit my teeth, resisting the absurd urge to check my phone, even though he doesn't even have my number.

I tap my fingernails against the side of my glass, contemplating ordering another. But something feels off. Not that I care. I don't. But it's weird, isn't it? He should be here.

And then, a creeping feeling of betrayal.

A ridiculous, unwanted flicker of disappointment.

I crush it immediately, dousing it with logic. Why would I even expect him to show? It's not like we're friends. Not like I actually wanted him here. This is a good thing. This is great.

I finish my drink, grab my bag, and leave without a backward glance.

I'm halfway through typing up a property listing when the bell over the estate agent's door chimes.

I know it's him before I even look up.

The air shifts. The temperature in the room rises a degree. The universe practically scoffs at my

pretence that I don't care. Or maybe I've just been spending too much time Aunt Edith.
He strolls in like he owns the place.
Like nothing happened.
Like I didn't sit there last night with my drink, waiting like a complete idiot for him to turn up.
I don't look up.
I don't even acknowledge him.
I keep typing.
Aiden whistles low under his breath. "You look like you're in a great mood."
Silence.
He tilts his head, clearly amused. "What, no 'good morning, Aiden'? No 'wow, it's so great to see you, Aiden'? No..."
I finally lift my gaze, fixing him with a glare so icy it could shatter glass.
He raises his hands in mock surrender. "Whoa. Okay. What's got you in such a..."
I cut him off. "Did you come here for a reason, or are you just here to waste my time... again?"
He falters, his expression shifting just slightly. "I..."
"Because correct me if I'm wrong, but you were the one who suggested I meet you at the pub last night. And you were the one who conveniently didn't show up."
His brows knit together, the faintest crease forming between them. "I got held up."
I huff a sharp laugh. "Of course you did."
He leans against the desk, arms crossed. "I did. Something came up at the farm."

I arch a brow. "So, what, you couldn't send a carrier pigeon? Smoke signals? Some vague telepathic message?"

His lips quirk. "I didn't realise you'd be so eager to see me."

*Oh, fuck this guy.*

I snap my laptop shut, standing up so fast my chair nearly topples.

He looks amused, which only pisses me off further. "You know what, Aiden? I don't know what game you think we're playing but let me make one thing perfectly clear." I step around the desk, closing the space between us. "I'm not one of your small-town girls who's going to trip over her own feet just because you flash that irritatingly charming grin of yours."

Aiden watches me, something unreadable in his gaze.

"I don't care if you show up. I don't care why you didn't. And I certainly don't care about whatever bullshit excuse you're about to give me. So do me a favour and just stay out of my way."

Aiden presses his lips together, his expression unreadable.

For the first time ever, he doesn't have a comeback.

He just gives a slow nod, pushing off the desk. "Duly noted."

And then he leaves.

And I tell myself, I was the one who won that exchange.

# Chapter 5

Aiden

There's something about Northwood Dale in autumn that makes you feel like you've stepped into a bloody postcard. The air smells like cinnamon and crisp leaves, the warm glow of lanterns dances off the cobbled streets, and everywhere you turn, there's something straight out of one of those cheesy Hallmark movies that Brynne makes Ethan suffer through.

It's all too cozy, too homely, too... much.

And maybe I'd be enjoying it more if I wasn't doing my level best to avoid the one person I haven't been able to stop thinking about for the last few days.

Alex Whitehorn is here.

Because of course she is.

It's the Harvest Festival, and the whole town turns up. Stalls are lined up along the streets, fairy lights strung between them, vendors calling out to passersby with warm cider and caramel apples. Kids are running around with sticky fingers and hay in their hair, and a band plays some old folk tune near the village square.

It's nice. Annoyingly nice.

And it would be even nicer if I wasn't skulking around like a guilty bastard trying to avoid a woman who probably wants to throttle me with her perfectly manicured hands.

Ethan nudges me as we wander through the crowds. "So. We're talking about it, right?"

I keep my eyes on the stall ahead. "Talking about what?"

"The fact that you stood up the most terrifying woman in town, and now she's here."

Brynne grins, sipping from a steaming paper cup. "I can't believe you actually stood her up Aiden. Like, are you actively trying to get yourself buried on a hillside?"

"I didn't stand her up, Brynne. I just got tied up."

"Exactly, and you'll be the one tied up when she drops you in a shallow grave. She's got money, power, and a jawline that could cut glass. She's basically a Bond villain."

"She's not a villain," I mutter, then clear my throat. "She's just... deeply unpleasant."

Ethan huffs a laugh. "You like her."

I shoot him a look. "I don't."

Brynne gestures towards the far side of the street. "Oh, good. Then you won't mind the fact that she's right there."

I follow her gaze and shit.

Alex is standing a few feet away, over by the roasted chestnuts stall, her hair catching the glow of the lanterns overhead. She's dressed in something casual but annoyingly expensive looking, a wool coat cinched at the waist, dark jeans tucked into sleek boots. She's holding a paper cone of chestnuts, her fingers peeling one delicately as she listens to something the vendor is saying.

I should walk away. I should turn around and leave before she sees me.

Too late.

Her gaze flicks up, locking onto mine.

Then, because she's Alex, her expression shifts into polite disinterest, like she's looking at a particularly unremarkable tree. Still ignoring me I see.

Fine. If that's the game she wants to play.

I take a step forward, closing the distance between us. "Roasted chestnuts? Didn't have you pegged for a festival-food kind of girl."

Alex peels another chestnut with surgical precision, popping it into her mouth. "And I didn't have you pegged for a coward, but here we are."

Brynne chokes on her cider.

Ethan mutters, "Oh, Christ."

Alex glances between them, then back to me. "Oh, I see. You've brought reinforcements. Are they here to hold your hand?"

I grin. Can't help it. "I don't need anyone to hold my hand, Trouble."

Her brow lifts at the nickname, but she doesn't comment on it. Instead, she offers me a chestnut from her paper cone. "Well, since you're here, I suppose I can extend an olive branch."

I take the chestnut, but I don't break eye contact. "What's the catch?"

"No catch." She smiles sweetly. "I just want to see if you're actually capable of swallowing something, including your pride."

Brynne elbows Ethan and whispers, not at all discreetly, "Oh my god, the chemistry."

Ethan sighs. "For the love of... can we just get some damn food?"

Alex rolls her eyes. Indifferent to our presence, indifferent to the conversation.

Brynne grins at me before dragging Ethan towards the cider stall, leaving me standing there with Alex, the smell of roasted chestnuts between us and something unspoken crackling in the cold autumn air.

I pop the chestnut into my mouth, chewing slowly. Alex watches me expectantly.

I swallow.

"Not bad," I say.

Alex tilts her head, eyes gleaming with something unreadable. Then she straightens and tosses the last of her chestnuts into the bin beside her.

"Well, as fun as this has been, I'm leaving. Enjoy the festival, Aiden."

Without another word, she turns and disappears into the crowd.

Something flares inside me. Irritation, frustration, hell, maybe even guilt.

"Wait," I call after her.

She pauses, glancing over her shoulder. Not expecting me to actually try.

I exhale sharply, running a hand through my hair. "I got held up at the farm the other night. One of the cows was calving. I had to help Dad."

Her lips part slightly, and for a split second, I think she might be softening.

Then she blinks, and the ice returns to her eyes. "Oh. How convenient," she says flatly.

My teeth clench. "It's the truth, Alex."

She hums like she's considering it. Then, "Well, it must have been very serious if it kept you from fulfilling your side of a deal."

"What is your obsession with deals?"

She looks at me, a hard glare that burns through me, "Because a deal reveals the measure of a person and you, Aiden, have been found wanting."

And then she's gone.

I exhale harshly, running a hand through my hair.

Brynne reappears at my side, cider in hand. "So, just to recap, you stood her up, and she *still* came over to flirt with you?"

Ethan chuckles. "More like challenge him to a duel."

I shake my head, my jaw tightening. "She's impossible."

Brynne smirks, taking a sip of her drink. "And yet, you're still standing here watching her walk away."

I scowl. "Shut up, Brynne."

She cackles, nudging Ethan. "Oh, she's good. She's very good."

Ethan just sighs, shaking his head. "You're both absolute fucking nightmares."

# Chapter 6

Alex

Aunt Edith's house is a world of its own.
The kind of place that doesn't just exist in Northwood Dale but seems to have been grown from the land itself, roots tangled deep beneath the floorboards. It's a mismatched, cluttered, undeniably warm space, filled with herbs hanging from the rafters, antique trinkets, and shelves so overflowing with books that they've started to spill onto the floor in uneven stacks.
The house smells like lavender and rosemary, a little bit of cinnamon, and whatever potion Aunt Edith has been brewing on the stove all afternoon.
Tonight, it's chicken stew, rich and peppery, steaming in mismatched bowls as we sit at her little wooden table, the one she claims is 'enchanted' because it's never wobbled, despite missing a chunk from one of its legs.
A candle flickers between us, the wax dripping lazily down the brass holder, pooling at the base like melted gold.
"So," Aunt Edith says casually, breaking apart a hunk of crusty bread with her delicate, ring-covered fingers. "When are you and that gorgeous blonde

man going to admit that you're madly in love and get it over with?"

I choke on my stew.

Setting my spoon down, I pinch the bridge of my nose, willing myself not to engage in this absolute nonsense. "Aunt Edith."

"Yes, dear?" She dips her bread into the broth, entirely unbothered.

I inhale deeply. "I am not in love with Aiden Gage."

She hums. "Of course not."

"I'm serious."

Another nonchalant hum like she's humouring a child who just insisted the tooth fairy isn't real., "And yet you can't seem to stay away from him. I saw you both at the festival, sharing your chestnuts."

I glare at her. "It wasn't like that. He's insufferable. Cocky. Arrogant. He calls me Trouble, for God's sake."

She grins, eyes twinkling. "Oh, I quite like that."

I exhale sharply, resisting the urge to drop my forehead against the table.

"I'm serious," I say again, quieter this time. "He's exactly the sort of man I could never want."

"Ah," Aunt Edith muses, breaking off another piece of bread. "So you've given it that much thought, have you?"

I pause, my spoon halfway to my mouth.

She smiles knowingly.

I scowl.

That's the thing about Aunt Edith. She never pushes, never pries. She just... knows. Knows when to step back, when to prod, when to sit and wait for the truth to spill out all on its own.

So I focus on my stew instead.

"I haven't given him any thought at all."

"Mm." She chews thoughtfully. "And yet, here we are, discussing him over dinner. Again."

I huff. "Because you brought him up."

"Yes, and you're awfully defensive for someone who supposedly doesn't care."

I grip my spoon tighter.

Edith sips her wine, far too pleased with herself. Then, as if sensing she's pushed just far enough, she changes the subject entirely. "So, have you thought about whether you're going to buy a house here or not yet?"

I stare at her, relieved for the change in topic. "I...what?"

She shrugs. "Well, dear, you are staying, aren't you?"

I nearly choke again. "Yes, I'm staying but it's a lot of upheaval. There's a lot to consider."

"Oh, I just assumed. I mean, it's not like you have anything to go back to in London."

I gape at her. "I don't, although technically I suppose I still live there."

She waves a dismissive hand. "Oh, nonsense. You existed in London. Existing and living are two very different things. Here, you actually live. You breathe fresh air. You eat home-cooked meals. You share chestnuts with handsome farmers at the Harvest Festival..."

Samantha Todd

"Oh my God." I groan, dropping my spoon with a clatter. "Enough with the chestnuts."
She grins, utterly delighted.
I fold my arms. "If I was ever going to buy a house, it would probably need to be in a busier town."
She nods, as if considering this. "So you could pretend to enjoy it as much as you enjoy being here."
I glare. "I don't pretend to enjoy anything."
She smirks. "Oh, I know, dear. That's the problem."
I open my mouth to argue, but she just dips another piece of bread into her stew, entirely unbothered.
I scowl and grab my wine glass instead, gulping half of it down.
There's a comfortable silence for a few moments, just the soft clink of spoons against bowls, the occasional crackle from the old fireplace.
Then, because she can't help herself, Aunt Edith casually says, "You do look nice together, though."
I slam my wine down. "AUNT EDITH."
She cackles, utterly delighted with herself, and pops another piece of bread into her mouth.

Later, when the dishes are stacked neatly in the sink and the fire crackles low in the hearth, we settle into the living room.
Aunt Edith is curled up in her favourite armchair, crocheting something indistinctly colourful, her glasses perched on the tip of her nose. The dim lighting makes the space glow, soft and flickering, with old fairy lights strung up around the

bookshelves, their bulbs humming faintly like fireflies trapped in glass.

I'm curled on the sofa, a book in my lap, my bare feet tucked under me.

It's... peaceful.

Comfortable.

Simple.

It's the kind of quiet night I crave but rarely allow myself.

Aunt Edith glances up from her yarn, watching me for a little too long.

"What?" I ask, flipping the page without looking up.

She loops another stitch, her bracelets jingling softly. "Nothing, love."

"Liar."

She chuckles, setting her crochet down for a moment. "You just... seem settled here."

I hesitate.

She's not wrong.

It's warm here. Easy. A far cry from my previous life. Something so wonderful in the mundane, the simple.

But I don't say that.

Instead, I smirk. "Don't get sentimental on me, Edith."

She gasps theatrically, clutching her chest. "Sentimental? Me? I'll have you know, I am a hard-hearted crone."

I snort, shaking my head.

"Besides," she continues, grinning now. "The last thing I need is to get attached to you being here, only

for some handsome blonde farmer to come along and..."
I slam my book shut. "I'm going to bed..."
She cackles, picking up her crochet again.
*Bloody Aunt Edith.*

# Chapter 7

Aiden

There's something about starting with a blank page that makes me want to set fire to the whole damn thing.
It's just a rocking chair.
It shouldn't be this bloody difficult.
But here I am, five sheets of paper deep, all crumpled into frustrated balls on the floor, and staring at the sixth, pencil poised, not a single damn idea coming to me.
The problem is the spindles.
I need them delicate enough to keep the chair from looking like a bloody medieval torture device,
but sturdy enough to withstand years of wear.
I tap my pencil against the edge of the workbench, exhaling hard. The whole workshop smells like wood shavings and sawdust, the air thick with the scent of oak and cedar. Tools are scattered everywhere, and the morning light filters in through the high windows, catching the suspended dust in the air, making it look like the place is brimming with magic instead of my rapidly deteriorating patience.
I take another stab at it, dragging the pencil along the paper.
Angle the rockers slightly more curved.

Maybe thin out the armrests so they don't look so...
Fuck.
Too thin.
I rip the page off and crumple it, launching it at the growing pile of rejected attempts.
Maybe I should just scrap the whole thing. Make a plank of wood with four legs and call it art.
I rub my jaw, rolling my shoulders, stretching my arms over my head. The chair will happen. It just has to sit in my head a while before I get it right.
That's how this always goes.
I stare at the blank page again, chewing the inside of my cheek, feeling the itch of something else in my mind.
Something, or rather, someone, that I'd rather not be thinking about.
I tell myself not to do it.
Tell myself to focus on the goddamn chair.
And yet.
Alex Whitehorn.
The thorn in my side. The bane of my existence.
The woman who has taken up permanent residence in my head, rent-free, with a smirk on her lips and an attitude sharper than a chisel.
Trouble.
I exhale sharply, shaking my head as I lean back against the bench.
I'm not an idiot.
I know the signs.
I know what it means when a woman gets under your skin like this, when you find yourself lingering in

places she might be, when you start wondering about things you shouldn't be wondering about.
Like what she looks like when she first wakes up. Or what she'd sound like saying my name in the dark.
I drag a hand through my hair, muttering under my breath. This is getting ridiculous.
She's not interested in me.
She's made that very clear.
And, more importantly, I am not interested in her.
Not in her smoky voice.
Not in her biting wit.
Not in her ridiculously perfect mouth.
I sit forward, gripping the pencil, determined to shake this nonsense out of my head.
I enjoy my quiet life. I'm here to do my work on the farm, build things that last, stay out of trouble.
I don't need a high-maintenance, infuriatingly posh woman barging into my thoughts like she owns them.
So, I press the tip of the pencil back to the paper, force my mind to focus on the curve of the spindles, the lines of the chair, the balance of the rockers.

It becomes quickly evident that the design isn't going to happen today. Some just fly out of my head easily, like they're half built already, some take longer to mature. Those are the days that I find the most frustrating, the one's where there is nothing for it but to just step away from the design desk and put yourself in a different space. Something to clear the mind.

Samantha Todd

So that's what I'm doing.
The bell above the corner shop door jingles as I step inside, rubbing a hand over my jaw. My patience for this week is running on fumes in general. Everything just feels like it's going fucking wrong. The designs are stalled, my favourite pig had to be put down, I had an argument with my dad when he confronted me about 'growing up' and 'getting out there'. I just need some space. A reset. A cold drink. A fucking snack. A distraction before I say or do something that I'll regret.
I reach for a bottle of water when the bell jingles again.
I glance my head around.
*Fuck my life.*
Of course it's her. Had to be fucking her.
"Everywhere I go, there you are," Alex's voice is clipped, sharp enough to cut. "Everywhere except where you say you'll be."
I tighten my grip around the bottle. Of course she'd show up now. Of course, fate would throw her back at me just when I was deciding whether or not to be done with this whole thing.
I force myself to stay calm, to keep my voice even. "Not everything is about you, Alex."
"No?" She tilts her head, arms crossing. "Because you certainly made it seem that way when you practically begged me to have a drink with you."
I exhale sharply, shoving the bottle onto the counter a little too hard. The old man behind the till glances between us but wisely decides to mind his own business.

"Are we still on this? I told you; I got caught up."
"And I told you," she leans in slightly, her voice low and venomous, "that I don't care."
I shake my head, laughing bitterly. "For someone who says that they don't care, you mention it quite a lot."
She shoots me a look that's filled with burning venom. I'd be concerned if I had the energy to give a shit.
"I don't play games Aiden."
"Well that's fucking rich."
Her eyes narrow. "Excuse me?"
I step closer, closing the space between us, but keeping my voice level. "You talk about games like you're above them, but you've been playing one since the second you walked into this town."
She scoffs, looking away for a moment before snapping her gaze back to mine. "Oh, enlighten me, Aiden, what game exactly am I playing?"
"This." I gesture between us. "This constant push and pull. You flirt, then freeze me out. You engage, then act like I'm the most irritating person on the planet."
"You are the most irritating person on the planet."
"Right back at you sweetheart."
Her lips part slightly, as if she's about to snap back with something clever, but she doesn't.
She hesitates.
And that? That's enough to light the spark of a fire I'm not sure I want to put out.
I step even closer, lowering my voice. "You act like you don't care, but you do, don't you?"

She swallows. Just once. Just enough that I notice. But then she recovers, her chin lifting slightly. "Don't flatter yourself, Gage."

I smile, slow and knowing. "Too late."

The air between us is electric, the silence crackling with something neither of us wants to name. But then she shakes her head, steps back. The moment's over, and just like that, she's back to the Alex I'm used to, guarded, cold, untouchable.

"Next time you want to waste someone's time," she says, brushing past me, "find some other unsuspecting victim."

"Don't flatter yourself darling" I mimic.

With a look that could kill, she storms out of the shop, leaving nothing behind but the scent of her shampoo and a frustrating tangle of emotions in my chest.

I watch her go, jaw clenching.

Fuck Alex Whitehorn. Fuck her ice-princess persona and her bullshit snide remarks. Fuck whatever this is.

I'm over it.

I finish up the day on the farm and resolve that the only way to get over my Alex-encounter is to get under (or on top of) someone else. In this non-existent town, the only place for that is the pub. Let's just hope that she hasn't sold another property today. Two encounters in one week with the Whitehorn-Witch is manageable, three would just send me over the edge.

The pub is busy for a Thursday, bustling with all manner of locals. It started doing food not long ago, so they now get clientele from other villages which suits me fine. In fact, it suits my current purposes perfectly.

I get a drink at the bar and then spot my friend Preach over in the corner sitting with Dane and Tugsy. All nicknames of course. Preach, because his dad is the local vicar; Dane because he had a Great Dane growing up that was a total lunatic and Tugsy because his last name is Tugman. If I'm honest, sometimes I completely forget what their actual names are.

"Alright lads?"

"Gage! How you doing?" Tugsy gives me a firm handshake with his pudgy hands.

"Yeah, good mate, just thought I'd come in and see who was about."

Preach eyes me quizzically. He can always tell when something isn't quite right. He's known me long enough. "Saw you talking to that Alex-girl in the shop earlier, sounded pretty heated."

'Ah, it was nothing, just another run in with the Ice Queen."

Dane smiles, his slightly crooked teeth making it appear off-centre, "Wow, has Aiden Gage finally found someone immune to his charms?"

"Couldn't give a fuck mate, she's just some annoying city girl who thinks she's got attitude."

I'm lying.

She's more than that.

But I'm not about to tell these guys that.

"Well anyway, you've arrived at the right time to settle a debate. I was just saying to Tugs that a goose would end him," Dane says, shaking his head. "You ever seen those bastards when they get territorial?"
Tugs scoffs. "I could take a goose."
Preach snorts. "Oh yeah? Go on then, next time you see one down by the lake, let's see you square up."
Tugs puffs out his chest like the absolute knobhead he is. "Bet you twenty quid I could knock one out."
I grin. "Mate, I'd pay good money to watch you try."
"Anyway," Preach says, dragging his fingers across the condensation on his pint glass. "Some of us actually have skills, unlike Gage here, who spends his time wrestling pigs and driving a tractor."
Tugsy chokes on his drink, Dane laughs, and I just shake my head.
"Jealous, mate?" I smirk. "That I actually work with my hands instead of sitting in front of a screen hacking into God-knows-what?"
Preach arches a brow. "You say that like I don't have the power to ruin your life from the comfort of my sofa."
Dane whistles low. "Jesus. You say that like it's a joke, but we all know it's not."
Preach grins, raising his glass. "I prefer the term 'highly skilled digital entrepreneur,' thank you very much."
The laughter flows, when the door opens, and in walks the ice-queen herself followed swiftly by her Aunt Edith. Edith's dressed in her usual mismatched colourful layers, gesticulating wildly about her about some nonsense. I actually quite like Edith, always

have done. She's definitely what you would call 'The town nutter' but she's actually pretty endearing and her endless rantings and ravings about moon cycles can be quite funny if you don't take them too seriously.

But the best part? Alex doesn't look my way, not once. Just orders a glass of wine (no sales today then) and sits down at the very far end of the bar. Good. Stay there for all I care.

"Your girlfriend just walked in" Tugsy says with that tell-tale glint in his eye.

"She's not my fucking girlfriend" I say, taking a deep sip of my beer.

"Well, if you're not going to bother, do you mind if I give it a go?" Dane pipes up.

"Mate, you'd need the jaws of life to be able to crack that one" I say flatly, no hint of amusement in my tone, "but by all means, give it your best shot." I say, sweeping my arm out in her direction.

"Alright, fuck it. I will" he says, standing and straightening his shirt which is already crumpled from sitting all day in his tractor.

*This should be good.*

Exactly twenty-five seconds later he's back.

"So? How did it go?" I ask, a smirk pulling across my face involuntarily.

"Told me to go fuck myself and then Edith gave me a bloody crystal. Told me to try again when Venus was in ascendant or some shit." He sits down heavily on his chair causing it to screech against the floor, holding his palm upwards to reveal a pink quartz stone.

"Yeah, well I did warn you."

I'm still smirking at Dane's failure when I stand to grab another drink. The pub is filling up now, bodies pressing into one another as the space shrinks, conversation growing louder.

I move to the bar, slipping through the gaps between groups of people, but as I reach it, someone else does too.

Of course, it's her.

Alex slides in next to me, clutching her empty glass with one hand, the other perched on her hip like she's about to lay into me already.

For a brief second, we stand side by side, waiting. The air thickens. The bartender is serving the other end of the bar, taking his sweet time, which means we're stuck here, shoulder to shoulder, pressed together by the crowd.

I glance down at her, a smirk tugging at the corner of my mouth.

"Miss me, Trouble?" I ask, tilting my beer in her direction.

She exhales sharply, not looking at me. "You know what? You're exactly like I thought you'd be."

I arch a brow. "That right? And what's that?"

Her lips curve up in something almost resembling a smile, but there's nothing sweet about it. It's razor-sharp. "All charm and no substance."

I hum, tapping my fingers against my glass. "And here I thought you liked charm."

She snorts. "Your idea of charm is making everything into a joke."

"Maybe you're just allergic to fun," I shoot back, my voice deliberately light. "Tell me, do you actually enjoy being miserable, or is it just a hobby?"

She huffs, turning away slightly, but the movement presses her closer to me instead of further away. The pub is packed now, people jostling at our backs, forcing us even closer together. I catch a whiff of her perfume, vanilla, with something warm and sharp underneath.

Dangerous.

She lets out an aggravated breath, her shoulder brushing my chest. "You are insufferable."

"And yet, here you are. Again."

She tenses at that, finally flicking her sharp gaze up at me. "Not for you," she says flatly.

"Course not," I say smoothly. "I'd be too much fun for you anyway."

Her nostrils flare, but before she can retort, the bartender appears. She steps forward quickly, ordering her drink and ignoring me like I no longer exist.

I chuckle, stepping away once I get my own order. "Enjoy your night." I say, walking back to my table. Her response is lost in the hum of voices and clinking glasses, but I feel her glare burning into my back as I go.

Good. Let her hate me.

# Chapter 8

### Aiden

I had offered to walk her home as her Aunt had left a little bit before, leaving her alone with her Mafia-romance book. I'm not a complete prick after all. But in her usual and not entirely unexpected way, she had flatly refused.

I leave the pub shortly after her. Stepping out into the crisp autumn air. The remnants of a hot summer still fresh in the air. Autumn's always been my favourite time of year. I don't know whether it's the colours or the way the light catches everything. I like how it smells, that sounds weird, but autumn has a scent to it. And I won't be told otherwise.

"Hello stranger!"

I turn around to see Lucy, her red hair falling around her shoulders as she rests her hands on her now bulging belly.

The shock in my face must have been evident. I'd heard that she was pregnant but actually seeing it in the flesh is different.

She walks up and gives me an affectionate kiss on the cheek, her arms lingering on my shoulders.

"Lucy! Wow, you look amazing!"

"Awww, thanks. I feel like a fucking whale, but not long to go now." She beams. Pregnancy suits her. Her

father was less than pleased when she couldn't tell him who the father was, but that seems to have died down now. He was telling Dad the other day about how excited he is to become a 'PopPop' (which to me sounds like some kind of lollipop or TikTok dance trend, but hey, to each their own).
"I'm pleased for you Luce."
"Thanks Aiden. Anyway, I've got to get going, I'm meeting a friend inside."
I eye her stomach warily, she laughs, "Don't worry, just a diet coke for me!" She makes her way to the door, "Nice to see you Aid."
And it was nice to see her. Two years of a casual fling doesn't just go away overnight. I'm pleased for her. But I can't lie that the thought of Lucy being a mum doesn't absolutely terrify me. Lucy, the first girl to buy a round of shots, the last one at the bar, the first to dance on tables and the girl that most of the young guys in this town have *known* in one way or another, about to be a mum?? If anything gives me pause on whether there is a benevolent god, that would be it. But I guess, everyone has to grow up sometime.

As I wander down the street, I notice Alex in the doorway of the estate agents, fiddling with the lock. At first, I don't think much of it, she's probably just forgotten something inside. But the three guys walking towards her make me pause.
I don't immediately recognise them, but as they step into the streetlight, I do. They used to run with Mark (who still hasn't been seen or heard from). But their

association to that shit-stain alone is enough to make my blood boil.

I start walking before I've even processed the scene. Alex still hasn't noticed them. She's too busy cursing under her breath at the lock.

The first guy steps forward, casual, like he's just out for a smoke. But I see the way his eyes rake over her, see the smirk tug at the corner of his mouth.

"Need a hand, sweetheart?"

Alex stiffens. I see it.

She turns, her expression cold, her tone even colder. "I'm fine."

"Aw, come on now," the second guy chimes in, stepping closer. She scrunches up her nose at his breath that probably reeks of whiskey and bad decisions. "No need to be so frosty. We're just being friendly."

"Didn't realise we were holding a fucking reunion," I say, my voice casual but laced with steel. "Shame Mark couldn't make it."

The first guy turns, sizing me up. His eyes narrow. "Gage."

I nod. "Tommy."

Alex exhales, a quiet breath of relief she probably doesn't even realise she let slip.

The second guy grins, cracking his knuckles. "This isn't your business, mate."

I step up to him, close enough to see the busted blood vessels in his nose, close enough to smell the cheap whiskey and stale sweat clinging to his shirt.

"See, that's where you're wrong." My voice is low, lethal. "Because she's my business."

Alex shoots me a look, but I don't take my eyes off the guy in front of me.

Tommy lets out a laugh, loud and mocking. "Ah, I get it. You're fucking her?"

My jaw tightens. My fists clench.

He holds up his hands in mock submission, "Hey Gage, I get it, I'd like to have a go on that tight, posh cunt as well."

That does it, without hesitation, I throw the first punch.

It connects solidly with Tommy's jaw, and the crack echoes through the night.

He stumbles back, but the second guy is already moving.

I barely have time to register the flash of movement before a fist slams into my ribs. A sharp burst of pain rips through my side, but I don't go down. I twist, driving my elbow into his stomach, and he doubles over with a grunt.

The third one lunges before I can fully reset. His knuckles catch me square across the cheekbone, rattling my skull. My vision momentarily blurs, but I recover fast.

I see him winding up for another swing, he's slow, too drunk to fight properly, and I duck, catching him with an uppercut that sends him sprawling onto the pavement.

Tommy has recovered, wiping blood from his mouth. His eyes blaze as he charges at me again, but this time, he doesn't aim for me.

He goes for Alex.

Samantha Todd

She's standing too close. Too distracted by the chaos to react fast enough.
His arm swings, wild and sloppy, he's not trying to punch her, but she's in the space where his hit is about to land.
I see it happening before she does.
And something inside me snaps.
I surge forward, stepping in front of her just as she instinctively throws up her hands.
My fist meets Tommy's ribs before his can reach her. He lets out a sharp grunt of pain, staggering back. My knuckles are already bruised, my ribs aching like a motherfucker, but I don't stop.
I grab the front of his jacket and slam him against the brick wall. "Try that again," I growl, my grip tightening around the fabric. My face is inches from his, my breath hard and uneven. "See what fucking happens."
His hands scramble at my arm, his chest heaving as he tries to push me off. But I don't let go. I want him to understand. To feel how close he just came to something worse than a bruised jaw.
The fight doesn't last much longer.
They're drunk. I'm sober. And I've got something they don't, purpose.
By the time it's over, one of them is groaning on the pavement, one is limping away, cursing under his breath, and Tommy, well, Tommy is coughing against the bricks, barely holding himself up.
I finally step back, my chest still rising and falling hard, my knuckles aching, my ribs burning.
Alex is staring at me, wide-eyed.

I shake out my hands, rolling my shoulders, trying to loosen the tension coiling through me. "You okay?"
She blinks, nodding slowly. "Yeah."
I nod back, running a hand through my hair. "Good."
Then, just as I go to walk away, she grabs my arm.
I look down at her.
She swallows, something unreadable in her expression.
"That was so fucking stupid." Her voice is quieter than I expect.
I let out a sharp laugh, wiping the blood from my nose with the back of my hand. "You're welcome, Alex."

# Chapter 9

Alex

"Seriously, Aiden, what the fuck were you even thinking?"

I wet a washcloth in the back toilet and bring it out to where he sits on one of the desks, his legs spread wide, hands resting on his thighs, like he owns the damn place. His shirt is rumpled, there's a small cut above his brow, a bruise just breaking across his jawline and his knuckles are raw.

Weirdly, he looks good.

Infuriatingly, annoyingly, ridiculously good.

Like some stupid action-movie hero who just saved the damsel and is waiting for his reward.

Only, I'm not a damsel. And he sure as hell isn't getting rewarded.

"You know," he says, voice dripping with sarcasm, "most people, and I recognise that you will inevitably be different, would thank someone for helping them out in a situation like that."

I fold my arms, fixing him with a glare. "I didn't need help. Specifically, not yours."

His lip curls, but before he can say anything, I press the damp washcloth to his cheek.

He winces.

"Ah, shit."

"Oh, don't be such a baby."

"Have you ever been punched in the nose before?" he grits out.

"Shocking as it may be, no, I have not ever been punched in the nose before."

"Then you have no idea how it feels."

*Still being a baby, then.*

I shake my head and keep working, the washcloth now stained pink from the dried blood. His skin is warm beneath my fingers, solid, the heat of him radiating against my hand as I tilt his face slightly. His jaw is firm under my touch, all sharp angles and rough stubble.

I ignore the strange, inconvenient awareness prickling up my spine.

"If you'd just minded your own business," I mutter, "you wouldn't be in this situation."

"And if you had let me walk you home from the pub, like I fucking asked, you wouldn't have been in *that* situation."

His voice is edged, his frustration curling through the words like smoke.

I snap my gaze up to his. "I could've handled it."

His green eyes blaze. "Yeah, sure you could."

A muscle in my jaw ticks. "I don't need you to fight my battles for me."

His nostrils flare, his expression shifting to something dark and unreadable. He doesn't move for a second, just watches me, watches my hands as they press the ice pack to his nose, watches the slight crease in my forehead as I focus.

His voice is lower when he speaks again. Rougher.

Samantha Todd

"I realise that this might be a foreign concept to you, Alex, but did you ever stop to think that maybe I wasn't fighting for you?" he murmurs.
I blink, "Then who the fuck were you fighting for?"
He huffs a humourless laugh. "I hate guys like that. Guys who think they can intimidate women into whatever the hell they want. So yeah, I stepped in. Because I wanted to. Particularly those fucking guys. Mark's friends."
"Who's Mark?" I ask.
"Doesn't matter. Just some fuckwit psycho…" His eyes fall on the far wall, as if a memory burns there. Something he doesn't want to remember.
So I do what I do best.
I give him an out.
I deflect.
"Well, congratulations," I deadpan, pulling back, flicking the bloody washcloth at him. "You successfully bruised your own ribs to settle a vendetta."
Aiden exhales sharply, rubbing a hand over his face. He mutters something under his breath, something like unbelievable, and swings his legs off the desk, standing up.
The movement forces me to step back, because suddenly he's too close, and I hate that I even notice.
The scent of him, pine, sweat, something warm and all Aiden, lingers in the air between us.
His chest rises and falls.
I swallow.
A second passes.

Then another.
And then—
"Fuck this. I'm going home," he mutters.
"Which is what you should've done from the beginning," I snap back, because I have to say something, anything, to break the tension between us.
He heads for the door, not looking back.
"Fuck you, Alex!" he calls over his shoulder as it slams shut behind him.
I stare at the door for a long moment, my pulse still uneven, my mind still swimming.
Why did he step in like that?
I could have handled the situation. It's not like I'm not used to being hit on by drunk, disgusting men. I know how to deal with them. I know how to handle myself.
What I don't know is how to deal with a guy like Aiden Gage, someone who thinks he has to protect me.
Who makes me feel like I want to let him.
I don't need protection.
I don't want him.
I don't want anything.
I run a hand through my hair, exhaling sharply.
There's a tiny, infuriating part of me that is silently, stubbornly...
Grateful.
But I'll never tell him that.
I'd never hear the fucking end of it.

Samantha Todd

What I do hear is the sound of the siren just after he leaves and the telltale red and blue lights screeching to a halt.
Fuck.
I race outside just in time to see Aiden being handcuffed and put in the back of the police car.

# Chapter 10

Aiden

Yes, it was stupid.
Yes, it was not a moment I would say I'm especially proud of.
And yes, it landed me a night in the local police cells and an assault charge that I'll have to answer to in court.
Luckily, Brynne had bail money.
And an absolute fucking arsenal of lectures locked and loaded.
"You realise you're a fucking idiot, right?" she rages as she drives me back to the farm, one hand gripping the wheel way too tight. "Your dad is going to go absolutely ape-shit, and don't even get me started on Ethan finding out."
"Yes, I'm aware that big brother is likely to have an opinion," I mutter, rubbing at my aching muscles.
One thing about police cells? They sure as shit aren't comfortable.
And I already have a fucking headache.
Actually… I have two.
One from the punches I took.
And one from the incessant nagging of the woman beside me, who is now determined to make sure I fully absorb the consequences of my actions.

Samantha Todd

What is it with women at the moment?
"Look," she exhales sharply, shaking her head, "I know you like this Alex girl, but is she really worth an assault charge, Aiden?"
Her grip on the steering wheel tightens as she jerks the truck around a bend, and I brace against the door.
Each turn feels like a countdown to the absolute bollocking I'm about to get from Dad.
I sigh heavily, letting my head thunk against the window. "First of all, I don't like her..."
Brynne scoffs.
I ignore it.
"...and second of all, those guys were Mark's friends, so they had it fucking coming."
Brynne visibly stiffens, her breath held tightly. It's been ages since *that night*, the night we never speak about. She's fine, she's stronger, she's processed it. But I can't imagine that that shit goes away very easily and like a storm at sea, it can rear up when you least expect it to.
I continue, "They were goading me, and they weren't exactly being gentlemanly towards Alex, in case you missed that part."
Brynne's silent for a minute, "I didn't miss that part, Aiden. I also didn't miss the part where you threw the first punch and pounded them into the fucking pavement."
I roll my eyes. "It wasn't quite that dramatic."
"It was that dramatic!" she exclaims, throwing one hand up in exasperation. "Do you ever think things through!"

## Raising the Gage

I open my mouth.
She cuts me off.
"Actually, don't answer that."
I sigh again, running a hand down my face. My ribs ache. My knuckles are raw. And my dad is probably waiting at home with a shovel and a grave plot.
This is not shaping up to be a good day.
As we pull into the driveway, the farmhouse stands in the early dawn light, innocent, peaceful, as though it hasn't been waiting all night to bear witness to my execution.
Brynne kills the engine and exhales.
"Good luck," she mutters, not sounding even remotely sympathetic.
I give her my best puppy-dog eyes. "You're not coming in?"
She snorts. "Absolutely fucking not."
I sigh. "Coward."
She grins. "Dead man walking."
I groan and drag myself out of the truck, trudging up the porch steps like a man marching to the gallows.
As soon as I open the front door...
"AIDEN JAMES GAGE!"
*Fucking hell.*
Dad's voice rips through the house like a gunshot, and suddenly, I am twelve years old again, caught red-handed sneaking out past curfew.
I barely get one foot inside before Dad storms in from the kitchen, shoulders squared, jaw tight, eyes fucking lethal.
I prepare myself.
And then I brace myself.

Samantha Todd

Because this?
This is gonna be bad.
"What in God's name were you thinking?!"
Dad roars, throwing his hands in the air.
I hold up a pacifying hand. "Dad, I can..."
"No, you can't!" he cuts me off, striding towards me like he's about to shake the stupidity out of my head. "Because there is no rational fucking explanation for you getting arrested for a bar fight at your age, Aiden!"
I rub the back of my neck. "Technically, it wasn't in the bar."
"I don't give a shit if it was in a fucking boxing-ring, Aiden, that's beside the point!"
Yeah.
That tracks.
He rakes a hand through his hair, his movements jerky, his anger barely contained. "You're twenty-four years old, Aiden. Twenty-fucking-four! And you're still acting like some dumb, reckless kid who thinks consequences don't apply to him!"
"That's not..."
"You think this is funny?" His voice drops, low and dangerous. "You think this is a joke?"
Fuck.
That tone is what gets me.
That's not just anger.
That's disappointment.
And that?
That hits deeper than a punch ever could.
"Dad, I..."

"You could have killed someone, Aiden!" His voice cracks.
And suddenly, I realise.
He's not angry. Not really. He's genuinely scared.
Not about the fight.
Not about jail.
But about me.
About what I'm turning into.
His hands are on his hips, his chest heaving, his fear barely masked beneath his frustration. "You need to grow up, son. You need to. Because this?" He gestures at me. "This isn't a life."
I swallow hard.
Dad lets out a sharp breath and pinches the bridge of his nose, his voice tired when he speaks again. "What are you even fighting for anymore, Aiden?"
I blink.
And for a second, I don't have an answer.
My gaze flicks away, out towards the porch, where the morning light spills golden across the fields.
I don't know.
I don't fucking know.
Dad exhales, shaking his head. "Fix this, Aiden."
And with that, he turns, walking away, leaving me standing in the wreckage of my own stupidity.

# Chapter 11

Alex

I stare at the pages of the open book in my lap, but I haven't read a single word. The main character, Cade Barron, might be the perfect man on paper but it's not him I'm thinking about.
And my mind is certainly running in circles.
Running around Aiden Gage.
The name is like an itch I can't scratch.
I shouldn't care. I don't care.
But still, an assault charge?
I sigh and pinch the bridge of my nose, exhaling slowly.
Stupid idiot.
I don't know why it's bothering me so much.
Yes, he was reckless. Yes, he was ridiculous to get involved in something that wasn't his fight. But part of me can't shake the fact that it was for me. Despite what he said.
I push the thought away before it can take root, snapping the book shut and setting it aside.
It's not my problem.
And it's not my concern.
But still...

Before I can spiral any further, the sharp click of the front door echoes through the office, and a cold weight settles in my stomach.

A shadow falls across the floor.

Carter Whitehorn steps inside.

He moves through the space with the slow, deliberate stride of a man who has never been denied anything in his life.

Tall. Immaculate. Not a silvered hair out of place. No hint of stubble. Dressed in a bespoke navy suit, not a single imperfection in sight.

The perfect businessman.

The perfect Whitehorn.

And my father.

I steel myself.

He stops a few feet away, glancing around the tiny office with barely concealed disdain.

"So," he says, his voice smooth as glass. "This is where you've been hiding."

I fold my arms and lean back against the desk, keeping my expression carefully neutral. "Not hiding. Living. And as if you didn't know where I was."

He hums, adjusting the cuffs of his shirt. "You always did like to be dramatic."

I bite the inside of my cheek, forcing myself to stay calm. "What do you want?"

His sharp blue eyes, so much like mine, flick back to me. "I think you already know."

Well, he's got me there. I do know.

And I know that there is no getting out of this conversation unscathed.

He steps forward, hands clasped behind his back.
"You've had your fun, Alexis. You've played house in this little village long enough."
My stomach tightens.
"And now," he continues, tone clipped, "it's time to come home."
I let out a sharp, breathy laugh. "Home?" I arch a brow. "You mean the prison you raised me in?"
His jaw tightens, but he doesn't take the bait.
"Your future is waiting, Alexis." He adjusts his cufflink again, a familiar tell of annoyance. "And I have arranged for you to meet with someone very promising."
There it is.
The words send a cold shiver down my spine.
I already know who it is before he even says it.
But still, I have to hear it.
"Who?" I ask, my voice deceptively calm.
My father tilts his head. "Miles Kensington."
I exhale sharply.
Bile rises in my throat.
Of course it's Miles.
Miles Kensington.
One of the worst men I have ever known. A self-entitled prick with a God complex, a coke habit, and a long list of women he's manipulated, cheated on, and discarded without a second thought. My teenage self included.
My father knows this.
He knows.
And he doesn't care.
Because Miles is a *Kensington*.

A perfect match for a Whitehorn daughter.
A merging of power.
A business deal, nothing more. I can fool myself into believing a lot of things but fooling myself into believing that this arrangement won't be lucrative in some ways for my father would be contrary to every fact I've ever known.
My skin crawls.
I will not marry *him*.
I will not let my father control my life like this.
I won't.
I lift my chin, meeting his gaze head-on. "No."
His lips press together. "Excuse me?"
I fold my arms. "I said no."
"You don't have a choice."
"I always have a choice."
He laughs, shaking his head like I'm some petulant child. "Alexis, you are twenty-three years old. You have a duty to this family."
I grit my teeth.
"Your mother would have wanted this," he adds smoothly, and I bristle.
"You don't get to use her against me." My voice is dangerously quiet.
He sighs, mock patience written all over his face. "You are being so very difficult, darling. It's already done; the engagement is practically set. You just have to return to London, and we can forget about this whole countryside business and move forward."
And that's when it hits me.
The way out.
The one thing that will make him back off.

I school my expression into perfection, tilting my head slightly.

"I'm afraid I can't marry Miles," I say smoothly.

Carter lifts a brow. "And why not?"

I let the words sit for a beat.

Then, with a small, satisfied smile, "Because I'm already engaged."

There's a beat of silence.

His entire posture shifts. His spine snapping into place like someone just cracked a whip against his back.

The air crackles.

His face hardens. "What?"

I shrug, feigning nonchalance. "You heard me."

His eyes narrow. "And to whom are you supposed to be engaged?"

I smile sweetly.

To the last person in the world he would ever approve of.

"His name's Aiden. Aiden Gage. I met him when I first moved here and we're... we're in love" I practically balk at that last part, we're the furthest from *in love* you could possibly be!

His jaw locks.

His hands clench into fists at his sides.

And for the first time in my life, I see genuine fury in his eyes.

"And who the fuck, may I ask, is Aiden Gage?"

Without missing a beat I continue, "He's the son of a farmer."

He turns to my aunt as she bustles out of the back room.

"And you knew about this Edith?"
Without missing a beat Aunt Edith nods her head, "Oh yes Carter," her smirk is evident. She's always hated my father, and with good reason. He was never good enough for my mother and he never approved of my hippy-dippy aunt with all her crazy theories. "Like two stars orbiting each other those two."
He turns back to me, steadfastly ignoring her. "Alexis, I'm going to pretend this conversation has not happened. I'm staying at the hotel the next village over for one night. You will meet me there at 7pm sharp with your bags and you will return to London with me. You will marry Miles and that is all there is to say on the matter."
With that he turns, adjusting his cufflinks again and stalks out of the door.
"I guess you had better go and inform your fiancé that he's... well your fiancé..." Edith says, her smile beaming. "And before your father does." She nudges me gently on the arm.
*Fuck, fuck, fuck. What have I done?*
I can't say that I've entirely thought this through.

# Chapter 12

Alex

The second I step out of Edith's battered 1989 Ford Fiesta; I regret everything.
Not the lie, I stand by that. I'd rather fake-marry a farmer than let my father sell me off like cattle.
But coming here, to this farm, to him?
That's the mistake.
The smell hits me first, mud, manure, and masculinity, before my gaze lands on Aiden-fucking-Gage, standing by the pig pens, arms folded across his broad chest, looking very much like someone who wants to kill me.
His bruises are worse in the daylight. Purple, swelling, a testament to his own stupidity, and for the briefest moment, I feel… guilty.
Not guilty enough to back out of this insane plan, but guilty enough to not insult him immediately.
His moss-green eyes flick up as I slam the car door shut, and his brows pull together in confusion before settling into something closer to exasperation.
He shakes his head, muttering under his breath. *"Of course. Of-fucking-course it's you."*
I ignore that.
Instead, I stride across the dirt, my boots sinking into the godforsaken farmland with every step. I stop

a few feet from him, arms crossed, chin lifted, my heart hammering so hard I'm surprised he can't hear it.

*Right. How do I phrase this so he doesn't tell me to go fuck myself?*

Aiden wipes his forehead with the back of his hand, eyes narrowing. "Come to berate me some more, Trouble? Or did you hear I got arrested and just couldn't wait to rub it in?"

Not the best start.

I take a slow, measured breath. "Actually, I came to offer you a deal."

He barks out a laugh. "Oh, this should be fucking *good.*"

I don't react. I can't.

Instead, I say the words that I know will catch his attention.

"I can make your charges disappear."

That shuts him up.

I see it in the way his jaw ticks, the way his arms loosen slightly, how he suddenly doesn't know what to do with his hands. He scoffs, folding his arms again, but there's something uncertain in his expression.

"Oh yeah? And how exactly do you plan on doing that, Your Majesty?"

"I know people." I say simply. "Powerful people."

His lips twist. "That's not reassuring."

"Look, Aiden, it doesn't matter how," I say impatiently. "All that matters is that I can get rid of this problem for you. No court case. No fines. No record."

He narrows his eyes. "And what do I have to do in return? Sell my soul to the devil? Or have you collected enough hapless bastards' souls this week"
I ignore the insinuation that I'm, in fact, the devil. I mean it's not like I've been an angel since we met.
*Here we go.*
I square my shoulders, force my face into something impassive, and drop the bomb.
"You have to pretend to be my fiancé."
Aiden stares at me.
I wait.
He laughs.
Not just any laugh.
A deep, full-bodied, hands-on-his-hips, throwing-his-head-back laugh.
"Sorry," he wheezes between breaths. "I could've sworn you just said…"
"I did." I cut in.
His laughter dies instantly.
His expression shifts, eyes scanning my face, waiting for the punchline.
When he realises, I'm serious, his amusement vanishes.
"You're out of your fucking mind."
"Probably." I exhale, rolling my shoulders back. "But that doesn't change the fact that I need you."
His lips twitch, like he wants to smirk but is too baffled to commit to it.
"That might be the first honest thing you've ever said to me."
I grit my teeth.

"My father is trying to marry me off to some absolute silver-spooned arsehole," I say flatly, not bothering to sugarcoat it. "Tonight, I'm meeting him at the Regent-on-Dale Hotel at 7pm to convince him otherwise. If I don't show up with a credible fiancé, he will bulldoze over me and make the decision for me."

Aiden's brows shoot up. "And you picked me?"

"Well, it's not like I have a long list of willing candidates." I shoot back.

He rubs his jaw, wincing when he catches a bruise. "So, let me get this straight. You want me to sit across from your apparently terrifying, clearly very rich, arsehole of a father…"

"Correct."

"…and pretend that we're madly in love."

"Yes."

He blinks at me.

Then, voice flat as hell, "No."

I resist the urge to strangle him. "Aiden…"

"Nope." He holds up a hand. "Not a fucking chance."

My patience snaps. "Oh, for fuck's sake, Gage…"

"You don't even like me!"

"Well, yeah, that's why it's called *acting*."

His nostrils flare, but I see it, that glimmer of hesitation. The part of him that knows he doesn't have a choice. This is his only way out.

Aiden runs a hand through his hair, muttering curses under his breath before finally—finally—looking at me.

"What do I get?"

I sigh. "Other than your freedom?"

"Yes Alex, in order to pretend to be in love with you I'm going to need far more than just my freedom."
I consider.
Then, because I know him, "Free drinks for a month."
Aiden's eyes flicker.
I pounce.
"Any time, any place. You just say the word, and I'll cover it."
His lips press into a line, like he's trying not to be tempted.
I take it up a notch.
"And..." I tilt my head, smirking slightly. "Since we'll be engaged, and this has to be believable, you can kiss me whenever you want."
His eyes darken.
*Bingo.*
His shoulders sink, and I know I have him. He might hate me; he might find me infuriating (he wouldn't be the first) but he still wants me.
"Fine," he mutters, voice low and reluctant. "But if this goes sideways..."
"Oh, don't worry." I cut in, already turning on my heel to head back to the car. "It absolutely will. But I will hold up my end of the bargain."
I hear him groan behind me.
And then I turn, "Wait."
Aiden nods at me, his face suddenly dead serious.
"We need to do something about your face."
I step forward, studying the damage. The bruises, the busted lip, the dark circles under his eyes from a night in a police cell.
He looks like a walking bar fight.

And there's no fucking way my father will believe that I'm in love with a man who looks like he just lost an argument with a metal chair.

*Fuck.*

"Do you have any makeup here?" I ask, grimacing.

Aiden's expression sours immediately.

"Oh, you've got to be fucking kidding me."

# Chapter 13

Aiden

I'm not entirely sure how I got here.
One minute, I was cleaning out the pig pens like a normal, functioning adult. The next? I'm sitting in my own damn kitchen, having Brynne's discarded concealer smeared onto my face by the most aggravating woman alive.
Alex looks... different like this.
Less like the cold, untouchable ice queen and more like someone who's just had her entire world knocked off balance.
She's fidgety, distracted, her normally composed exterior slightly cracked, and for some reason, I find that deeply entertaining.
"So, let me get this straight," I say as she dabs aggressively at my cheek, eyes narrowed in frantic concentration. "One minute, I'm public enemy number one, and the next, I'm your fiancé."
She doesn't look at me.
"Fake fiancé," she corrects, like that makes this any less ridiculous.
"Right. My mistake."
She steps back slightly, arms folded, eyes scanning my face like she's critiquing a goddamn oil painting.
I raise a brow. "Well? Do I look presentable?"

Her lips press together. Then, with zero hesitation—"No."

I grin. "Careful, sweetheart. If you keep staring at me like that, I might start thinking you actually enjoy looking at me."

She ignores me (*shocker*) and instead mutters, "We need to make sure we sell this. If we're going to pull this off, we have to act like we've been together for years. That means we need to know everything about each other."

Before I can respond, she grabs my chin, pulling my face this way and that, checking how the concealer looks under different angles.

*Jesus Christ. Woman's manhandling me like a fucking show pony.*

"My father is never going to believe that I'm the type of girl who gets engaged in less than twenty-four hours."

I smirk, lips smooshed between her fingers.

"You literally are that type of girl, though."

She scowls, stepping back with a huff, hands on her hips.

"In this particular circumstance, yes. But this isn't real. So how do you take your coffee?"

I chuckle. "Well, you'd already know that if you had been in my kitchen, wearing my t-shirt at 8 a.m."

Alex's expression doesn't change.

Deadpan. Utterly unimpressed.

"Are we really going to go through this again, Aiden?"

I sigh dramatically. "Fine. Black, no sugar."

Her nose scrunches like I just told her I drink engine oil.

Samantha Todd

"God, you're so fucking predictable."
I grin. "Let me guess, you only use coffee filters?"
She flicks her auburn hair over her shoulder and pulls out a chair, looking every bit like a woman about to school me on my own existence.
"Actually, I use a French press."
I groan. "Of course you fucking do."
"Refined tastes, Gage. You wouldn't understand."
I shake my head and get up, grabbing a beer from the fridge, because if I'm going to be subjected to this nonsense, I'm doing it half-cut. I pop the cap off and take a slow sip, watching her across the table. She watches me back, unimpressed. "You know, most civilised people would offer their fiancée a drink."
I gesture toward the fridge with my beer bottle. "Be my guest, princess. You know where it is."
She scowls. "How very chivalrous."
I smirk. "I tried the white knight routine with you yesterday. I got beaten up and now we're engaged. I can't say it went well. So if you want more white knight material, sweetheart, you should go for a Kensington."
She mutters something under her breath that sounds suspiciously like "fucking Kensington's", but before I can ask, she squares her shoulders and moves on.
"What side of the bed do you sleep on?" she asks, eyes narrowing.
I pause mid-sip.
"Do you honestly think your dad is going to ask that?"

Alex leans forward, her voice tight with impatience. "If we're going to make this believable, we have to be prepared for any question that might come up."
I roll my eyes. "And you think what side of the bed we sleep on is high-priority interrogation material?"
She stares at me. Unblinking. Unrelenting.
*Jesus Christ.*
"Fine," I sigh, dragging a hand through my hair. "I don't have a side. I just sprawl out."
She smirks. "Figured as much. I don't have a side either, just whichever side the door isn't on."
I frown. "Why?"
She shrugs, eyes flicking to the table as she picks at her fingernails.
"I just don't like sleeping by the door, I guess."
It's the first real, unscripted thing she's said all afternoon.
No sass. No bravado. Just matter-of-fact honesty.
I study her for a second.
"You are quickly becoming one of the weirdest women I've ever met."
Alex's lips twitch.
"Coming from you, Aiden, I'll take that as a compliment."
I shake my head, taking another sip of my beer.
*This is going to be a long fucking night.*
"What's your favourite band?" I ask, coming back to sit with her.
"Linkin Park, easy."
*Well, I didn't see that coming.*
"Hybrid Theory or Meteora?" I press.
"Hybrid Theory obviously."

*Now we're getting somewhere.*
"Well, fuck me, with information like this, we don't stand a chance of getting caught."
She leans forward, taking hold of my arm in a vice like grip, "Listen, you have no idea what my father is like. You have no idea what you're walking into. The less jokes you make now, the easier this will be later."
I snatch my arm back and grab my beer, "If you're father is anything near as witty as you, I'm sure I'll be fine."

# Chapter 14

Alex

When we pull up outside the hotel, I can already see my father's car parked outside. A sleek black Mercedes as unforgiving and pompous as its owner. Inside, the hotel bar hums with quiet sophistication, a low murmur of conversation, the clinking of crystal glasses, the muted shuffle of polished shoes against mahogany flooring.

It smells of old money and expensive deception, where people in finely tailored suits sip whiskey, they pretend to enjoy and shake hands with men they secretly despise.

My father fits into this world seamlessly.

Aiden?

Not so much. But then that's half the point, I guess.

I spot him immediately.

Carter Whitehorn, my father, sitting at the bar like he owns the place.

Which, to be fair, he probably could if he felt like it. The Regent-on-Dale Hotel is exactly his kind of place. Expensive, pretentious, designed to cater to people who pretend they hate being catered to.

He's drinking Macallan 25, because, well of course, he is. Nothing but the most expensive scotch available will do for Carter Whitehorn.

Samantha Todd

His suit is immaculate, his cufflinks gleam, and his expression is unreadable as he watches Aiden and me approach.
I can already feel the judgement radiating off him. Aiden wearing an open-collar shirt and blazer with jeans looks disastrously out of place in this environment, a true fish out of water. But it was the only thing he had that wasn't a band t-shirt or a checked flannel shirt. The bruises are still slightly visible underneath the right lighting but the coverup we found actually did a remarkably good job. So long as Aiden doesn't wipe his face, we should be all good.
I force myself to smile sweetly, linking my arm through Aiden's and leaning in slightly.
*Showtime.*
"Dad," I say smoothly, "this is Aiden. My *fiancé*." The word almost lodges in my throat.
Aiden, to his credit, doesn't even flinch.
He extends a calloused, work-worn hand toward my father, his usual cocky grin just slightly tamed.
"Sir," he says in that lazy tone of his. A lock of his blonde hair falling over his forehead.
Dad doesn't take his hand immediately. Instead, he stares at it, as if expecting it to turn into a farm tool or something equally beneath him.
Eventually, he shakes it.
Firm. Calculated. A silent warning wrapped in politeness.
Aiden just grins wider.
*Fucking idiot.*

Dad gestures to the two empty seats. "Sit," he says simply.

We do.

A well-dressed waiter appears immediately.

"What can I get you, sir?" he asks my father.

Dad gestures toward Aiden with a pointed smirk. "Why don't we start with my future son-in-law?"

Aiden doesn't miss a beat. "Whiskey and Coke."

I close my eyes briefly.

I swear, I hear my father's soul physically die.

"Whiskey. And Coke?" my father repeats, like Aiden just ordered a tequila shot in a cathedral.

Aiden leans back lazily, throwing an arm over the back of my chair, completely unbothered.

"That's right," he says. "Preferably with plenty of ice."

I almost laugh at the way my father's nostrils flare.

*Oh, this is going to be painful.*

Dad waves the waiter off. "Make that two Macallan 25s," he says, before shooting Aiden a pointed look. "Neat. And a glass of Sauvignon Blanc."

My father turns to me. "So, tell me Alexis, sweetheart," he says, his voice dripping with disapproval, "how exactly did you meet your... fiancé?"

Aiden beats me to it.

"Oh, you know, the usual way," he says, smiling. "Girl walks into town, boy instantly falls in love, girl pretends she hates him to keep things interesting."

I kick him under the table.

He doesn't even flinch.

Dad's lips press together.

"Hm." He takes a slow sip of his drink, assessing Aiden like he's some rare, unimpressive breed of cattle.
"You're a farmer, I understand?"
Aiden nods. "A farmer's son."
My father's gaze flicks to me.
"Honest work I suppose. And you, my dear, have suddenly found agriculture fascinating?"
I smile sweetly. "Turns out, I have a thing for manual labour."
Aiden just about chokes on his whiskey.
My father just ignores him.
"And tell me, Aiden, do you have aspirations? Or is shovelling pig shit your lifelong ambition?"
I feel Aiden tense slightly beside me.
There it is. The insults wrapped in pleasantries.
The subtle knives hidden in silk.
Aiden leans forward, resting his elbows on the table, completely unfazed.
"Actually," he says, "I make furniture."
Dad raises an eyebrow. "Furniture?"
"Yep. Wooden furniture. Tables, chairs, that kind of thing." Aiden shrugs, like it's no big deal. "It started as a hobby, but now I'm thinking about selling them."
I turn to him sharply.
"What?"
He shrugs, a smirk forming at the corner of his lips.
"Yeah, well. I figured I was decent enough with my hands."
The effort it takes not to roll my eyes nearly gives me a headache.
Dad, of course, looks unimpressed.

"And this... enterprise of yours. Is it profitable?"

Aiden smirks. "I guess it depends on how you define profitable, sir. I'm not swimming in private jets, but I can make a damn good rocking chair."

I snort.

My father does not.

He sighs, swirling his drink. "Alexis, my dear, if this is some kind of rebellion, I assure you, it's unnecessary. I'm only looking out for your future."

I resist the urge to roll my eyes.

"Of course, Dad," I say dryly. "Nothing says concern for my well-being like trying to marry me off to a coked-up, cheating hedge-fund brat."

My father smiles. "Miles comes from an excellent family, Alexis. You know that."

"Yes, and an even better drug dealer."

Aiden snorts into his whiskey.

My father's jaw tightens. "This little engagement stunt will not last, Alexis."

I tilt my head. "Why not?"

"Because you and I both know you would never seriously commit to someone so... ordinary."

I feel Aiden tense again.

*Oh, hell no.*

Before I can open my mouth, Aiden leans forward, flashing his most infuriatingly cocky grin.

"Yeah, that's what she said at first," he says smoothly. "Then she saw me without my shirt on, and... well, here we are."

I choke on my drink.

My father stiffens.

Samantha Todd

Aiden just sits back, looking positively delighted with himself.
A beat of silence.
Then my father sighs, rubbing his temples. "I need another drink."
*Yeah, buddy. So do I.*
This might actually kill him.
I almost feel bad.
Almost.

The evening drags on like some kind of slow-motion train wreck I can't escape from.
Aiden, to his credit, is playing the role disturbingly well.
He's charming, quick-witted, and somehow managing to match my father's level of bullshit with an effortless ease that is both infuriating and utterly impressive.
Every time Dad throws a thinly veiled insult, Aiden counters with a grin and some half-sarcastic remark that makes me want to kick him under the table... again.
The waiter refills my glass for what feels like the fiftieth time, and I swirl the wine absentmindedly, my head already buzzing.
My father, for his part, hasn't let up once.
Not that I expected him to.
He's been testing Aiden all night, pushing, prodding, waiting for him to crack, to slip up.
Aiden hasn't.
Which, annoyingly, only makes him
more obnoxiously smug.

Dad finally downs the last of his whiskey and pushes back his chair.

"I'm going to the restroom," he announces, adjusting his cufflinks. He turns his gaze to Aiden, cool and assessing. "Try not to embarrass yourself while I'm gone."

Aiden, without missing a beat, flashes his most charming, infuriating grin.

"I'll do my best, sir."

My father exhales sharply, then stalks off toward the restroom.

The moment he's out of earshot, I turn to Aiden, ready to explode.

"You need to dial it back," I hiss.

Aiden leans back lazily in his chair, arms folded behind his head. "Dial what back?"

"The..." I gesture wildly, "...this. The you of it all. The cocky, infuriating charm offensive."

His lips twitch. "Oh, Trouble, if you think this is me on the offensive, you really need to get out more."

I groan, pinching the bridge of my nose. "You're enjoying this, aren't you?"

He smirks. "Immensely."

"Of course you are." I sigh, swirling my wine. "It's a miracle he hasn't tried to have you forcibly removed yet."

Aiden tilts his head, studying me.

"He's hard on you."

I blink at him. "What?"

He shrugs, his smirk dimming slightly. "Your dad. He's a grade-A prick, but I'm guessing this isn't a new development."

Samantha Todd

I look away, my grip tightening around my glass.
I hate how easily he sees through the situation. Hate it more than anything.
"It's just how he is," I say dismissively.
Aiden hums, like he doesn't quite believe me.
I take a long sip of wine, desperate to change the subject.
"So," I say, clearing my throat. "Furniture making?"
He grins, clearly amused by my sudden interest.
"Yep."
I arch a brow. "You? Building chairs?"
He shrugs. "Stranger things have happened."
I scoff. "Like what?"
He leans in slightly, his voice dropping to something low and teasing.
"Like you sitting here pretending not to find me ridiculously attractive."
I choke on my wine.
"Go fuck yourself, Gage."
His smirk widens. "I would, but I'm a little busy being your loving, doting fiancé."
I glare at him. "Loving and doting fiancés don't start bar fights."
He shrugs. "In my defence, I was protecting your honour."
"Oh, please," I scoff. "You were looking for an excuse to throw a punch."
"Maybe," he admits, tilting his glass toward me. "Or maybe I just didn't like the way that arsehole was looking at you."
My stomach flips, but I ignore it.
Instead, I roll my eyes. "You are so…"

"Charming?"
"Infuriating."
"Same thing."
Before I can respond, Dad returns.
He adjusts his cuffs, standing beside the table, and fixes Aiden with a long, assessing look.
"I'm hosting a business gala in London next weekend," he announces. "Important people. Old money. Politicians, CEOs, men who shape the very foundation of our economy." He picks up his glass again, rolling it in his palm. "I assume you'd be out of place."
Aiden doesn't miss a beat, "You should be careful with assumptions."
My father's brows lift, amused. "Well then you won't mind proving me wrong."
Aiden tilts his head. "How so?"
"You'll be attending."
I tense.
I know exactly what this is. A test.
Aiden thinks this invitation is about me, about seeing if he's 'worthy' of dating Carter Whitehorn's daughter.
It's not. This isn't about me at all.
Dad wants to see if Aiden sinks or swims in a room full of sharks.
He's setting him up to fail.
Aiden stretches his fingers against the rim of his glass. "Do I get a plus-one?"
Dad smirks. "You already have one." He lifts his drink in mock salute. "Welcome to the family, *son*."

And just like that, he pulls his jacket off the back of the chair pulling it on, buttoning it with precise movements.

He turns to me, his gaze unreadable. "We'll talk soon, Alexis."

Then, with a final glance toward Aiden, something wordless and calculating, he strides toward the exit.

The moment he's out of earshot, I drop my forehead into my palm.

"Well," Aiden mutters, taking a long sip of his drink. "That was fun."

I lift my head, staring at him. "You have no idea what you just signed up for."

His grin is infuriatingly lazy. "Oh, sweetheart…" He leans in slightly, voice low and teasing. "I think we both know I thrive under pressure."

I groan, rubbing my temples.

This is a disaster waiting to happen.

Aiden Gage, in the heart of high society, surrounded by men who will eat him alive the second he puts a foot wrong.

And worst of all?

I think the prick is actually going enjoy it.

# Chapter 15

Aiden

I toss my arm over my eyes, exhaling sharply into the darkness.
Tonight was a hell of a thing.
The ceiling of my bedroom stares back at me, bathed in the dim glow of the outside lights. The faint hum of night-bugs drift through the cracked window, the scent of hay and damp earth settling into my bones like an old friend.
Familiar. Comfortable.
Which is more than I can say for the fucking circus I'm about to walk into.
I don't get nervous. I never have. But even I can't ignore the sheer absurdity of the situation.
A week from now, I won't be elbow-deep in tractor grease or fixing fences on the farm.
Nope.
Instead, I'll be suited up in a room full of billionaires and trust-fund babies, trying to convince Alex's father that I belong there.
Which I don't.
And that's what pisses me off the most.
Not because I give a shit about fitting in, but because that slimy bastard in a three-piece suit thinks I should care.

Samantha Todd

Carter Whitehorn looked at me like I was a fucking experiment, something to be examined under a microscope before being dismissed entirely.
A farmer.
*'Honest work, I suppose.'*
The condescension in his voice still rings in my ears, and it takes everything in me not to let it crawl under my skin.
But it wasn't just the way he looked at me.
It was the way he looked at *her*.
*Alexis.*
Every time he said it, it felt like a loaded weapon.
Like he was reminding her exactly who she was.
Who *she* belonged to.
Not herself. Never herself.
And that? That doesn't sit right with me.
I've seen a lot of fathers in my time. Good ones. Shit ones. Absent ones.
Ben Gage? He's a good man. He's never tried to control us, me, Ethan, Brynne. He let us become who we are, gave us the space to make our own damn choices, even if he didn't agree with them.
But Carter?
Carter Whitehorn doesn't give a shit about who Alex is, only who she's supposed to be. What she can do for him and his fucking stuck up empire. A mere pawn in his game.
And Alex, God, I could see it. The way her spine stiffened under his scrutiny, the way her voice flattened, perfectly measured, perfectly poised. Like she was reverting to muscle memory.

Like she was used to being nothing more than a product of his expectations.
And I hate it.
I hate that I can still hear his voice in my head. Hate that I keep seeing the way her fingers tightened around her glass every time he spoke.
Hate that I actually give a shit about any of this.
I should be pissed off at her.
She's dragged me into this mess, forced me into playing house with her, mocked me at every damn turn, and yet...
I sigh, scrubbing a hand through my hair.
Edith had been waiting at the doorstep when I dropped Alex off, that ever-knowing smile plastered across her face like she'd been expecting us. Which, knowing her, she probably had.
"You two look like the perfect couple," she'd said, voice dripping with that cryptic, meddling amusement she seemed to thrive on.
I don't think Alex even dignified it with a response. Just let out a long, slow exhale like she was re-evaluating every choice she'd ever made.
Meanwhile, I just smirked and told Edith she had impeccable taste.
Because say what you want about Aunt Edith—and trust me, I could say a lot—but she was loyal to Alex to a fault. And not just in the passive, 'supporting from the sidelines' kind of way. No, Edith was actively and enthusiastically fucking with Carter at every opportunity, and I had to respect that.
And that just makes me like her even more, despite all of her eccentricities.

Samantha Todd

Apparently, Alex has an apartment in London. Bought for her when she turned eighteen, because of course it was. I can't even imagine casually being gifted a goddamn apartment. But I suppose when your father's worth more than some small countries, it's just another transaction. A name scribbled on a deed. A neatly tied-up asset.
So, that's where we'll be staying.
It's not that I hate London. It's fine, I guess. I don't mind it in small doses. But it's too much. Too loud. Too fast. Too many people walking too quickly to god-knows-where, earbuds in, blank-faced, wrapped up in their own bullshit. No one looks at each other. No one stops to just breathe. It's the exact opposite of home.
And now, I have to throw myself into this chaos, put on a suit, and pretend to be someone I'm not for an entire weekend.
Oh yeah. And apparently, I don't even own a fucking suit.
I did—past tense—until Ethan and I got into a fight in the front yard, and I ripped the sleeve. No idea what the fight was even about now, but I'm guessing it was something stupid. It usually is.
Somehow, I don't think turning up to this event in a suit with a patch on the sleeve is going to cut it. Carter Whitehorn might be a soulless bastard, but I doubt even he could stomach that level of fashion atrocity at one of his precious events.
So now, on top of everything else, I have to go fucking suit shopping.
All because I punched a guy.

Okay, fine. Three guys.
And now, for my sins, I have to put on a suit, smile through gritted teeth, and make polite conversation with a bunch of pricks who drink whiskey that costs more than my truck—and wouldn't dare put Coke and ice in it.
Who knew, right?
My phone buzzes beside on the nightstand beside me, illuminating the room in a dull blue glow.

Ethan:
*So let me get this straight. You stood her up. Then got in a fight. And now, somehow, you're engaged?*

Aiden:
*Fake engaged.*
*It's a deal. She gets Carter off her back; I get my name cleared. Simple.*

Ethan:
*Right. Simple. Nothing complicated. Definitely no underlying sexual tension.*

Aiden:
*Shut up, Ethan.*

Ethan:
*So, when's the wedding? Can I bring Brynne?*

Aiden:
*There is no wedding, you dickhead.*

Samantha Todd

Ethan:
*And does Alex know that?*

Aiden:
*Fuck off.*

Ethan:
*Speaking of love, I assume you haven't told Brynne about this yet?*

Aiden:
*Absolutely not. Because I value my life.*

Ethan:
*Oh, I'm fucking telling her!*

Aiden:
*Ethan, I swear to God.*

Ethan:
*Relax. I'll wait until you're safely out of punching range.*

Aiden:
*Awesome, thanks.*

Ethan:
*You're really going to London for this?*

Aiden:
*Yeah.*

Ethan:
*And you're staying at her place?*
*...In the same bed?*

Aiden:
*Not a chance.*

Ethan:
*Interesting.*

Aiden:
*...*

Ethan:
*Just taking mental bets on how long it'll take before you break that rule.*

Aiden:
*Go to hell.*

Ethan:
*Already there, mate. Just watching you dig your own grave.*

Aiden:
*I actually do hate you.*

Ethan:
*Love you too, bud. See you tomorrow, got some news of my own.*

Samantha Todd

He goes offline immediately afterwards, and I put the phone back. I hadn't considered the one bed scenario and had never thought to ask if there was more than one room. Surely there will be? I can't imagine Alex Whitehorn being willing to share her space with anyone, let alone me.
Fuck this just got more complicated.

# Chapter 16

Ben

The morning air is crisp, carrying the scent of damp earth and hay as I lean against the back porch railing, sipping my coffee. The sun hasn't long been up, but Aiden's already out in the yard, kicking at a stray rock with the tip of his boot, hands stuffed deep in his pockets.

Something's on his mind.

That alone isn't unusual. Aiden's always been one to let his thoughts roll around inside him like a loose wheel, rattling the frame but never coming off entirely. But today?

Today, that wheel's about to shake itself loose.

I push off the railing and walk toward him.

"You're up early," I say, though I already know the reason.

Aiden snorts, rolling his shoulders. "Yeah, well. Got a lot to do before I go off and become a high-class socialite."

I raise an eyebrow. "That what they're calling it now?"

He grins, but it doesn't reach his eyes. "Yep. Heading to London, schmoozing with the elite, rubbing shoulders with men who probably own islands."

"And pretending to be engaged to a woman who's about as interested in marriage to you as a cat is in taking a bath."

His grin falters just a little. I catch it.

"It's not real, Dad," he says, voice light, too light. "It's just a bit of fun. A business transaction. A way for her to get her old man off her back."

I study him for a long moment. "And what do you get out of it?"

He shrugs, rocking back on his heels. "I get my assault charge magically wiped away and a chance to see what the rich folk do for fun. Win-win."

I don't say anything for a moment.

Aiden's always been like this. Always laughing, always joking, because if he doesn't, then he might have to sit with the truth.

And the truth?

This isn't just a deal for him.

"You're playing a dangerous game, son."

He rolls his eyes. "Oh, come on. Dangerous? What's the worst that happens? I wear a suit, smile at a few of London's finest, pretend to be hopelessly in love with the ice queen, and then we part ways when the plan works. No harm, no foul."

I let out a long breath. "Aiden... you ever ask yourself why you're so willing to do this for her?"

His face tightens, just for a second. "Because I made a deal."

"You don't give a damn about deals. You never have."

He opens his mouth, probably to spout off some smart remark, but the sound of a car rolling up the drive cuts him off.

Brynne steps out first, her usual confident stride making its way up the steps before I notice the glint of something on her hand.

A ring.

Well, I'll be damned.

Ethan follows behind, his usual quiet presence settling into place beside her.

"Morning, boys," Brynne says, a knowing smile on her lips as she lifts her hand and waves just a little too purposefully.

Aiden catches it before I do. His head snaps down, eyes narrowing at the ring before his face lights up in a way only he can pull off.

"Well, would you look at that," he drawls, stepping forward and grabbing her hand. "The demon king finally made an honest woman out of you."

Brynne rolls her eyes, but there's no missing the happiness there. "He did."

I look over at Ethan, who watches her with that same quiet intensity he always has, but there's a softness there now, something settled, something sure.

I clap a hand on his shoulder. "Proud of you, son."

He nods, something like gratitude flickering in his eyes.

Brynne turns to me next. "And you, Ben? You got any fatherly words of wisdom?"

I smirk. "Just don't let him drive. He's got a lead foot."

Ethan snorts.

But the moment is short-lived.

Brynne turns back to Aiden, her gaze narrowing. "Now, back to the actual pressing matter. This is a bad idea, Aiden."

He groans, dragging a hand through his hair. "Christ, not you too."

"Yes, me too!" She throws up her hands. "This is going to end in disaster. You don't fit in that world, Aiden, and I don't mean that as an insult. You're going to stick out like a sore thumb, and that man, her father, he's going to eat you alive."

"He can try," Aiden mutters.

Ethan watches him carefully. Not saying anything. Just observing.

He knows his brother.

Knows him better than anyone.

And the way he looks at him now?

He knows why Aiden's doing this.

But he also knows there's no talking him out of it.

Instead, he just sighs, shaking his head. "Try not to get yourself arrested again."

Aiden grins. "No promises."

I take another long sip of my coffee.

"So have you two set a date?" I ask, my eyes on my eldest son.

"No, not yet, we just want to enjoy being engaged at the moment." Brynne says, her smile beaming. Something has shifted ever since they moved in together. The house is quieter, a little lonelier if I'm honest, but their happiness is palpable and as a father, that's all you want for your children. To be happy. Brynne irons out Ethan's hard edges and Ethan sharpens Brynne. Their dynamic exposes the harsh reality of both of them and their different personalities compliments the other perfectly. Now if only my youngest son could find someone as up to the challenge. But that might be asking too much.

# Chapter 17

Alex

The scent of polished leather and cedarwood lingers in the air, the rich, masculine fragrance of old money and timeless elegance. The walls of Beauregard & Sons are lined with dark mahogany shelves, neatly pressed shirts stacked like high-rise buildings, an array of silk ties draped over brass fixtures. It's the kind of place that reeks of prestige, of men who have their suits hand-stitched in Milan and their shoes polished by someone who calls them 'Sir' without any irony.

Aiden Gage, standing in the middle of it all, could not look more out of place if he tried.

"I look like a bloody penguin."

His voice is full of disdain, his reflection scowling back at him in the gold-trimmed mirror that takes up half the wall.

I sigh, pinching the bridge of my nose. "You do not look like a penguin."

He turns, raising an eyebrow. "No? Maybe a polar bear then?"

I roll my eyes. "Polar bears are white, Aiden."

He grins. "Yeah, but they have black noses. So, technically, there's some contrast."

*Jesus. This man.*

"You're impossible." I mutter, stepping forward and adjusting his jacket with firm, precise tugs, smoothing the fabric over his broad shoulders. Unfortunately, that means I also feel the firmness of said shoulders. And the way the suit fits him like it was made for him.

Which, I suppose, it was.

*Damn it.*

Mr. Beauregard, the owner and tailor, watches over us with mild amusement from behind his round spectacles, his silver moustache twitching with the faintest of smiles. He's a frail-looking man, but his sharp gaze and the way he moves with measured precision tells me he's been in this business for decades. His measuring tape is slung over his shoulder like a badge of honour, and the navy three-piece suit he wears is impeccably pressed, not a wrinkle in sight.

"You're going to need at least one good suit for this, Aiden. If you want my father to take you seriously, you can't go looking like you just rolled off the back of a tractor."

He smirks. "Now, see, that's where you're wrong, Trouble. The tractor aesthetic is what makes me charming."

"Charming is the last word I would use to describe you."

"You wound me," he gasps, clutching his chest like I just stabbed him with a dagger.

I step back, crossing my arms. "You just have to get through one night in London without making an absolute fool of yourself. You think you can manage that?"

Aiden tilts his head, considering. "Hmm. No promises."

I groan, turning to Mr. Beauregard. "We'll take it."

The tailor chuckles, beginning to fold up the spare jackets when the shop door bursts open, and in sweeps Edith, draped in an offensively large patchwork shawl and absolutely covered in beads.

"There you are, my little cosmic wanderer!" she exclaims, throwing her arms wide.

Aiden coughs into his fist to cover a laugh.

I glare at him.

"You know, Alex," Edith continues, completely unaware of the murderous energy rolling off me, "I stopped by the crystal shop, and the owner says that you and your betrothed," she wiggles her fingers in the air like a magician "are experiencing a celestial alignment!"

Aiden's eyes practically sparkle with mischief. "Is that so?"

Edith nods sagely, rifling through the dozens of trinkets and gemstones she's no doubt just purchased. "Oh, absolutely. The universe is practically vibrating with energy around you two."

"Yeah, vibrating with irritation," I mutter.

Edith ignores me completely, walking up to Aiden and placing a very large chunk of rose quartz in his hand.

"For love," she says solemnly.

Aiden grins, turning it over in his palm. "You hear that, Trouble? It's fate."

I snap the crystal out of his hand. "You're so lucky I need you for this."

Edith cackles, delighted.

Mr. Beauregard looks between the three of us, clearly entertained. "So, shall I wrap up the suit, or are we expecting another divine intervention?"

Aiden flashes his signature annoying-as-hell grin. "Nah, just a miracle if she doesn't murder me first."

Edith pats his arm. "Oh, don't worry dear. Murder would be very bad for your chakras."

*I swear to God, I need a drink.*

I cross my arms as I lean against the wall outside the suit shop, watching as Aunt Edith floats across the street, entirely enraptured by whatever monstrosity of a scarf she's currently admiring through the shop window.

"She's going to buy that one, isn't she?" Aiden mutters beside me, stuffing his hands into his pockets.

"Oh, without a doubt." I sigh, following Aunt Edith's delighted expression as she holds a particularly gaudy purple and gold scarf against her neck, her rings clinking as she examines her reflection.

Aiden shifts beside me, rolling his shoulders against the somewhat more forgiving fabric of his t-shirt and checked shirt, looking every bit like a man who has just been released from a straitjacket.

I inhale deeply, bracing myself.

"Okay," I say, turning to face him. "Let's talk about the gala."

He tilts his head. "The gala?"

"Yes," I huff. "The pretentious, shallow, soul-draining event we're attending."

He smirks. "You're really selling it, sweetheart."

I ignore the pet name. "You need to know what you're walking into."

He exhales, tilting his head back against the brick wall. "Alright, hit me."

I cross my arms. "The room will be full of people who are too rich to care about anyone but themselves. They're fake. Every single one of them. Their smiles are rehearsed, their compliments are laced with poison, and their eyes are always watching, judging, waiting for a misstep."

Aiden raises an eyebrow, unimpressed. "Sounds delightful."

I nod, deadpan. "Oh, absolutely. They'll drink obscenely expensive champagne, they'll whisper behind gloved hands about whoever isn't in the room, and they'll talk about charity like it's a novelty instead of a necessity."

Aiden watches me for a moment, an unreadable expression flickering across his face.

And then, he smirks. "But you know all this because you're one of them."

The words are like a slap, but I don't flinch.

Instead, I tilt my head, meeting his gaze with equal measure of steel.

"Yes," I say, voice sharp. "I grew up with them. I was educated with them. I probably even dated some of them."

His smirk widens, but I cut him off before he can say something infuriating.

"And *that*," I continue, stepping closer, "is exactly why I know how vile they are. Why I've made it my mission to never be like them."

Aiden's expression shifts, like he wasn't expecting me to say that. Like he's seeing something else in me for the first time.

But then he grins, that boyish, cocky smirk that makes me want to punch him square in the face.

"Alright, Ice Queen," he says, rolling up the sleeves of his suit jacket, clearly already over this conversation. "Teach me your ways."

I exhale sharply, biting back my irritation.

"So back to our getting-to-know-each-other conversation…"

Aiden leans against the wall, watching me with a lazy smirk.

"I don't need to learn anything, sweetheart," he drawls. "I already know you."

I scoff. "Oh really?"

He nods, grinning smugly.

"You only drink whisky when celebrating and wine the rest of the time. Coffee is a must, and you take it white with one sugar. You hate small talk, but you love to argue. You pretend to be cold and untouchable, but you care more than you let on. You grew up surrounded by money, but you never felt like you belonged in it. And despite everything, despite your whole *I hate men and their egos* attitude" he pauses, tilting his head, "you keep finding yourself around them."

I blink.

*Ok, so that was pretty accurate.*

"Alright, Mr. Observant," I say, crossing my arms. "Let's see how much *I* know about *you*."

Aiden grins, stepping closer. "Oh, this should be good."

I tap my finger against my chin, feigning thoughtfulness.

"You like instant coffee," I start, eyeing him pointedly.

"Because it's quick," he shrugs. "I have a life to live, Alex."

I roll my eyes. "You don't believe in fancy things."

"That's just called being practical."

"You sleep in the middle of the bed like a starfish."

His smirk widens, "Have you been watching me sleep?"

I ignore the jab and continue. Leaning in slightly, watching him carefully.

"You love your family more than anything, and you'd do anything for them," I say, my voice quieter now.

Aiden stiffens, his smirk flickering.

I tilt my head, watching him closely.

"You don't like talking about yourself," I continue. "You hide behind jokes and charm, but it's mostly a front."

His jaw tightens.

I soften my voice, just slightly.

"And you don't let many people in. Not really."

For a moment, he doesn't move.

And then, he smirks again, like I didn't just say something undeniably true.

"Well," he says, his voice laced with amusement, "aren't you just a little psychic?"

I roll my eyes, stepping back. "You're impossible."
"And you're a pain in my arse, fiancé."
We glare at each other, tension humming between us like a live wire.
"Oh, for heaven's sake, just kiss already!"
We both whirl around to see Edith standing behind us, a ridiculous scarf draped over her shoulders, holding a shopping bag full of more scarves.
Aiden snorts. "Told you she was gonna buy one."
I pinch the bridge of my nose. "Aunt Edith, I swear..."
She waves a hand, entirely unbothered. "Come along, lovebirds. Let's get lunch before Aiden faints from the sheer horror of wearing designer clothing."

# Chapter 18

Aiden

The café is the kind of place that only exists in small towns, where the tables are a little too close together, the scent of fresh bread and vanilla lingers in the air, and the matronly waitress behind the counter knows everyone's order before they've even sat down.

Sunlight spills through the wide bay windows, catching on the mismatched china teacups that clatter against their saucers as plates are served. Handwritten chalkboard menus display the day's specials in looping, uneven script, homemade quiche, beef stew, and scones the size of my damn fist.

A bored-looking teenager, no older than sixteen, leans lazily against the till, chewing gum with the enthusiasm of a corpse while scrolling through her phone. She doesn't even look up as Edith makes a very grand gesture of removing her shawl and declaring, "Oh, I feel the energy in this place today!"

Alex sighs deeply, palming her face like this is some sort of ordeal, before sliding into the booth across from me.

"What energy?" I ask, trying and failing to keep the amusement out of my tone.

Edith looks at me knowingly, like I'm the biggest idiot in the room. "Aiden, darling, the *energy*."
*Well, that clears that up then.*
Alex clearly doesn't have the patience for any of this today. She busies herself by stirring a sugar cube into her tea, though she doesn't even take a sip.
"So," Edith continues, lifting her cup delicately, the picture of regal eccentricity, "did I ever tell you about Alex's mother?"
Alex visibly stiffens.
"She was wild," Edith says fondly, eyes distant, like she's looking back at a different time entirely.
"Always wanted more. Not just money or status, something bigger. A life that meant something."
Alex flicks her gaze away, pushing the sugar cube around with her spoon.
"She met Carter at university," Edith continues, oblivious to the tension creeping into Alex's frame, "and he had everything. The money, the connections, the name." Her lip curls slightly. "And she thought that was the 'something more' she was looking for."
I glance at Alex.
Her jaw is tight, her hands a little too still.
She doesn't want to hear this.
I get it. I get closed off in discussions about my mother too. My Dad always says it's my defence mechanism. The truth is it just hurts to talk about her.
Edith carries on oblivious to the obvious rising tension.

"And so, she chose it," Edith sighs, leaning back into the booth, "chose him. And for a while, it worked. Or it looked like it worked."

Alex abruptly stands.

"I'm going to the bookshop." Her voice is carefully neutral, but I can hear the thread of tension woven through it.

She doesn't wait for us to respond before striding across the street.

I watch her go, pushing through the door of a small, dusty bookshop, probably to find another mafia romance to distract herself with.

Edith doesn't say anything for a moment, just watches her niece disappear into the shop before taking a sip of her tea.

"She doesn't like talking about her mother," I say eventually.

Edith snorts. "She doesn't like talking about anything… in case you hadn't already noticed"

*Can't argue with that.*

I settle back into the booth. "So, what happened?"

Edith exhales, running a hand over the beaded bracelets stacked on her wrist.

"Cancer," she says finally.

I blink. "Shit."

*Same as my mother.* A depressing connecting factor I have finally found with Alex and one that neither one of us will likely ever discuss.

*Perfect.*

She nods, her expression saddened, but not bitter.

"By the time they caught it, there wasn't much they could do."

The waitress appears with our plates, soup for Edith, a ridiculously overstuffed sandwich for me and some salad with chicken for Alex. As soon as she leaves, Edith continues.

"And a good job as well, because not long after, she passed, Carter's indiscretions came to light."

My brows pull together. "Indiscretions?"

Edith lets out a low, unimpressed hum. "A whole parade of women. All lithe and young, all eager to please. He never loved her, not really. For Carter, love is a transaction. A merger, if you will."

A cold bitterness pools in my stomach.

"I take it Alex knows."

Edith huffs a laugh. "Oh, she knows. And she's spent her whole life trying not to repeat her mother's mistakes."

I chew my sandwich a little slower.

"So what," I say after a minute, "she doesn't do relationships?"

Edith arches an eyebrow, stirring her soup. "She doesn't do *risk*."

That lands.

I glance across the street, through the window of the bookshop, and spot Alex standing by a shelf, running her delicate fingers over the spines of romance novels like she's searching for an escape route.

She doesn't do risk. But this? This fake engagement? This whole elaborate charade she's roped me into? It's the biggest risk of all.

I take another bite of my sandwich, watching Edith as she carefully stirs her soup, lost in thought.

Samantha Todd

For a woman who spends most of her time raving about moon cycles and "celestial energy shifts", there's something oddly grounding about her.
She's warm, in a way that feels familiar, like sitting by a fire in the dead of winter, listening to the kind of stories that only people who have really lived can tell.
She pushes her spoon around the bowl before finally looking up at me.
"You're staring," she says, voice teasing.
I smirk. "You fascinate me, Edith."
She grins, her face crinkling with deep laugh lines, the kind only people who have smiled their way through an entire lifetime can have.
"Well, aren't you just full of charm?" she says, picking up her spoon again. "You should be careful, Aiden Gage, or you might end up *meaning* half the things you say."
I let out a low chuckle, shifting in my seat.
"Tell me about your life," I say, leaning forward. "I don't know much about you beyond the fact that you're apparently an *oracle* and that you've got a questionable taste in scarves."
She gasps, clutching her chest dramatically, "How dare you! My scarves are sacred!"
I grin, but she waves me off, tucking a loose curl of silver-streaked brown hair behind her ear.
"Oh, alright. Let's see... I was married once," she muses, her voice soft with nostalgia, but not regret.
That throws me for a second.
I blink. "You were?"

She nods, reaching for a napkin and absently folding the edges, smoothing them over like she's pressing the memory into place.

"Yes," she sighs, "to a painter. A true artist. Flighty, restless, his head always somewhere between the clouds and the bottle of whatever red wine he had in his bag."

I can't help but laugh. "Him? *Too flighty* for *you*?"

Edith grins. "I know, I know. The irony is not lost on me."

She shakes her head, taking a sip of tea before continuing.

"But the thing is, Aiden, as much as I believe in energy and soul connections, I also believe that people need balance. And he and I were like... two dandelion seeds in the wind. Floating. Free. But never rooted."

I consider that, swirling the ice in my drink.

She shrugs. "So, we let each other go. And it was the right thing."

I tilt my head. "Did you love him?"

A slow smile tugs at her lips, something far away in her gaze.

"I did," she says simply. "But not the kind of love that lasts. The kind that *teaches* you something before it moves on."

I let that settle.

Edith is a hippie, through and through, long, flowing skirts, countless beads and rings, a mound of curly greying hair that seems to have a mind of its own. She's always draped in colourful layers, stacked in enough handmade bracelets that she jingles whenever she moves.

And yet, despite all that, she's probably the most inherently wise person I've ever met.

I like her.

I really, really do.

"So," I say, leaning back, "what brought you to Northwood Dale?"

She grins, tapping her spoon against her plate.

"I wanted to sell something with a soul."

I quirk an eyebrow. "So you chose houses?"

She nods solemnly, as if it's the most obvious thing in the world. "Of course, houses have souls! They hold the echoes of the families that lived in them before. They carry memories, love, heartbreak. Haven't you ever walked into a house and just *felt* something?"

I blink. "Uh... sure?"

She huffs. "That's the soul, Aiden! That's the imprint left behind."

I shake my head, laughing.

She's completely ridiculous. And yet somehow, she makes it work.

Before I can say anything else, the bell over the door chimes.

Alex strides back inside, a paper bag of books clutched in her hands, her auburn hair catching the afternoon light streaming through the window.

Her eyes narrow suspiciously when she sees the two of us still deep in conversation.

"I can feel you talking about me," she says dryly, slipping into the seat beside Edith.

I smirk. "Relax, we were talking about *ghosts*."
"Close enough," she mutters.
Edith beams at her, clearly unfazed. "What did you get, darling?"
Alex pulls out a couple of titles, stacking them neatly beside her plate.
I glance at them, immediately recognising the dark, brooding covers.
A slow grin spreads across my face.
"Oh, Alex," I say, my voice dripping with amusement. "Another mafia romance? Really?"
She doesn't look up.
"Don't start," she says, flipping through the pages absently.
"I'm just saying," I smirk, "for a woman who claims to be so immune to men, you sure do love books about women falling at the feet of morally grey bad boys."
Edith laughs outright, while Alex levels me with a glare so sharp it could gut a man.
"I will shove this book so far up your arse, Aiden Gage."
I grin. "Ooo, should I call you *sir* after?"
She kicks me under the table causing me to choke on my drink.
Edith just smiles, sipping her tea like she's watching the best entertainment she's had in years.
"Right, stop bickering you two. Honestly, it's like sitting with a couple of love-struck teenagers." She says, spooning soup into her grinning face.
Alex just scowls and picks at her salad.

# Chapter 19

Alex

I hear Aiden exhale sharply as we step through the lobby of my building.
Yeah. He's impressed.
Even though he desperately doesn't want to be.
The polished marble floors gleam under the golden light, a vast chandelier dripping with crystal catching the reflection of the lavish entrance below. The walls are adorned with large-scale modern art, pieces my father no doubt had a hand in 'investing' in, because nothing in this world can exist without some form of strategic deal attached to it.
Aiden shifts beside me, suit bag slung over his shoulder, looking wildly out of place in this world of pristine wealth and silent judgment.
The concierge, a man in a perfectly pressed black suit with silver streaks at his temples, greets me with a polite nod.
"Miss Whitehorn, welcome back."
I return his nod, stepping towards the lift as he signals for one of the bellhops to collect my bags.
Aiden hesitates, gripping the strap of his suit bag a little tighter.
"Uh, no need," Aiden mutters quickly, adjusting his grip on his own things. "I got it."

The bellhop looks startled at the idea of someone *carrying their own luggage* but steps back obediently.

I press the lift button, casting Aiden a glance.

"You could have let him carry it."

"I can carry my own shit," he mutters. "Rich people and their damn…" he stops himself, rolling his eyes. "Whatever. Just show me the damn penthouse."

I stifle a smirk, stepping inside as the lift doors slide open.

The ride up is silent, except for the smooth jazz playing softly from the speakers. I know Aiden is dying to say something, probably something snarky, but he keeps his mouth shut.

When we step into my apartment, I hear him exhale sharply again.

I smirk as I drop my keys onto the marble entryway table.

"Go on," I say, not even looking at him. "Say it."

Aiden lets out a low whistle.

"This place is fucking ridiculous Alex."

I smile to myself, striding into the massive open plan living room, flicking on the sleek, modern lights that flood the space in a soft glow. The apartment is all glass and steel, the floor-to-ceiling windows overlooking the expansive London skyline.

The living area is decorated in a minimalist style, full of designer furniture that I didn't pick out, and pristine décor that has never once felt like home.

Aiden wanders further in, his head tilted back as he takes in the massive crystal chandelier hanging above the dining table. His boots echo against the polished wood floors, and I already know I'll find dirty footprints trailing behind him.

"You lived here?" he asks, a little too incredulously.

I shrug. "Technically."

He raises an eyebrow.

"It was a gift," I explain.

He lets out a bark of laughter. "Yeah, I remember you saying, but fuck me!"

"It was my 18$^{th}$ birthday," I add by way of explanation, as if that helps.

Aiden shakes his head, clearly baffled.

"Jesus," he mutters. "I got a toolbox for my 18$^{th}$."

I smirk, crossing my arms. "I bet you loved that toolbox."

He tilts his head, pretending to consider. "Still use it to this day."

I roll my eyes, stepping further inside. "Come on, I'll show you where you're sleeping."

Aiden follows, but as I swing open the guest bedroom door, disaster strikes.

The room is half-painted, the furniture is covered in plastic, and painter's tools are scattered across the floor.

I close my eyes, pinching the bridge of my nose. "Fuck."

Aiden leans in slightly, surveying the scene with amused curiosity. "So… what, you hosting a DIY show in here?"

I sigh. "I forgot it's being redecorated."

Aiden swings his suit bag onto the ludicrously expensive Italian leather couch and stretches his arms overhead with a lazy smirk.

"Well," he says, flopping down onto the cushions with a satisfied groan, "I've gotta say, if this is my punishment for getting into a fight, I might start throwing punches more often."

I cross my arms, eyebrow arching. "You think that's funny?"

He tilts his head, grinning unapologetically. "I think it's hilarious."

I glare at him before turning on my heel. "There's no way in hell I'm sharing my bed, so you'll have to sleep here."

"Oh, no," Aiden deadpans, sprawling out across the couch. "Please don't make me sleep on the absurdly soft, obscenely expensive, leather monstrosity in the middle of your penthouse. I simply couldn't bear it."

I huff, crossing my arms. "It's hardly a monstrosity."

"Alex, I could park my truck on this thing and still have room to stretch out." He pats the armrest. "Seriously, sweetheart, don't lose sleep over me. This sofa's probably worth more than my entire house."

"Don't be ridiculous."

He shrugs. "I'm not. This thing's gotta be at least ten grand, right?"

I hesitate for half a second too long.

Aiden barks out a laugh. "Are you shitting me? You actually have a ten-grand sofa?"

"I..." I shake my head. "It was a gift."

"Yeah?" His grin is infuriating. "From who, the King of England?"

I roll my eyes. "If it makes you feel better, I had no say in any of the furniture."

"Ah, right," Aiden nods sagely, mock understanding in his eyes. "Of course. Must've been tough, forced into luxury. I don't know how you survived."
I throw a death glare in his direction. "So, you're sleeping here, aren't you?"
He chuckles, stretching again. "Gladly." Then, with a lazy smirk, he adds, "I mean, I was gonna offer to share, strictly for warmth, but I know you're a woman of class and dignity, so I'll keep my hands to myself."
"Right," I say flatly. "Because that was the main concern here."
"I'm just saying," he shrugs, arms folded behind his head, "some women would be delighted to have me as their bedmate."
I snort. "Well, it's a shame I'm not one of them."
Aiden puts a hand over his chest dramatically, feigning heartbreak. "You wound me, Alex."
I shake my head. "You'll survive."
"Barely."
I turn toward the hallway. "I'll get you a blanket."
"Don't rush. I think I need a minute to mourn my rejection."
I don't dignify that with a response.
Instead, I walk toward my bedroom, shutting the door behind me with a soft click.
And suddenly...
I hate it.
The silence. The stillness.
I glance around my pristine, perfectly curated room, cool neutral tones, immaculate bedding, art pieces

carefully chosen to match the aesthetic of the space and feel nothing.
This place is not a home. Not like Aunt Edith's.
I close my eyes for a second, inhaling deeply.
I can almost smell it. The warm, herbal scent of simmer pots bubbling away in the kitchen, the faint aroma of old books and parchment, the comforting clutter of history layered in every corner.
This apartment?
It's cold.
It has no soul.
I smirk to myself, sinking onto my bed, finally understanding what Edith meant about houses having hearts.
Because this one doesn't.
And I miss hers.

# Chapter 20

Alex

The smell hits me first.
Warm, rich, buttery. Hints of garlic and herbs, the subtle saltiness of something being cooked on the stove.
For a moment, I forget where I am.
Eyes still closed, I inhale deeply, my stomach immediately protesting with a low grumble. The sound of oil sizzling and the faint, rhythmic chopping of a knife against a wooden board filter in from the kitchen.
My eyes snap open. I must have fallen asleep when I'd laid down for a bit. Shit.
Aiden.
What the...?
I push back the covers and pad out into the ridiculously sleek kitchen, rubbing the sleep from my eyes.
And there he is.
Standing at the stove, barefoot, sleeves rolled up to his elbows, stirring something in a pot like he belongs here.
Like he's done this a hundred times before.

The sight is so domestic, so utterly out of place in my world, that I actually freeze in the doorway, momentarily stunned.

Aiden fucking Gage... in my pristine, designer kitchen.

Cooking.

I shake off the weird warmth pooling in my chest and cross my arms, leaning against the doorframe.

"Are we running a pop-up restaurant now?"

He doesn't even turn, just grins at the stove. "Good evening, sleeping beauty."

I scoff. "I was not asleep."

"You were snoring."

"I..." I pause, scowling. "I do not snore."

His smirk grows. "Hmm. Loud little huffs, then. Like an angry kitten."

I narrow my eyes at him.

He tilts his head, mock serious. "Actually, it was kind of cute."

Cute. I could kill him.

His grin widens, like he's already won. Infuriating.

I step closer, eyes darting to the pan sizzling on the stove. "What exactly are you doing?"

He stirs the risotto slowly, deliberately. "Cooking dinner. You had nothing but a bottle of champagne and a sad-looking protein bar in your fridge, Alex. That's a crime."

I roll my eyes and shrug my shoulders. "I don't cook."

"No shit," he mutters, shaking his head.

I scowl. "Excuse me?"

Samantha Todd

He gestures around the spotless, barely used kitchen. "This place is a goddamn museum. I don't think your oven has even been turned on."
I huff. "It has."
He gives me a knowing look.
"...Once. When the heating system broke down."
He smirks, turning back to the stove. "Thought so."
I shift on my feet, suddenly awkward, watching him move around my kitchen with ease. Like it's his. Like he belongs.
And I hate how... natural it looks.
How comforting it feels.
I push the thought aside and glance at the counter, where a cutting board sits with a whole onion waiting to be diced.
"You can at least help," he says, nodding toward it.
I wrinkle my nose. "What do I do with that?"
He blinks at me. "Are you fucking serious?"
"I don't cook, Aiden."
"Jesus Christ." He sighs, rubbing his forehead. "Alright, grab a knife from the block over there."
I do as I'm told, gripping the handle awkwardly, trying to figure out the best way to cut it.
Aiden watches me for about five seconds before groaning in horror.
"Oh, for fuck's sake, stop!"
Before I can protest, he's behind me.
Close.
Too close.
His fingers tighten around mine, guiding the knife to the onion. His voice is low and teasing.

"What, you gonna tell me I should just sit pretty and drink wine while you cook?" I challenge, trying to ignore the way my pulse is hammering.

His lips tilt up into a smirk, his stubble grazing my cheek as he leans in.

"No," he murmurs. "I was going to tell you to watch your damn fingers before you lose one. You're dangerous with a knife."

I exhale, but it's shaky as hell.

He lifts a hand, gently brushing a stray curl from my face, tucking it behind my ear. The touch is casual, but my skin burns where his fingertips graze me.

He notices.

Because his eyes dip to my lips for a second, just a second.

And suddenly, my breath is caught somewhere between irritation and something much worse.

He leans closer, voice like gravel and smoke.

"Your hair smells good," he mutters.

My stomach flips.

"Shut up," I snap automatically, my voice entirely too breathy.

His chuckle is low. "See? Angry kitten."

And that's it.

I wrench away, spinning on my heel, my pulse going haywire.

Aiden just grins, like he knows exactly what he's doing to me.

Like he enjoys getting under my skin.

I scowl at him, heart still racing, and grab a glass of wine.

"I would be great at cooking," I say, trying to sound indifferent. "If I had the time."
His chuckle is soft, almost indulgent.
"Right. And I suppose, in your glamorous life, you never had time to dice an onion?"
"Nope."
"You're hopeless."
"And yet, somehow, I've survived."
He laughs quietly, turning his attention back to the stove.
"Alright," he says, a little too casually, "You're officially banned from handling sharp objects from now on. You just sit pretty and watch the expert at work."
I exhale, rolling my shoulders, shaking off whatever the hell that was. I sink onto a stool at the kitchen island, watching as Aiden moves around the kitchen, back to that easy confidence.
Even I can admit that the risotto smells incredible. He babbles on telling me it's a family recipe and that if I like it there's a chicken dish that he'll try next.
The sound of the wooden spoon scraping against the pan fills the silence, the warm glow of the stove casting soft shadows against the marble countertops.
And for the first time in a long time… this place doesn't feel so cold. So empty.
I take a slow sip of wine, watching him.

# Chapter 21

Aiden

Alex Whitehorn is terrified of The Ring.
And I find it adorable as fuck.
She's currently half-buried under a plush blanket on the far end of her ridiculously expensive couch, her knees pulled to her chest, a cushion clutched to her face like a shield.
"Jesus, Alex, it's just a movie."
"Just a movie?" she hisses, eyes peeking over the top of the cushion. "Aiden, a cursed videotape that literally murders people in seven days is not just a movie."
I smirk. "It's fiction."
Her glaring eyes flick to mine. "That's what the people in the movie say right before they die."
I let out a slow laugh, stretching an arm over the back of the sofa. "So let me get this straight. You can face down a father who wants to sell you off like a racehorse at auction, you can talk shit to me without batting an eyelid, but a creepy little girl crawling out of a well has you ready to relocate to another country?"
Alex stiffens, glares harder, and then turns back to the screen. "Shut up. Just... shut up."

I chuckle under my breath, letting my eyes drift over to her again.

It's not just the terror that I find strangely endearing. It's the way she looks right now.

Curled up in the soft glow of the television, her long auburn hair draped over the cushion, her sharp, elegant features relaxed for once.

And the biggest shock of all?

Her pyjamas.

Pink and white polka dots.

*Pink*.

I never had her pegged as a pink kind of girl.

In fact, I was convinced she slept in some sleek black satin bullshit, something effortlessly expensive, the kind that barely covers anything. Not fucking country-girl, Hallmark-movie, my-grandmother-bought-these-for-me-for-Christmas polka dots.

I tilt my head, openly smirking at her. "Nice PJs."

She doesn't take her eyes off the screen. "I swear to God, Aiden."

"No, really. It's cute." I gesture at the fabric on her trouser legs. "Did you steal them from a thirteen-year-old?"

She turns her head slowly, like something out of *The Exorcist*, all murderous intent and narrowed eyes.

I grin. "I just didn't think pink was your colour."

She sighs deeply and rubs her temples. "Yes, Aiden. I normally sleep in a diamond-encrusted ball gown, but I thought I'd dress down for the occasion."

I grin, adjusting the couch cushion behind my head. "Well, I appreciate the effort."

She mutters something about wanting to smother me with a pillow and turns back to the movie.

I should be watching the screen too, but my eyes drift to her again.

Because this is different.

Comfortable.

I never would have guessed that watching a horror movie with Alex, of all people, would be so easy.

That I'd enjoy seeing her like this, so unguarded, so normal.

Or that I'd find it so fucking hot.

I shift slightly, gritting my teeth at the memory of earlier, of her pressed against me in the kitchen, her hair smelling like coconut and vanilla, my body reacting like a thirteen-year-old with his first Playboy magazine.

*Fucking hell.*

I went too far.

And I knew it the second I leaned in.

That damn scent had been like a shot of heroin straight to my dick, and I'd had to bite back every urge to turn her around, pin her against the counter, and see just how deep her ice runs.

And now here we are.

She jumps slightly as the TV flickers, gripping the cushion tighter, her big brown eyes going wide.

God help me, I enjoy this way too much.

"Alex." I lean in slightly.

She flinches. "What?"

I lower my voice to a whisper. "She's right behind you."

Samantha Todd

She yelps, flinging the cushion at me. "YOU FUCKING ARSEHOLE!"
I burst out laughing, catching it mid-air.
She glares daggers, cheeks slightly flushed, her hands tight fists in her lap.
"Unbelievable," she mutters under her breath.
I smirk, tossing the cushion back onto the couch.
"You can relax, city girl. If Samara shows up, I'll fight her off for you."
She rolls her eyes, crossing her arms. "You'd probably flirt with her first."
I grin, pretending to think about it. "Maybe. She seems like she's got unresolved trauma. I'm great with emotionally unavailable women."
Alex snorts. Actually snorts.
She immediately masks it, grabbing her wine glass and turning back to the screen. But I caught it. And that is something I'll be storing away for later.
Who would I be if I didn't have a little ammo in my arsenal?

The smell of fresh coffee fills the apartment as I lean against the counter, watching the French press work its magic.
Yes. A French press.
Because I remember how Alex likes her coffee, and as much as I love pissing her off, I also pay attention.
The apartment is quiet, the kind of quiet that comes just before a storm. Because tonight is the Gala, and we both know what's coming.
I hear her door open, followed by the soft padding of her bare feet on the hardwood floor.

And then she appears, rubbing a hand over her sleep-mussed hair, her pink polka dot pyjamas scruffy from a night of sleep. Fundamentally looking ridiculously good for someone who just woke up.

I glance at the clock. 8.00 AM.

I smirk, crossing my arms. "Well, well, well. Look who finally made it into my kitchen for coffee in the morning. Only thing missing is you in my T-shirt."

She pauses, blinking at me groggily. Then she rolls her eyes so hard I'm surprised she doesn't fall over. "If I weren't half-asleep, I'd tell you to shut the fuck up."

"I'm just saying, I'm giving Aunt Edith a run for her money on the predicting things front!" I say, grinning.

She ignores me, dragging herself to the counter and freezing when she spots the coffee. Her eyebrows lift slightly.

I nod at the French press. "Go on. Say it."

"Say what?" she mutters, reaching for a mug.

"That I'm the best fake fiancé a girl could ask for."

She snorts. "Let's not get carried away."

I chuckle under my breath as she pours herself a cup. I lean over the counter pouring in some milk and throwing in a sugar cube alongside it. Something flashes across her eyes, but she quickly masks it, taking a long slow sip like she actually enjoys it. Like she's impressed but won't admit it.

I lean against the counter, watching her, because watching her is becoming a fucking problem for me. She still looks half-asleep, her hair a mess, the slight smear of leftover mascara shadowing her eyes. And I

shouldn't be noticing how good she looks like this, but my brain doesn't seem to give a shit about what I should or shouldn't be doing.
So I clear my throat and say, "So tell me about him."
She blinks, looking up over the rim of her mug. "Who?"
"The prick your father wants you to marry."
Alex stiffens slightly, lowering her coffee.
She hesitates, like she's considering brushing me off.
But then she sighs, leaning against the counter, tapping her perfectly manicured nails against the ceramic.
"Miles Kensington."
The name alone sounds like a trust fund and a cocaine habit.
"We dated in sixth form," she continues, her voice steady but laced with something sharp underneath. "He was trouble. A rich, spoiled, entitled arsehole who thought he could do whatever he wanted because of his last name."
"And let me guess," I say, tilting my head. "He did?"
She huffs a quiet, humourless laugh. "Yeah. He did."
I wait, watching her closely, because she's not done yet.
"He cheated," she says after a moment, swirling her coffee absently. "Multiple times. Did coke at every opportunity. Thought being 'young, rich and reckless' excused being a total twat."
I grip my mug tighter, a slow burn working its way up my spine. I don't know why I'm angry, but I am.

Because I know Alex now, at least enough to know that she doesn't give her trust easily.

And this prick took it for granted.

I take a slow sip of my black coffee, keeping my voice even. "And let me guess. Your father still thinks he's a catch?"

Alex lets out a dry laugh, shaking her head. "Of course. He has the right connections, the right background, the right family name. That's all that matters."

I exhale sharply, rubbing a hand over my jaw. "And this arsehole, he'll be there tonight?"

She nods. "Without a doubt."

Something inside me tightens.

Because I haven't even met Miles Kensington yet, but I already want to punch him in the face.

I drain the rest of my coffee, setting the mug down a little harder than necessary.

Alex watches me, expression unreadable, before quirking an eyebrow.

"What?" she asks.

I stretch lazily, rolling my shoulders. "Nothing. Just can't wait to meet him."

She smirks. "Please don't punch him in the face Aiden."

I grin. "No promises, sweetheart."

# Chapter 22

Alex

The moment we step through the grand gold-plated doors of the Kensington Ballroom, I
remember exactly why I left this world behind.
The opulence is suffocating.
The vast space is all marble floors and crystal chandeliers, the light from a thousand candles bouncing off the walls like a Monet painting. Women draped in silk and diamonds, men in bespoke suits worth more than a small house, all of them sipping champagne and exchanging smug, meaningless conversations.
This is the world I was raised in.
And it makes my skin crawl.
"Jesus," Aiden mutters beside me, straightening the black tie I forced him to wear. "Did we just step into the season finale of *Succession*?"
I let out a snort I shouldn't, then quickly mask it with a sip of champagne handed to me by a white-gloved waiter.
Aiden, for all his complaints about dressing like a penguin, cleans up ridiculously well.
His dark suit is tailored to perfection, hugging broad shoulders and long legs, the crisp white shirt complemented perfectly by the pale blue tie at the

collar, just enough to add that signature 'charming rogue' effect. He looks so at ease, so casually out of place yet completely unbothered by it, that I almost hate him for it.

And then, of course, he leans in and ruins it.

"By the way," he murmurs, his breath warm against my ear, "you never told me I'd be escorting a Bond girl tonight."

I shoot him a look, but his gaze rakes over me anyway—slow, appreciative, lingering.

My dress is black satin, floor-length, plunging neckline, backless. Classic. Timeless. Strategic. If I have to suffer this godforsaken evening, at least I'll look damn good doing it.

"Wipe the smirk off your face, Gage."

"Not my fault you look like sex and sin," he says easily, grabbing a flute of champagne from a passing waiter. "I mean, the poor blokes in this room are already struggling with fragile egos, now they have to compete with me? Rough night for them."

I sigh. "You're insufferable."

"Yeah," he muses, sipping his drink, "but admit it, you'd be bored without me."

Before I can fire back, a familiar chill creeps up my spine.

My father.

We don't see him at first, but I can feel his presence before his imposing frame steps into view.

He's wearing his usual charcoal three-piece, not a hair out of place, holding his scotch like he owns the whole damn city.

Aiden tenses beside me, no doubt sensing the shift in my posture.

My father's lips curl into a smirk as his sharp blue eyes rake over Aiden, assessing. Calculating.

"Well," he drawls, "isn't this quite the picture."

Aiden's smile is blindingly charming as he extends his hand. "Carter, mate. How's business?"

My father's eyes the outstretched hand like it's a rotting carcass, before shaking it briskly, his grip undoubtedly crushing.

Aiden just grins, completely unfazed.

Dad turns his attention to me. "Alexis. Stunning, as always."

I clench my jaw at the deliberate use of my full name, but before I can say anything, Aiden's hand lands on my waist.

I swear my breath hitches.

A bold move. Possessive. Protective.

My father notices. His jaw tightens just slightly.

Interesting.

He watches Aiden like he's trying to find the angle.

"Tell me, Mr. Gage, how are you finding London? Bit different from the muddy fields of Northwood Dale, I imagine."

Aiden grins. "Oh, you know, Carter, mud's all the same when you're standing in it long enough."

I turn my face slightly to hide my smirk.

Something in my father's jaw flexes as he fidgets with his cufflinks.

Checkmate, Dad.

"Well," he finally says, "I hope you'll enjoy yourself tonight. Try not to embarrass my daughter."

The implication is clear. Don't fuck this up.
Aiden doesn't blink. "Oh, don't worry. I plan on being unforgettable."
My father stares him down a moment longer, then downs the rest of his scotch and walks away.
I let out a slow breath.
Aiden turns to me, expression annoyingly smug. "Think I'm growing on him?"
"Like a parasite," I mutter, scanning the room.
The usual faces are here.
The Kensington's. The Rutherford's. The Mont crofts.
All well-bred, old-money aristocrats who only tolerate each other because of mutual investments and exclusive ski resorts.
Aiden follows my gaze. "Alright, Trouble. Give me the rundown."
I smirk. "You just want ammo, don't you?"
His dimples flash. "I'm here to cause chaos. Educate me."
So I do.
I tell him about Miles Kensington, my charming yet degenerate ex, currently chatting up a socialite's wife across the room.
About Daniel Rutherford, who once got so drunk at Ascot, he pissed himself in front of the Queen.
About Sophia Montcroft, who "studied abroad" for a year but was actually in Switzerland getting a nose job, among other rejuvenating surgeries.
Aiden listens intently, his eyes flickering with amusement.

"Jesus," he mutters, shaking his head. "I take it back. This isn't *Succession*—this is a fucking soap opera."

I clink my glass against his. "Welcome to the circus, Gage."

He smirks. "Let's burn it down, shall we?"

I had thought, no, I had known, that bringing Aiden to this event was going to be an unmitigated disaster.

I had prepared myself for cringing through every interaction, for holding my breath every time he opened his mouth, for the smirks and whispers and the carefully veiled insults.

I had not prepared for him to thrive.

And it's throwing me completely off my game.

We move through the lavish ballroom, and I introduce him to faces I've known my whole life, people who sneer at anything they deem lesser. They take one look at Aiden, his casual demeanour, his easy smirk, his very presence, and they assume they have the upper hand.

They are sorely mistaken.

First: Miles Kensington.

The slimy bastard is exactly where I expected him to be, loitering near the bar, charming the hell out of a banker's wife. His hair is a little too perfect, his suit a little too tailored, his expression that exact mix of arrogance and sleaze that I have spent years avoiding.

He turns when he sees me, grinning like the devil himself.

"Well, well, well," he drawls, "Alexis Whitehorn, gracing us with her presence."
I resist the urge to gag at the sound of my full name. Miles' sharp gaze slides to Aiden, eyes flicking from his broad shoulders to his slightly messed up hair, assessing, calculating.
"You must be the pig farmer," he smirks, swirling the amber liquid in his glass.
Aiden's grin is unbothered. "And you must be the poor sod who lost her."
Miles stiffens.
I blink.
*Holy shit.*
Aiden claps him on the back, all false camaraderie, his voice mockingly sympathetic. "Tough break, mate. But don't beat yourself up, I'm sure it wasn't the coke addiction that did it."
Miles' nostrils flare.
I bite the inside of my cheek so hard I nearly draw blood.
Next: Daniel Rutherford.
The man is already three drinks deep, sloshing his whiskey slightly as he gestures wildly to some unsuspecting investor.
Aiden leans in, whispering, "That's the guy who pissed himself in front of the Queen?"
I nod.
Aiden grins and rubs his hands together. "Right."
We approach, and Daniel turns, eyes bloodshot but still laced with the usual superiority complex.
He sneers at Aiden. "And you are?"

Aiden extends a hand, cheerful and disarming. "Aiden Gage. Alex's fiancé. Heard you're quite the man of legend."

Daniel preens, delighted. "Ah, yes, my reputation tends to precede me."

Aiden smirks, taking a sip of his champagne. "I mean, not everyone can say they left such a lasting impression on the monarchy."

Daniel freezes.

Aiden keeps a completely straight face.

I nearly choke on my drink.

Finally: Sophia Montcroft.

She's standing with a group of other well-manicured women, all adorned in glistening jewellery and judgement. Her nose is suspiciously perfect, her smile polite but predatory.

She eyes Aiden like he's something she's thinking about purchasing.

"And what is it that you do, Mr. Gage?"

Aiden grins, tilting his head slightly. "Oh, a bit of this, a bit of that. Farming mostly."

Sophia giggles, flicking her hair over her shoulder. "How… quaint."

Aiden smiles wider. "Oh, but enough about me. Tell me, what was it like studying abroad? Changed your life, among other things, I would imagine?"

Her expression stiffens ever so slightly.

I swear I see a vein twitch in her temple.

I grab Aiden's arm and steer him away before I lose my composure entirely.

He is having far too much fun.

I weave through the ballroom, dodging more elitist nonsense, and I realise something...
I'm actually impressed.
Aiden is doing alarmingly well.
I watch him from across the room, champagne flute in hand, fingers absently running over the delicate stem. I had expected, no, I had prepared, for his inevitable slip-up. The moment when the sheer weight of the room pressed down on him, when the polished veneers of these people would become too much. When he'd say the wrong thing to the wrong person, and the sharks would smell blood in the water. The wolves would descend.
Except... he doesn't say the wrong thing.
He's charming. Disarmingly so. He listens, really listens, his sharp green eyes locked onto whoever is speaking, nodding in the right places, asking just the right questions. And when he speaks, it's not the bumbling, out-of-place country boy that my father had predicted. It's not the brash, reckless man who threw punches in the street only days ago.
No, this version of Aiden is sharp. Calculated. A tactician in a borrowed suit.
He's got Lord Everett practically belly-laughing over some joke that I didn't catch. Christ. Everett doesn't laugh. He smirks at best. But here he is, nearly spilling his overpriced scotch, clapping Aiden on the back like they're old friends.
To my left, Mrs. Gainsborough, who I had last seen openly weeping at a charity event because the caviar wasn't the right grade, leans into her husband and murmurs, "I quite like him."

Samantha Todd

Like him?
Like him?
My father's associates don't *like* people.
They *tolerate* them for the sake of business. They manipulate them. They network and barter and negotiate their way into stronger alliances. And yet here they are, genuinely taken with Aiden Gage of all people.
I take a sip of my champagne to mask my surprise. But my father has noticed it too.
I catch Carter Whitehorn watching from the far side of the room, his lips pressed into a thin line. His hand swirls his glass absently, though I know his mind is turning a mile a minute. He wasn't expecting this. He had been hoping for Aiden to fail. To prove that he didn't belong.
But Aiden is proving him wrong.
Again.
And I can see that it's *infuriating* him.
I smirk into my drink.
There's something unnerving about watching Aiden seamlessly slip into this world. He's supposed to be the outsider. The rough-around-the-edges farm boy with dirt under his nails and no time for politics. But here? He fits, somehow. Not in the polished, effortless way that the others do, but in a way that demands respect.
He doesn't pander or preen.
He's just... *Aiden*.
And I think that might be the secret.
I force myself to look away as he finishes some story about the village pub, and Lord Everett wipes tears

of laughter from his eyes. He pats him on the back as he begins walking over to me. But as I turn, feigning indifference, I meet a pair of familiar, dark eyes across the room.

Miles Kensington.

Shit.

His lips curl into a knowing smirk, his expression all amusement and condescension. The same as it always was. He tilts his glass toward me in mock salute before taking a sip, never breaking eye contact.

A cold, familiar dread creeps up my spine.

Aiden was holding his own in this room of sharks. But this?

We barely make it to the other side of the room when my father intercepts us. His face is unreadable, his scotch still untouched in his glass.

"You seem to be making quite the impression," he says, his tone dripping with disdain.

Aiden beams. "It's a gift."

My father studies him for a long moment, then downs the rest of his drink in one swift motion.

"I'm hosting a dinner next weekend at my home. A select few business partners and other important people. I expect to see you there."

I freeze.

Aiden doesn't know what this means. But I do.

My father isn't just inviting him. He's testing him.

Again.

To Aiden, it sounds like just another event.

To me, I know it means that this Gala was merely the warmup. The real test is yet to come.

Aiden, clueless and cocky, grins. "Wouldn't miss it for the world, mate."

My father smiles coldly, and it feels like a warning.

And then, just like that, he walks away.

The tension lingers long after he's gone.

Aiden turns to me, looking entirely unbothered.

"So… how bad did I fuck up just now?"

I sigh. "You have no idea."

I down the rest of my champagne and grab his arm, steering us towards the exit.

"We're leaving."

Aiden grins. "God, I thought you'd never ask."

As we step outside into the cool London air, he slides his hand around my waist once more, smug as hell.

"Be honest," he murmurs. "You're a little bit proud of me, aren't you?"

I roll my eyes. "You're tolerable at best."

His laughter echoes down the street as we disappear into the city, heading towards the nearest dive bar.

# Chapter 23

Aiden

This is more like it.

The low hum of music, the clinking of glasses, the comforting dimness of the bar, it's all a stark contrast to the gala. No pretence here, no overpriced champagne or people eyeing me like I'm an experiment gone wrong. Just normal people, having normal conversations, drinking normal drinks.

And Alex.

She sits across from me, her black gown looking entirely out of place in a bar like this, but somehow, she still looks like she belongs. Or maybe I just want her to.

Her hair is looser now, a few stray tendrils falling from the intricate updo she spent too long perfecting earlier. The stiff posture she held all night has melted away, replaced by something softer, something... *relaxed*.

I like her like this.

Less Ice Queen, more just... Alex.

She takes a sip of her whiskey and coke, then sets the glass down with a clumsy little *thunk*, blinking at it like she hadn't meant to drop it so hard. I bite back a grin.

"Getting a little tipsy there, Trouble?"

She narrows her eyes, sitting up straighter, trying to regain some composure. "I— I'm *perfectly* in control, Gage."

Except she trips over the last word slightly, and my grin breaks free.

"Oh yeah?" I lean in, elbows on the table. "Say 'perfectly in control' five times fast."

She rolls her eyes. "I am not playing this game."

"You can't." I smirk. "Because you're tipsy."

She huffs, taking another sip. "You're insufferable."

"And yet, here we are."

That earns me a *look*, but I can tell she's fighting off a smile. She stirs the ice in her glass absentmindedly, gaze flicking to me as if she's studying me.

"You did well tonight," she says finally, and there's no teasing in her tone. Just something quiet. Thoughtful.

I cock a brow. "I know."

She groans, tossing her head back. "God, you're unbearable."

I chuckle, taking a slow sip of my drink. "You're the one who dragged me into this world of suits and overpriced scotch, sweetheart. You don't get to complain when I excel."

She mutters something under her breath that I don't quite catch but sounds suspiciously like *cocky bastard*.

I lean back in my seat, watching her, letting the moment settle between us. She's still holding herself together, still *composed*, but there's a warmth in her now. The sharp, biting edges are dulling.

I tilt my head. "You seem more comfortable here."

She swirls the ice in her drink, considering. "What, then at a place where everyone is calculating their next power move and waiting for someone to fail? Gee, I wonder why."

I smirk. "So, what I'm hearing is, you're a secret dive bar girl."

She scoffs. "Don't push it, Gage."

But I see the way she settles deeper into her chair, like she's finally letting herself breathe.

She's beautiful like this.

Carefree, uninhibited, slightly flushed from the whiskey.

She catches me staring and raises a brow. "What?"

I shake my head, taking another sip. "Just thinking."

She hums, resting her chin on her hand, elbow propped on the table. "About what?"

"Just... trying to figure you out."

She smirks, tilting her head. "And?"

I exhale through my nose. "I don't think I ever will."

Something flickers across her face, something unreadable. But then she smirks. "Good."

The conversation flows easily after that.

We talk about everything and nothing. How bad the music in here is, the worst first dates we've ever been on, how Tugsy once got chased across the village by an angry swan and has never lived it down. Alex laughs, really laughs, when I mimic his terrified shriek, and it does something funny to my chest.

By the time we're halfway through our second round of drinks, she's laughing more freely, her walls lowered enough that I can see glimpses of the girl she could be when she's not constantly fighting to prove something.

And fuck me, she's adorable when she's drunk.

"You have dimples," she says suddenly, pointing at my face.

I blink. "Uh. Yeah?"

She squints at me like she's just made a groundbreaking discovery. "Why have I never noticed that before?"

I smirk. "Probably too busy hating me."

She hums, pursing her lips. "That does sound like me."

She takes another sip of her whiskey and coke, but misjudges the angle, nearly missing her mouth. She frowns at the glass like it personally betrayed her.

I shake my head, biting back a grin. "How many of those have you had, Trouble?"

She sets the glass down with extreme precision, like she's trying to prove a point. "Not enough to be drunk."

I tilt my head. "Uh-huh. So, you're just naturally this uncoordinated?"

She scowls, but the effect is ruined when she hiccups. She slaps a hand over her mouth, eyes wide.

I chuckle. "I stand corrected."

Her eyes narrow, and then, without warning, she leans in, her elbow resting on the sticky bar top, her chin propped in her hand. "You know," she says, voice slow and considering, "I think I like you better when I've had a few drinks."

I raise a brow. "Oh yeah?"

She nods solemnly. "Mmhmm. You're... less annoying."

I grin. "And you're more honest."

Her eyes flick over my face, slow and lazy, lingering just a little too long on my mouth. She tilts her head. "Your jaw is really sharp. Like, offensively sharp."

I huff a laugh. "Offensively sharp?"

"Yes," she says, waving a hand, almost knocking over her glass. I steady it before she can. "Like, it should come with a warning. 'Beware: May cause intrusive thoughts.'"

I raise both brows, smirking. "Intrusive thoughts?"

She exhales dramatically, falling back against the stool. "Forget I said anything."

"Oh no." I lean in slightly, my voice dropping just enough to make her blink. "By all means, continue. I'd love to hear about these... thoughts of yours."

Her cheeks flush, whether from the alcohol or the conversation, I'm not sure, but she shakes her head. "Not happening, Gage."

I shrug, feigning indifference. "Shame. You had me curious."

She mutters something under her breath, but before I can ask, she straightens, pointing a finger at me again. "Anyway, back to the dimples."

I grin. "What about them?"

Her eyes drop to my mouth again, then flick back up. "They make you look... dangerous."

I blink, thrown for a second. "That's not usually how dimples work."

She frowns, as if she's genuinely trying to puzzle it out. Then she waves her hand again. "No, but, like... it's the contrast. All cocky and gruff and then Bam! Dimples! It's disarming."

I chuckle, shaking my head. "You're a real lightweight, aren't you?"

She hums, propping her chin in her hand again. "Maybe. Or maybe I just feel... good right now."

Her voice dips slightly, a little softer, a little slower. I watch her, my smirk fading just a fraction.

She exhales, looking down at the ice melting in her glass. "No pressure. No expectations. Just... this."

I don't say anything for a moment, just study her. She's relaxed in a way I've never seen before. Her guard is down, her shoulders loose. She's here, in this moment, with me. Not planning her next move, not calculating the next battle she has to fight.

Just here.

It does something to me.

"So, what you're saying," I finally say, keeping my voice light, "is that I should just keep you in a constant state of tipsy so you'll tolerate me?"

She laughs, tilting her head, eyes sparkling. "Wouldn't be the worst idea."

Her knee brushes mine under the bar. Neither of us move away.

I glance at her half-finished drink. "You done?"

She makes a face. "One more sip."

I watch as she takes it, then promptly shudders.

I smirk. "That bad?"

She groans, setting the glass down with finality. "I think I need food. Greasy food. Fried food." She pokes my arm. "Feed me, Gage."

I chuckle, pushing off the stool. "Come on then, Trouble. Let's get you something before you start waxing poetic about my bone structure again."

She rolls her eyes, wobbling slightly as she stands. I catch her elbow, steadying her.

Her breath hitches just slightly.

For a second, just a second, she looks at me like she's really seeing me.

Then she shakes her head, mumbling, "Let's go before I change my mind."

I grin, leading her out into the London night, the warmth of her lingering against my palm.

# Chapter 24

Alex

The first thing I register is warmth.
The kind of warmth that isn't just from a blanket, but from something solid, something alive.
The second thing I register is weight. A heavy, steady pressure draped across my waist.
The third thing I register...
*Oh, fuck.*
My eyes snap open, and for one horrifying second, I don't breathe.
Aiden's arm is wrapped around me.
His very muscular, very heavy arm.
And I'm in bed. With him.
Panic spikes through my chest, my breath hitching as I slowly, very slowly, tilt my head to look at him. He's still asleep, his broad chest rising and falling with slow, even breaths, his face relaxed in the kind of peace I imagine he never lets himself have when he's awake.
He looks... good like this. Soft.
But that's beside the point.
The point is, I have no idea how the fuck I got here.
A careful glance down confirms that I'm still in my polka dot pyjamas. That's something. Aiden, too, is fully clothed, his t-shirt rumpled, his jeans slightly

unbuttoned like he had been about to change and then never finished.
Okay. So, no naked disasters.
That's good.
Still, I need to get out of here.
With painstaking precision, I begin to lift his arm, sliding out from under it inch by inch until I'm free. He shifts slightly but doesn't wake, mumbling something unintelligible under his breath before turning onto his back.
I hold my breath until I'm safely in the bathroom.
I grip the edges of the sink, staring at my reflection in the mirror.
My hair is a mess, my eyeliner smudged, my lips slightly swollen, probably from a combination of dehydration and pressing my face into a pillow all night.
I groan, squeezing my eyes shut.
"What the fuck, Alex?" I whisper to myself.
I try to retrace the events of last night. The bar. The drinks. The laughing. The way we got comfortable. The way my stomach had fluttered when he looked at me a certain way, like we were actually becoming friends.
But then what?
I press the heels of my palms into my eyes.
I don't do this. I don't wake up in bed with men. Even if, technically, nothing happened.
Still gripping the sink, I force myself to take a slow, steady breath. Then another. It's fine. It's nothing. Just a little too much whiskey and a moment of weakness.

Samantha Todd

I blink at myself.
God, I look like hell.
Without thinking, I grab my makeup wipes, scrubbing away the smudged mascara beneath my eyes, then reach for my lip balm, swiping a layer over my lips. It's only when I pause, hand halfway to my hairbrush, that I realise what I'm doing.
I freeze.
I'm tidying myself up.
Why?
Aiden doesn't care how I look. I don't care how I look in front of Aiden. I've spent the last few weeks making sure he knows I don't give a single fuck about his opinion of me.
So why does the thought of walking back out there with my hair looking like I've been electrocuted and my face an absolute disaster suddenly make me feel vulnerable?
I exhale sharply, shaking myself.
This means nothing.
I don't care if Aiden sees me like this.
Still, I grab the brush, pulling it through my hair a few times before throwing it back onto the counter like it personally offended me. I quickly run some toothpaste over my teeth to avoid morning breath and with my chin lifted and my dignity firmly reinstalled, I march out of the bathroom.
Time to go and face the inevitable.
When I return to the bedroom, Aiden is awake.
He's sitting up, lazily propped against the headboard, arms stretched above his head in a way that does far too much justice to his biceps. His t-

shirt rides up slightly, revealing a sliver of tanned skin.

I quickly look away.

"Morning, Trouble," he drawls, voice thick with sleep. "You look like you've seen a ghost."

I fold my arms, ignoring the way my stomach flips at the roughness in his tone. "What the fuck happened last night?"

Aiden smirks, rubbing a hand over his face before stretching again. "You tell me."

"I don't know," I snap. "That's why I'm asking you."

He exhales a chuckle, clearly enjoying my panic far too much.

"Well," he says, tilting his head, "you got *very* drunk. And then you insisted—insisted—that you weren't scared after watching *The Ring*, but about five minutes later, you started clutching my arm like I was the only thing standing between you and eternal damnation."

I glare.

He grins.

"And then you may or may not have begged me..."

"I did not beg."

"Oh, you definitely begged," he says, smirking. "Practically whimpered, really. Told me you *couldn't possibly* sleep alone because the scary movie demons might crawl out of your TV and take you."

I stare at him, horrified. "You're making this up."

Aiden holds up a hand. "Scout's honour."

I pinch the bridge of my nose.

He leans forward, his voice softer now, teasing but not unkind. "Relax, Trouble. Nothing happened. I

tucked you in, you held onto me like a barnacle for the first ten minutes, then you rolled over and passed out. That's it."
I let out a breath I didn't realise I was holding.
Aiden watches me closely. Then, too quietly, he says, "Would it have been so bad if something had happened?"
My head snaps up.
His eyes flick over my face, something unreadable in them.
My throat goes dry.
"I...I just mean," I stumble, "it's good to know that I wasn't stupid enough to..."
"To what?" he challenges, a slow, knowing smirk pulling at the corner of his mouth.
I scowl. "Never mind."
He leans back against the pillows, arms behind his head, looking for all the world like he's the most relaxed man on earth. "Just say the word, Trouble. If you want something to happen..." He winks.
"Absolutely not," I snap, marching toward the door.
He laughs as I storm out, but I swear, as I close the door behind me, I hear him murmur...
"We'll see about that."

The scent of freshly brewed coffee fills the kitchen, rich and inviting, curling through the air like an unspoken truce. Aiden leans against the counter, arms crossed, watching as I push the plunger down on the French press.

He smirks. "You know, Trouble, I think this is the longest I've ever seen you in a kitchen without looking completely lost."

I arch a brow, pouring the coffee into two mugs. "Well, I had to learn how to make coffee since the person who usually does it in this apartment was apparently raised in a barn."

He snorts, reaching for the mug I slide toward him. "Joke's on you, I was. And my coffee's phenomenal."

I roll my eyes, taking a slow sip of mine. He watches me over the rim of his mug, and for once, his expression is almost serious.

"So." He sets his coffee down. "Seeing as I have a couple of weeks off and Edith is forcing us to 'soak up the London experience,' what's the plan?"

I exhale dramatically. "Well, there's plenty to do. Art galleries, theatres, museums…"

"Christ, could you sound any posher?"

I glare at him over my mug. "Fine. What do you want to do?"

His smirk is pure mischief. "You're the guide, Trouble. Show me your city."

And somehow, between his teasing and my reluctant amusement, it's decided. We're spending the day together. Voluntarily.

God help me.

The Tower of London is packed with tourists, all herded together like medieval cattle, eyes wide with historical fascination. Aiden has been smirking since we arrived, occasionally shooting me a look that I already know means trouble.

"So let me get this straight." He walks beside me, hands shoved in his pockets, his boots sounding far too casual against the ancient stone pathway. "King Henry gets bored, chops off his wife's head, and still has to deal with her ghost hanging around? Now that's some karma."

I sigh, exasperated. "Yes, Aiden, Anne Boleyn is famously one of the Tower's most notorious ghosts."

He grins. "And do people see her headless or...?"

"Honestly, I hope she's headless. I hope she bloody terrified him! Seems like the least he deserves after putting her through all that bullshit."

He chuckles. "Didn't peg you for a feminist history buff."

"Didn't peg you for someone who actually listens."

His smirk deepens, but he says nothing. Instead, he lets his gaze drift to the Beefeaters giving their usual tour to a group of wide-eyed American tourists.

"Alright, I have to ask," he says, rubbing his chin like he's actually contemplating something important.

"How much do they get paid to wear those ridiculous hats?"

I let out a short laugh. "Probably not enough."

"Do you think I'd suit one?"

"Absolutely not."

We banter all the way through the Tower grounds, lingering by Traitor's Gate, arguing about whether or not we'd survive in medieval times (I would, obviously), and wandering into the gift shop, where the real trouble begins.

The gift shop is small and overcrowded, crammed with history books, novelty mugs, and a questionable amount of bejewelled crown replicas. The air smells of aged paper and overpriced souvenirs, and I'm thumbing through a book on Henry VIII's wives when Aiden appears beside me, holding up a keychain with a tiny axe.

"Souvenir?" He grins, flipping it between his fingers with ease. "Figured it suits your general energy."

I snatch it from him, ignoring the way his fingers brush against mine. Warm. Rough. Too much.

"You're hilarious."

"I really am."

I roll my eyes, about to say something undoubtedly cutting, when suddenly, a woman with a huge backpack barrels past, jostling me hard, straight into Aiden.

His hands come up fast, gripping my arms to steady me, his fingers pressing into my skin, solid and unyielding. My own hands land against his chest, the heat of him bleeding through his shirt, and just like that, the entire world narrows to this.

This single moment.

The gift shop fades away. The bustle of tourists, the clinking of trinkets, the hum of voices, it all dissolves into nothing.

Aiden doesn't move.

Neither do I.

I feel the rise and fall of his chest beneath my palms, steady but slightly uneven, like maybe I'm affecting him, too. His grip on my arms tightens, not rough, but firm enough that I can feel the callouses on his fingertips.

And when I finally lift my gaze to his, I find his smirk is gone.

His expression is different now, unreadable, intense. There's something flickering behind his eyes, something deep and electric, and my breath catches, my pulse stumbling over itself.

I should move. We should move.

But neither of us does.

His eyes flicker down to my lips, just for a second, just long enough to make my stomach flip, to make my skin prickle with awareness. And then, his hand moves. Slowly. Deliberately.

He reaches up, brushing a strand of hair behind my ear, his knuckles ghosting against my cheek as he does. A barely-there touch. A whisper of contact.

I stop breathing entirely.

His fingers linger, just for a second, before he lets his hand drop.

And then, as if some invisible thread has snapped, we both pull back at the same time.

Aiden clears his throat, rubbing the back of his neck, that cocky mask snapping back into place. "Jesus, Trouble. Try not to fall for me in a public place."

I scoff, shoving him lightly, pretending my entire body isn't on fire. "You wish."

But the comeback doesn't land quite right. My voice isn't as sharp as it should be. And Aiden?

He knows it.

I see it in the way his smirk lingers, in the way his gaze drags over me for half a second too long. In the

way his hand almost brushes the small of my back before he shoves it in his pocket instead.
The moment?
It was nothing.
I tell myself that again and again as we walk through the Tower grounds.
I tell myself that as Aiden resumes his relentless teasing, as I roll my eyes and fire back.
I tell myself that as we leave, as he throws an arm over my shoulder like we've always done this, like it's the easiest thing in the world.
I tell myself that as my heart thuds just a little too hard.
And I tell myself that, if I repeat it enough times, maybe it'll actually be true.
Maybe.

# Chapter 25

Aiden

Ethan:
How's my favourite future sister-in-law?

Aiden:
Piss off.

Ethan:
That good huh?

Aiden:
She's taking her sweet time getting ready. Pretty sure she's in there trying to figure out ways to kill me and make it look like an accident.

Ethan:
You do have that effect on people...

Aiden:
That's funny. You should do stand up.

Ethan:
Seriously though, how's it going?

Aiden:
Well, I haven't been castrated yet, so that's something.

Ethan:
Good to hear. What's she like when she's not trying to rip your head off?

Aiden:
Still trying to figure that out. But she's... interesting.

Ethan:
You like her.

Aiden:
Did you miss the part where this is FAKE?!

Ethan:
Sure. But I know you, Aid. And I know you're full of shit.

Aiden:
Go be engaged and stop bothering me.

Ethan:
Go be fake engaged and stop lying to yourself.

I launch the phone onto the sofa, scowling, right as Alex steps into the room.
She's... casual.
Her hair falls in soft waves around her shoulders, her jumper slipping just slightly off one. A hint of

collarbone, just enough to be distracting. Dark jeans hug her frame, stylish but not forced.
She doesn't look like the sharp, untouchable ice-queen I first met. She looks...
*Soft.*
And that's far more dangerous.
"You good, Gage?" she asks, arching a brow as she grabs her bag.
I clear my throat, pulling myself together. "You mean now that I've finished ageing a decade waiting for you?"
She smirks. "You survived. Barely."
She brushes past me, and I follow after her. Her soft footfalls from her casual sneakers squeaking slightly on the polished wooden floor.
I'm so screwed.

The second we step inside, I know I don't belong here.
It's the kind of place where the napkins are folded into weird little shapes, and the waiters wear those fancy white jackets that make them look like they should be sailing a yacht instead of serving pasta. There's soft jazz playing in the background, all smooth saxophones and slow piano, and the whole place smells like roasted garlic and expensive wine. The tables are dressed in crisp white linen, each flickering with candlelight, and the air is thick with the kind of quiet conversations that come with *old money*.
It's nice, I guess.
Just... not *me*.

Raising the Gage

Alex, though?

She fits in seamlessly.

She's cool and composed, sweeping through the room like she owns the place, her casual loose clothing still somehow hugging her curves just right. She's been here before, I can tell. The kind of girl who grew up in places like this, who knows which fork to use, who probably had a favourite Italian restaurant before she even had a favourite Disney movie.

I feel like a goddamn ox in by comparison.

Still, I pull out her chair like the gentleman I actually am and slide into the seat across from her, draping my jacket over the back of my chair as the waiter immediately appears with the kind of energy that suggests he *knows* he's getting a big tip.

He rattles off the specials in rapid, accented English, and I have to fight the urge to laugh when I see Alex's eyebrows raise slightly at the mention of *truffle-infused risotto with saffron foam*.

"Sounds delightful," she says, deadpan, closing the menu.

She's fucking with me.

I can tell.

I smirk, propping an elbow on the table. "Getting the foam, are you?"

She sips her water, eyes glinting. "I enjoy a bit of decadence in my meals, Gage."

The way she says 'decadence' makes something twist in my gut.

I roll my lips together and glance back at the menu. "Well, I'd hate to cheapen the experience." I slap the menu shut and shoot the waiter a grin. "I'll have the same."

Alex's lips twitch.

Round one goes to me.

We start with safe topics.

Alex asks about the farm, which I'm pretty sure she couldn't give less of a shit about, but she listens anyway. I tell her about the pigs, the cattle, about the way the seasons change the work, about how my dad could run the place with his eyes closed but still keeps meticulous records, probably just for the hell of it.

She nods, swirling the wine in her glass. Then she asks, "Is that what you want to do forever?"

The question throws me for a second.

Because yeah. The farm is my life.

But forever?

I take a slow sip of whiskey before answering. "I don't know. Maybe not just that."

Her head tilts slightly. "What else?"

I could brush it off. Make a joke.

But I don't.

Instead, I lean back in my chair, running a hand along my jaw. "Well, there's my furniture."

That gets her attention.

"Go on..."

"Well," I lean forward, resting my arms on the table, "I'd offer to show you my workshop, Trouble, but I think I'd have to actually like you for that."

Her lips quirk. "Good thing I'm irresistible, then."

I laugh. "Right. That's what I was thinking."

For a second, there's something else there.

Something not sharp and teasing. Just easy.
Then the food arrives, and the moment passes.

Dinner is good.
Too good.
The kind of meal that makes you want to lean back and groan in satisfaction, but I resist because, you know, manners.
We settle the bill and step out onto the quiet London street. The air is cool, fresh, the rain-slick pavement reflecting the glow of streetlights.
Alex walks beside me, tipsy off wine, her sneakers shuffling against the sidewalk.
She looks… relaxed. A little loose around the edges.
And I like it.
I like her like this. The sharpness dulled just enough. The tension unwound just a little.
"You okay there, Trouble?" I ask, sliding my hands into my pockets.
She exhales, giving me a sideways glance. "I am *so* full."
"Tell me about it," I chuckle. "You know, for someone so tiny, you really put it away."
She glares. "I savoured it."
I smirk. "Sure."
She nudges me with her elbow, and I don't think she realises it, but she's walking closer now.
And I don't move away.
I should.
I should create some space.
But I don't.

Samantha Todd

When we stop outside her apartment building, she turns toward me, still looking softer than usual, still loose from wine and candlelight and a damn good meal.
And then she just... looks at me. Not with her usual irritation. Not with that challenging glare she throws my way. Just... looks. Her gaze flicks to my mouth.
It's quick. Barely there. But I see it.
And just like that, I stop breathing.
Fuck.
This is a mistake.
A massive fucking mistake.
But I want to.
For the first time in a long time, I actually want to close the space between us. I don't know what possesses me, but I feel my feet moving, closing the gap. Close enough to see the delicate line of her collarbone, the way her breath catches slightly at my proximity.
I could kiss her. If this were any other 'date' I most definitely would, then I'd make some clever excuse to get upstairs and hear her soft moans breathing against my ear. I could just lean in.
She sways slightly, knocked off balance by the wine and I reach out, my hands settling on her waist, steadying her.
"Easy, Trouble" I murmur.
"Why do you always call me that?"
The question flickers between us, a match tossed into a room full of petrol.
I should answer quickly. Keep it light. A joke, a quip, something to diffuse the sudden charge in the air.

But I don't.
Instead, I lean in.
Not much, just enough that I can feel the warmth of her breath, enough that her scent, vanilla and coconut, mixed with something that's just her, fills my head.
"Because you are."
Her lips part slightly, her eyes locked on mine.
"You strut into my life with your smart mouth and your sharp edges, acting like you're too good for all of this, too good for me," I smirk, fingers flexing against the fabric of her sweater, "but you keep showing up, don't you? And every damn time, I can't seem to walk away."
She exhales, barely, the faintest brush of air against my lips.
The gap between us is tiny now.
The kind of distance that could be closed with a breath, a shift, a surrender.
I see it in her eyes. The war happening inside her. The fight between common sense and desire.
And for once, she isn't pushing me away.
For once, she isn't rolling her eyes or cutting me down with some perfect one-liner. She's just there, still, waiting, watching. And I swear to God, I'm about to kiss her.
I'm about to ruin everything.
Then...
The sharp chime of her phone slices through the moment like a goddamn blade.
Alex gasps, stumbling back a step, like the universe itself just slapped some fucking sense into her.

My hands drop from her waist instantly, and I drag in a slow, deep breath, shoving them into my pockets to keep from reaching for her again.

She fumbles for her phone, blinking rapidly, her fingers shaking just slightly as she stares down at the screen.

Aunt Edith.

Of course it's Aunt Edith.

She clears her throat, straightens, grips the phone a little too tightly. "I... I should take this."

I nod, jaw tight, heart still pounding. "Yeah. Yeah, you should."

She turns away, pressing the phone to her ear, voice slightly breathless as she answers.

And I just stand there, staring at the pavement, breathing.

Jesus Christ.

I need another fucking drink.

Or maybe just a brick to the face.

Later, when I'm sprawled out on the ridiculously soft couch, staring at the ceiling, I tell myself it was just the moment.

Just the wine, just the setting.

Just the fact that Alex is the most frustrating, infuriating, impossible, beautiful woman I've ever met.

Our back and forth, the biting wit and endless sarcasm. Is it all just a front or is it real? Sometimes she softens just enough that I can see the actual edges of her, the cracks in her ice-queen exterior, but then, just as quickly as it appears, she shuts it

down. Slicing through the moment with some cutting remark. But this time? She didn't do that. She didn't pull away. She didn't make an excuse or a snide retort. This time, when she looked at me like that, it was like she wanted me to kiss her...
Yeah.
I'm completely and utterly fucked.

# Chapter 26

Alex

I toss my phone onto the nightstand, exhaling sharply.

Aunt Edith had been her usual self, rambling on about how the moon was in some particularly amorous phase and how the energies around me were shifting. I'd brushed her off, but the worst part? She wasn't wrong.

I sit at the edge of the bed, staring at the door. The apartment is silent now. The hum of the city outside is faint, muffled by the thick glass windows.

But all I can hear is my own heartbeat.

Too loud. Too erratic. Too fucking stupid.

I run a hand through my hair, groaning. What the hell was that?

The way Aiden had looked at me tonight, the way his fingers had curled into the fabric of my sweater, the heat in his voice when he called me Trouble.

I swallow.

It was just the wine.

Just the moonlight.

Just the moment.

It doesn't mean anything.

And yet…

I look at the bed. At the expanse of soft, expensive cream-coloured sheets. At the empty space beside me. I hate how empty it feels.

It's not like I want Aiden in my bed. That would be...

I shake my head quickly, shutting that thought down before it can form fully.

But the living room isn't far.

Just a few steps, and I could see him. Just... talk. Maybe pick up where we left off, maybe...

No.

*Absolutely not.*

This is a fake arrangement. An act.

Aiden doesn't like me like that. Sure, he flirts, relentlessly, but that's just who he is. He likes the game, the push and pull, the banter. He likes getting under my skin.

And maybe, for a second, he thought about kissing me. But that was just the moment.

The lingering effects of the Gala.

The candlelight and drinks at dinner.

The fact we've been spending so much time together.

Nothing more.

Right?

I chew on my lip, folding one arm over my stomach and extending the other across the vacant space beside me. Running my hand over the ridiculously expensive sheets.

The smart thing to do is stay in this bed.

I should just go to sleep and forget that anything happened. Forget all about Aiden Gage and his irritatingly alluring personality. Forget about the way

Samantha Todd

his smile is slightly crooked when he finds something genuinely funny, usually something at my expense. Forget the way my stomach felt like a million butterflies had been let loose when he looked at me tonight. Just forget him.
But instead, I stand.
I don't know what I'm doing. My body moves before my brain can catch up. Before I can think better of it.
I reach for the door handle, grip it.
Breathe in. Breathe out.
I could go out there.
Just to talk. Just to…
No.
I let go of the handle like it burns, turning away sharply and throwing myself back into bed.
I roll onto my stomach, groaning into the pillow.
I hate this.
I hate that I'm thinking about him at all.
But I especially hate that I can still feel his hands on me.
His warmth against my chest.
The way his voice dipped low, gravelly, when he said, "Because you are."
I squeeze my eyes shut.
Tomorrow.
Tomorrow this will all be a distant memory.
Because it has to be.
But tonight? I could take care of this. I could rid myself of this aching need to be touched. I don't need a man to satisfy me, I never have. And honestly, with the men I've been with, if I left it up to them, I'd never have an orgasm ever.

I glide my hand down my front, over the delicate curve of my stomach and find the waistband of my pyjamas.

Listening out for any movement outside the door, I pull my pyjama bottoms down and spread my legs. If I'm going to do this, if I'm going to make myself come to thoughts of Aiden Gage, I'm going to take my damn time and enjoy it. Because it'll be the only time that me coming and Aiden Gage fall in the same moment.

Gently I slide my fingers up my lips, finding the soft opening already so wet and warm. My fingers dance over my swollen clit as I let out a shaky breath. But it's not enough.

I need more.

I need someone else's touch.

I need him.

I imagine it's not my fingertips running small circles around my clit, but his. His large, slightly rough hands gently teasing me. His face burrowed into my neck as he whispers filthy things. Things that would make me blush in the cold light of day, but things I need to hear brush against my ear while his fingers slide inside me.

First one.

Then two.

His body pressed over the top of me, pushing me deeper into the soft mattress as his thumb finds my clit again, caressing it with the practiced ease I know he has.

I feel the swell of it low in my core, building, as his words intensify. *"So fucking wet for me, Trouble."*

That deep voice dancing over my skin, igniting my blood. One hand slides up under my top and finds my breast, my nipple already hard.
*"Come for me Alex"* I imagine his words and can practically feel them against my ear, as I work my clit harder and faster, imagining how hard his cock would be pressed up against me. Imagining how much he would want to slide inside me, how much he would be holding back, how much he would want to taste me.
Oh god, the thought of him down there, his tongue sliding over my wet slit, flicking against my clit, his soft murmurs against my most sensitive place.
His fingers plunging in and out of me as his tongue runs circles around that bundle of nerves. Then his eyes catch mine and that's it.
I'm done for.
Pleasure crashes through me, white-hot and all-consuming, stealing the breath from my lungs as I bury my face in the pillow to muffle my cry.
I ride it out, body trembling, waves of heat rolling over me until I finally, finally go still.
I exhale, eyes fluttering open.
Holy. Fuck.
For a long while, I just lie there, chest heaving, fingers still resting between my thighs.
Then the reality of what I just did slams into me.
I just got myself off to Aiden Gage.
Aiden. Fucking. Gage.
I groan, dragging my hands over my face.
How the hell am I supposed to look him in the eye after that.

# Chapter 27

Aiden

London definitely has a certain charm. The streets are alive, at all hours of the day and night, with the hum of conversation, the occasional laughter spilling from riverside pubs, and the gentle ripple of the Thames reflecting the city around it.

Alex walks beside me, eating an ice cream, because apparently, after a couple of days of spending time with me, she's in need of a treat, a double scoop of vanilla of all things. The woman is impossible to figure out.

"Vanilla?" I glance at her, taking a sip of my drink.

"Seriously, Trouble? That's an old person's choice." She huffs, looking thoroughly unimpressed.

"Sometimes simplicity is better Aiden Gage. I take it you're not a vanilla fan?"

I smirk. "No, I just don't like eating something that tastes like a candle smells."

She nudges me with her elbow but keeps eating, unbothered. We've been walking along the embankment for about ten minutes, neither of us in a rush to get back to the flat. There's a cool breeze off the water, and it makes Alex's hair fly around her face in wisps.

"So," I say, leaning on the railing, watching the water lap against the stone. "I can't imagine what it was like growing up with a father like Carter."

Alex snorts, licking her spoon. "Oh, it was a dream. A childhood filled with warmth, laughter, and unconditional love."

I shoot her a look. "Oh yeah…"

She exhales heavily, staring out over the river. "It was… lonely," she admits. "He was always working. Always focused on business. I remember once when I was seven, I made him this card for Father's Day, full-on glitter glue, macaroni, the works."

I smirk. "Sounds very on brand for you."

She rolls her eyes but continues. "I left it on his desk. He came home late that night, saw it, and threw it in the bin. I found it there the next day."

I shake my head. "Jesus."

She laughs, but there's no humour in it. "Yeah, I learned pretty quickly that Carter Whitehorn doesn't have time for emotional nonsense." She lets out a slow breath, tossing the remains of her ice cream into a nearby bin. "It only got worse after my mother died."

I glance at her. She's not looking at me, just staring at the river, but there's something raw in her voice, something she usually hides behind sharp remarks and relentless bravado.

"He must have had some redeeming moments," I say, watching her carefully.

She tilts her head, considering. Then a small smile tugs at the corner of her lips. "There was one time…"

I raise an eyebrow. "Oh, this should be good."

"I was fourteen," she says, crossing her arms over the railing. "He was away on business, so I snuck out to go to this underground jazz club with some friends."

I grin. "You? A jazz club?"

"Shut up, I was going through a phase." She waves a hand dismissively. "Anyway, I came home at three in the morning, fully convinced I'd pulled it off. Until I walked into the house and saw him sitting in the dark, drinking a whiskey like some kind of Bond villain."

I let out a low whistle. "Busted."

"Oh, beyond busted. He was furious. Ranted about reputation, security, how if I wanted to act like some 'commoner' I should go live with Aunt Edith." She grins. "In hindsight, I should have taken that deal."

I chuckle, shaking my head. "And what was the punishment?"

"Boarding school."

I cough. "You got exiled?"

She shrugs. "I'd already embarrassed him with my teenage rebellion, might as well avoid having an audience for any future escapades."

I exhale, turning to lean my back against the railing, studying her. "So, you've always been a bit of a menace."

She smirks. "Of course."

I shake my head. "And here I thought I was the troublemaker in this relationship."

She turns to me, eyes bright. "Oh, don't flatter yourself, Gage. If anything, I'm the reason you have a record."

I grin. "I was arrested once. That's not a record. It's just a good story."

She laughs, and for a moment, the weight on her shoulders seems to lift. The city hums around us, the streetlights casting a soft glow over her face. She looks lighter here, softer somehow.

We stand there in silence for a beat, both staring out over the water.

The cool autumn breeze shifts and she tightens her jacket around her. The scent of some restaurant down the road carries on the wind as a barge passes past with tourists snapping sights of the landmarks. Something in my chest tightens.

I don't say anything for a long moment. Just watch her, this impossible woman who has somehow taken up permanent residence in my brain.

Then I reach over, plucking a stray bit of melted ice cream from her chin with my thumb.

She startles, eyes snapping to mine.

I hold her gaze, smirking. "You're a mess, Trouble."

She scoffs, rolling her eyes, but there's colour in her cheeks now.

"I was a menace as well," I say, swiftly moving the conversation on.

She raises an eyebrow, a smirk tugging at her lips. "Why am I not shocked to hear that?"

"Yeah, me and Ethan definitely gave poor Dad the runaround."

She smiles, looking out over the water. "Well, I guess growing up in the countryside, there was plenty to get up to. Stealing tractors, rolling around in haystacks..."

I cut her off with a grin. "Oh, there was plenty of that."

"That's not what I was referring to," she deadpans, shooting me a look.

I nudge her shoulder playfully. "I think you walked into that one, Trouble."

She rolls her eyes and flicks her hair back over her shoulder, tucking the loose strands behind her ear. I catch myself watching her, the way the streetlights that have slowly turned on as we've talked cast a warm glow on her skin, the way her eyes flicker with amusement, and something else I can't quite place.

"So, does that mean you've had lots of girlfriends then?" she asks, casual, but I don't miss the way she angles her body slightly toward me.

I turn sideways to look at her, leaning an arm against the railing. "A couple, nothing serious. Why? You jealous?"

"You wish," she shoots back without hesitation. "I can see it now, Aiden Gage, the heartthrob of Northwood Dale."

I chew on my lip, the smile teasing at the corners of my mouth. "Yeah, well, I did alright."

"But no one serious?" There's nothing behind the question, just genuine curiosity.

"Nah, it's not my style. I'm more of a lone wolf kind of guy. Breaking hearts but not keeping them."

Her expression shifts just slightly, something flickering behind her gaze. "It's lonely though. Being like that."

I pause, because she says it like she gets it. Like she sees me.

I shrug, turning my attention back to the river. "I could always find some company."

"Yeah, but there's a difference between sex and actually being with someone," she says, voice quieter now.

I glance at her. "And you would know?"

"Not really," she admits. "But there must be a reason why people do it. Some people spend their entire lives together, for God's sake."

"Yeah, poor sods." I exhale, shaking my head. "Can you imagine? Putting up with the same person every day, forever."

"I pity the poor girl who ends up with you," she says, shaking her head with mock sympathy.

I feign shock, placing a hand over my heart. "And the poor guy who ends up with you? Poor sod. He'll never know a moment's peace."

She laughs, a proper laugh, from deep inside, and something about it settles in my chest.

"Ain't that the truth," she says, shaking her head.

"Well, at least it would be interesting, I suppose." I muse, watching a loved-up couple walk past, all puppy-dog eyes and sweet touches.

Alex follows my gaze, something unreadable in her expression. "Yeah. Interesting."

We fall into silence, the city buzzing around us. The kind of silence that isn't uncomfortable, but something else entirely.

I could kiss her.

The thought hits me so suddenly I nearly flinch.

I could.

I could lean in, right now, in the middle of London, with the river stretching out beside us and the glow of the city casting golden light against her cheek. And I'd bet my last pound that she wouldn't pull away.

But I don't.

Because that's not our game. Not yet.

Instead, I nudge her shoulder again, breaking the moment before it swallows us both whole.

"Come on, Trouble," I say, smirking as I start walking. "Let's get you home before you start proposing to me."

She scoffs but falls into step beside me. "In your dreams, Gage."

# Chapter 28

Alex

The rain drums against the window in a steady rhythm, a grey, overcast sky swallowing the London skyline beyond the apartment.
I exhale sharply, staring into my coffee.
Tomorrow.
Tomorrow is dinner at that house.
A house that should feel like home but never has.
A house full of cold marble floors, silent hallways, and a father who will be watching my every move, waiting for me to fail.
When I'd left London after the rumours of the Miles Kensington betrothal had surfaced, I hadn't looked back. I hadn't worried about money, or what my life would look like. I just knew that I had to get out. I had to get away.
My father insinuating that he'd only just found me in NorthWood Dale was about as believable as a politicians promise before an election. He'd known where I was all along, I'd run to my Aunt's house for God's sake, not the moon! And a man like Carter Whitehorn knows where everyone in his life is at all times. One eye on the deal, the other on the dealer. He'd bided his time until the betrothal (and the obvious lucrative business deal behind it) was all but secure. Just shy of a year.

And so here we are. I got one year of experiencing what it could be like to just exist. To not be a pawn in your own father's never-ending game of monopoly. One lousy year and now I'm back. Attending Gala's and dinners all over again.
I take another sip of coffee, letting the bitterness sit on my tongue.
I should be preparing for it.
Mentally steeling myself for the inevitable war of words, the disapproving looks, the veiled threats Carter Whitehorn likes to lace between sips of hundred-year-old scotch.
Instead, my brain is busy thinking about something, or rather, someone, else entirely.
Aiden.
I roll my shoulders, trying to shake the thought of him off.
Since the almost-kiss-that-definitely-didn't-happen, and my wandering hands and overactive imagination, I've been careful. Too careful. I've avoided putting myself in situations where something like that could happen again.
And it's worked.
Sort of.
We've been to a few more sights. Walked along the Thames. Went to Covent Garden where Aiden insisted on watching a street magician while I rolled my eyes and pretended I wasn't entertained.
Things have slipped back into routine.
Banter.
Teasing.
Me pretending not to laugh at his dumb jokes.

Him pretending not to notice when I do.
But there's something underneath it now, something simmering that I don't know what to do with.
And maybe that's why I'm feeling… frustrated… again.
Not that I would ever admit that out loud.
But it's been a long time since I was physically with anyone. And that explosive orgasm, the slightly charged conversation down the by river, the lingering looks, none of it is helping.
Imagining Aiden with other women ignited something inside me that I hadn't anticipated. I don't know why I pried into his escapades and conquests.
I don't care, or at least I shouldn't.
But I guess I was just curious.
It's hard to imagine Aiden, with all his bullshit and constant teasing ever being like that with a woman, although I did a pretty good job of imagining it the other night. And from what he said, he never has been that open, that vulnerable. I don't know why that makes me feel slightly better. It shouldn't. I shouldn't give a shit. But now, and if I'm honest with myself, even slightly before now, my brain has been playing cruel tricks on me, because the only person I can think about is him.
I let out a breath through my nose, shutting my eyes.
No.
That's not happening. This is a fake engagement. A means to an end.
Nothing more.
Nothing complicated.

And sleeping with Aiden Gage? That would complicate the hell out of everything. I'm not saying it wouldn't be good. Aiden is most definitely the sort of man that is well practiced in that area and that just makes it even harder to resist in my current state.

Just as I'm about to mentally slap myself out of this ridiculous train of thought, the apartment door opens.

I glance over my shoulder just in time to see Aiden stroll in, shaking the damp from his hair.

His jacket is slung over his shoulder, his white t-shirt clinging just slightly from the drizzle outside, and his damn forearms, those fucking forearms, are on full display.

I swallow.

*Fucking hell.*

"Your lawyer's a miracle worker," he announces, kicking off his boots. "All charges dropped. Apparently, the judge owed him a favour."

I nod, setting my coffee down. "Yeah. It took some effort, but luckily, that effort paid off."

I hesitate.

It took a lot of effort. Strings were pulled. Calls were made. But it worked.

Aiden Gage is a free man.

Which means...

I chew on my lip.

Maybe this is it.

Maybe now he'll want to leave.

He has no reason to keep up this fake engagement anymore. No reason to deal with me.

"So..." I say carefully, keeping my voice neutral. "I guess that means you don't need to stick around anymore."

He tilts his head, watching me for a second too long. Something flickers in his expression.

Then he smirks. "Oh, Trouble, you think I'd leave you to suffer that dinner alone?"

My stomach flips.

I scoff, ignoring the strange, ridiculous relief that washes over me. "Oh, so you're in this for the long haul now, are you?"

He grins, stepping closer, tapping the tip of my nose with his finger like I'm some amused little house cat.

"Guess you're stuck with me," he murmurs, voice low and teasing.

I slap his hand away. "Unbelievable."

And just like that, we're back to our usual rhythm.

But for the first time, I let myself feel it.

The relief.

The warmth.

The knowledge that, for reasons I don't quite understand yet, I don't want him to leave.

# Chapter 29

Aiden

This is a bad idea.
I know it's a bad idea.
But when Alex turns to me, a mischievous spark in her eyes, and says, "Let's go out. Really go out. Celebrate you being officially crime-free." how the hell am I supposed to say no?
So here we are.
In a low-lit, slightly-too-loud London bar, tucked into a corner booth with drinks in hand, letting the world around us fade into the buzz of neon lights and bass-heavy music.
And Alex?
For the first time since I met her, she looks free.
Her hair is loose around her shoulders, the strap of her black lace camisole constantly dropping down and it's taking everything in me not to keep t picking it up. Her sharp brown eyes are softened by alcohol and amusement. She's tapping her nails absently against her glass, watching the bar with an expression that isn't calculating, or guarded, or exhausted.
She's just... here. Existing in the moment.
And fuck, it's infuriatingly attractive.

Samantha Todd

Not that I'm thinking about that.
(Not that I'm not thinking about that.)
She leans forward suddenly, tilting her head.
"Alright, tell me something."
I smirk, taking a sip of my drink. "You'll have to be more specific, Trouble."
She waves a hand, a little loose from the drinks, a little careless in the best way. "Something I don't know about you. Something real."
I tilt my head, watching her. "And what do I get in return?"
Her lips twitch. "The honour of knowing you've contributed to the betterment of my evening."
I snort. "Oh, well, in that case."
I pretend to think, swirling the amber liquid in my glass. "Alright. I used to want to be a race car driver."
Alex's brows lift in genuine amusement. "You?"
"Yep." I grin. "Five-year-old me had posters of Formula 1 cars plastered all over my bedroom."
She shakes her head, laughing. "Let me guess, Ethan wanted to be an astronaut?"
"Close. Firefighter."
She hums. "That tracks."
I lean forward, resting my arms on the table. "Your turn."
Alex takes a sip of her cocktail, eyes glinting over the rim of her glass. "I had a crush on my physics teacher when I was sixteen."
I choke on my drink. "What?"
She shrugs, laughing at my reaction. "He was intelligent, sarcastic, and kind of an asshole. I was clearly doomed from the start."

I wipe my mouth, shaking my head. "Jesus, Trouble, remind me to never leave you alone with Ethan."

She rolls her eyes, but she's laughing.

The conversation flows like that, teasing, bantering, little glimpses into who we actually are beneath all the walls and roles and expectations.

We talk about growing up. The shit we got up to as kids. The worst lies we ever told our parents.

Alex laughs, telling me a story about sneaking out to a concert one summer when she was seventeen, only to get caught on the way back in because she forgot to lock the front gate, and the wind blew it open.

She snorts. "My dad was waiting for me in the sitting room. I thought I was going to be murdered on the spot."

I laugh, imagining a younger version of her, already too sharp for her own good, already too headstrong to be controlled.

"See, this is why I never had a curfew," I say, taking another sip. "Couldn't get in trouble if no one expected me to be home at a certain time."

She hums, looking at me over her glass. "You really are a menace, aren't you?"

I smirk. "Oh sweetheart, you have no idea."

An hour later, we're a little drunk, a little ridiculous, and Alex has completely let her guard down.
She's laughing with her head thrown back, completely uncaring of the people around us, swaying a little to the music.

Samantha Todd

The song changes, and something upbeat and familiar blares through the speakers.
She lets out a delighted gasp. "Oh my God. I love this song."
I recognize the tune instantly.
I grin. "Don't tell me you're one of those people who screams the lyrics to songs in bars."
Alex raises a single brow. "You think I can't sing?"
I smirk. "I think you can't not make everything a challenge."
And just like that, she stands.
Takes my hand.
Drags me toward the open space where other people are half-dancing, half-stumbling along to the music.
And then, to my absolute fucking surprise,
Alex starts singing.
Loud. Dramatic.
Slightly off-key, but confident as hell.
It's ridiculous.
It's embarrassing.
It's the best fucking thing I've ever seen.
I laugh, shaking my head. "Jesus Christ, you're insane."
She twirls, actually twirls, arms up, eyes bright, auburn hair flying in all directions. "Come on, Gage, don't tell me you're scared."
And fuck it.
If Alex Whitehorn is going to get drunk and sing in a bar like she's never had a day of stress in her life, then I'm going to let her.

No teasing. No biting remarks. No cold reality waiting at the edges.
Just this.
So, I do the unthinkable.
I join in.
She gasps in mock shock when I start singing along with her, just as loud, just as ridiculous.
"You know this song?!" she exclaims.
I shrug, grinning. "Guess you don't know everything about me, Trouble."
We're moving, laughing, and for the first time in weeks, I forget what we are supposed to be.
The song ends, and we're breathless, laughing, still too close.
Alex sways slightly, the alcohol in her system making her steps uneven.
I instinctively reach out, steadying her with my hands on her arms.
Her smile falters for a split second as her eyes flick to mine.
Her skin is warm beneath my hands. The soft fabric of her top itching my fingertips.
We're close enough that I can feel the heat of her breath.
And suddenly, the noise around us fades.
Her gaze flickers, down to my lips, just for a second.
My grip tightens.
She blinks, shakes her head, and steps back.
I release her instantly, clearing my throat, masking the moment before it can become something real.
She exhales, a quick, sharp breath. "Right. More drinks?"

I chuckle, shaking my head. "You're going to be a nightmare tomorrow."

She grins. "Probably."

We stumble back over to the bar and Alex puts in the order, the noise of the bar drowning out her voice as she turns towards me, grinning wickedly.

"We're doing tequila," she announces.

I lift a brow. "Bold move, Trouble."

She shrugs, already reaching for the saltshaker. "If I'm going to endure a stuffy, suffocating dinner tomorrow night, listening to boring conversation and drinking overpriced champagne that I won't even be allowed to enjoy properly, then we're getting royally fucked up tonight while we still have time."

I chuckle, watching her pour with practiced ease. "Should I be concerned by how well you handle tequila?"

She grins, tossing me a lime wedge. "Shut up and drink, Gage." She raises the shot in the air, "To your freedom!"

I shake my head, "To *our* freedom!" Her eyes flick to mine briefly.

We lick the salt, down the shots, and bite into the lime, both wincing, both grinning through it.

"Fuck," I mutter, shaking my head. "Tastes like regret."

Alex licks the remaining salt off her thumb, eyes gleaming. "I don't regret a damn thing."

She waves at the bartender, signalling for another round.

I groan. "You're trying to kill me."

She smirks. "You're a big boy, you'll survive."

More drinks come. More laughter. More teasing. Somewhere along the way, I lose track of the number of shots we've done, the number of times she's rolled her eyes at me, the number of times I've caught myself staring at her.
And then…

We're stumbling through the apartment door, late, very late, drunk enough that walking in a straight line is an active challenge.
Alex kicks off her shoes, letting them land somewhere in the abyss of the entryway. She wobbles slightly, catching herself on the arm of the couch. "I think," she says, enunciating carefully, "I might be slightly drunk."
I snort, closing the door behind us. "Right there with you, Trouble."
She straightens, flicking her hair back in what I assume is meant to be a graceful gesture but only makes her sway again.
I step forward, catching her elbow.
She blinks up at me, eyes heavy-lidded, lips slightly parted.
Something shifts.
The drunken haze doesn't dull it, if anything, it makes it more palpable.
This heat between us.
The weight of her body close to mine.
She bites her lower lip, and I swear to God, it nearly undoes me.
"Aiden," she murmurs, voice softer now.
Fuck.

Samantha Todd

This is it.
The moment where we could cross the line. Where I could close the space between us, press her against the wall, kiss her senseless, feel her completely.
And she wouldn't stop me.
But she's drunk.
And so am I.
And fuck, if this is ever going to happen, it's not going to be like this.
I exhale sharply, forcing my grip on her to loosen, to become something steadier, something gentler.
I drag my thumb across her cheekbone, brushing a stray strand of hair back.
"You need to go to bed, Trouble," I murmur.
Her brows draw together slightly, lips parting as if to argue, but then, her exhaustion catches up with her.
Her body sags.
She lets out a small, defeated sigh.
I guide her toward her room, steadying her as she stumbles.
She flops down on the bed, face first, utterly unbothered by the world.
I chuckle. "Real elegant, sweetheart."
A muffled sound comes from the pillow. Something vaguely resembling "fuck off."
I shake my head, tugging the blanket over her.
And then, just before I leave, I hesitate.
Brush her hair from her face.
Watch her for just a second too long.
God help me, she's beautiful.

## Raising the Gage

I close her door gently behind me, then head straight for the bathroom.
Turn the shower on cold.
Very, very cold.
Because if I don't, I'm going to lose my fucking mind.
Because if I don't, I'll be thinking about the way she looked at me, the way she leaned into me, the way her breath caught.
Because if I don't, I'll be thinking about how badly I wanted to stay.
And that?
That's a problem.

# Chapter 30

Aiden

**Brynne:**
*Be honest, how many cold showers have you had?*

**Aiden:**
*None of your fucking business.*

**Brynne:**
*So, multiple then. Got it.*

**Aiden:**
*Seriously, do you and Ethan just sit around discussing my sex life?*

**Brynne:**
*Oh, absolutely. We take notes and everything.*

**Aiden:**
*You're insufferable.*

**Brynne:**
*And you're deflecting. Soooo… when are you going to admit that you're completely gone for her?*

**Aiden:**

...

**Brynne:**
*That's what I thought.*

**Aiden:**
*I don't need this from you right now.*

**Brynne:**
*Oh, you absolutely do. You're in deep, and you know it. And sooner or later, you're gonna have to stop pretending that this is just a game.*

**Aiden:**
*Know-it-all.*

**Brynne:**
*I'm just saying... I know what a man looks like when he's fighting a losing battle.*

**Aiden:**
*And what does that look like?*

**Brynne:**
*Like you, standing outside her bedroom door, thinking about going back in.*

**Aiden:**
*Jesus Christ, Brynne.*

**Brynne:**

*Just admit it, Gage. You're completely and utterly screwed.*

**Aiden:**
*Yeah, well, tell me something I don't know.*

**Brynne:**
*Fine. You left your tool belt at our place last week.*

**Aiden:**
*…That is not the same thing.*

**Brynne:**
*Debatable.*

**Aiden:**
*Goodnight, Brynne.*

**Brynne:**
*Sweet dreams. Oh wait, I bet you won't be getting much sleep, will you?* 😉

**Aiden:**
*Blocked.*

# Chapter 31

Aiden

Alex had rallied remarkably quickly this morning. Two cups of coffee and a hearty breakfast of bacon and eggs cooked my me of course, I'm not letting that girl go near the kitchen ever again, and she was right as rain.

The water runs hot against my skin as I rinse off the soap, steam curling against the frosted glass of the shower.

This is the only moment of peace I'm going to get tonight.

I already know it.

Because tonight isn't the Gala.

This isn't just a room full of cocky investment bankers and trophy wives in too-tight dresses.

This is Carter Whitehorn's house.

An intimate, private dinner.

Where everyone in attendance will be watching *us* like a goddamn hawk, waiting for cracks to appear.

Where Miles Kensington will be sniffing around, looking for any opportunity to throw me under the bus and steal Alex away.

Where Carter will be sat at the head of the table, picking me apart piece by piece.

Samantha Todd

I shut off the water, running a hand through my hair before stepping out onto the heated marble floor of Alex's ridiculously expensive bathroom.

"Alright, Trouble," I call through the wall as I grab a towel. "Tell me how bad it's going to be."

There's a shuffle from the bedroom. The rustling of fabric. A slight thump, probably Alex kicking something out of her way, or falling over. For someone so poised, she can be alarmingly clumsy.

"How bad do you think?" she replies dryly.

I grin, rubbing the towel through my hair. "Worse than the Gala?"

"Worse than the Gala."

"Great."

I hear her sigh through the wall. "This isn't some party where you can just charm your way through, Aiden. This is a test. The real test."

I frown, pausing. "A test?"

"Yes." A slight hesitation, then, "The Gala was a performance. This? This is a battlefield. The drinks reception before dinner will be… pleasant, but that's just so my father can assess you properly. He'll be watching for any slip-ups. Any tells. He wants you to fail."

I run a hand down my face. "Fucking hell, you make it sound like I'm about to go into an underground fight ring."

She laughs, and I can hear the eyeroll. "You're not. But you need to understand that this is going to be a far more intimate setting. Less people. More scrutiny. Every interaction will matter. Every glance, every touch, every word."

I don't respond immediately, pulling on my shirt instead. Buttoning it up, I glance at myself in the mirror, adjusting the collar.

"And Kensington?" I ask eventually, keeping my voice even.

There's a beat of silence.

Then, "He'll be watching too."

I clench my jaw. Of course he fucking will.

Which means that if he sees any hesitation, any crack in the foundation of us, he'll be the first to pounce.

I exhale, steadying myself.

I've played the game so far.

I can play it for one more night.

"You ready?" I call, stepping out of the bathroom, tie in hand.

Alex turns at the sound of my voice, and my mouth dries instantly.

*Holy shit.*

She's standing by the window, adjusting an earring, wearing the most Alex dress I could possibly imagine.

A sleek, effortless black cocktail dress.

Lace backing, the plunging neckline drawing my eyes exactly where I shouldn't be looking.

Her hair is up, but loose curls frame her face, teasing at her bare shoulders.

She looks...

I swallow.

She looks fucking incredible.

Alex catches me staring and raises an eyebrow.

"What?"

I clear my throat, shifting my weight. "Nothing. Just... uh... should I be worried that you look like you're about to eat me alive?"

She smirks. "You should be worried about my father. I am the least of your concerns."

I let out a breath, rolling my shoulders. "Right. Well, you don't make it sound daunting at all."

She hums, stepping closer, reaching for my tie.

My pulse spikes.

"Here," she murmurs, taking the fabric from my hands. "You're useless at this."

I stand perfectly still as she carefully fixes my tie, her delicate fingers brushing against my throat.

The scent of her shampoo, vanilla and coconut, that same goddamn drug that sends a signal straight to my dick is all I can fucking smell.

And she's close.

Not in the way she's been before, not in our usual bantering, sparring way.

This is easy.

Comfortable. Almost familiar.

And it rattles me.

Because when was the last time someone did something for me? Something small. Something like fixing my tie, like it was the most normal thing in the world?

"Thanks," I murmur, voice lower than I mean it to be.

She hesitates for just a second.

Then, she leans in, pressing a quick kiss to my cheek.

And it's nothing.

Just a brief brush of lips.

Soft.
Barely even there.
But my entire fucking brain short-circuits. Any other woman, this would be it, the moment where I would grab her, dinner be damned, rip that dress off of her and throw her down on the bed. This would be the moment that my usually quite strong resolve would shatter. That I would take what's mine and have her whimpering my name. But not with Alex, this is an arrangement, this isn't real. Even if it feels suspiciously so.

By the time I register what's happened, she's already pulling away, already grabbing her clutch from the bed.

"Let's get this over with," she says lightly.

I blink.

Then, snapping back to reality, I shake my head and follow her to the door.

"Jesus, Trouble," I say, forcing a grin to hide the fact that I still feel off-kilter. "Didn't know you were so into me."

She snorts. "Oh, shut up Gage."

But as we step out of the apartment, I swear I see the tiniest smirk tug at her lips.

# Chapter 32

Aiden

The house, if you can even call something this ridiculous a house, rises out of the ground like some kind of neo-classical monstrosity.
White stone. Towering columns. Carved archways. The kind of house that doesn't belong in a bustling, overcrowded city like London, but exists anyway, because money has a way of bending reality.
And this place?
This place simply oozes money.
A grand staircase sweeps up to the front entrance, lined with pristine hedges that probably have their own gardener. The driveway is lit up like a fucking airport runway, showing off a handful of expensive cars that probably cost more than my entire farm.
I glance at Alex.
She's stoic as ever, but I can see the tightness in her jaw. The way her fingers clench around her small, black clutch.
Like she's steeling herself. Resigning herself to whatever torture lies beyond the vast glass doors. Steadying her resolve.
For this.

## Raising the Gage

For him. Daddy-fucking-dearest.

The front doors are opened by some guy in a full butler's suit. Actual tails. He bows his head slightly as we step inside, and I have to fight every instinct not to burst out laughing.

Because what the fuck even is this place?

The ceilings are impossibly high, draped in intricate chandeliers. The walls are lined with gold-framed paintings of old dead people, the kind that have been in the family for centuries. So long that those that currently live here probably don't even know who the hell they are. There's a fucking grand piano sitting off to the side, as if someone might casually break into a concerto over cocktails. Which in this kind of environment I wouldn't be at all surprised.

And the guests?

Dressed to the nines.

Suits that look like they were tailored to within an inch of their lives. Dresses that cost more than my truck. And jewellery, dripping in diamonds, in emeralds, in the kind of old money wealth that reeks of generational privilege.

If dinner at my house is done in pyjamas and yesterday's flannel, this is the goddamn opposite. This is a bloody wedding reception. A completely different world.

And all of them—*every single one*—are looking at us.

Like we're the entertainment for the evening.

Or more likely, like *I'm* the entertainment.

*Come on then you rich bastards. I'll give you a fucking show.*

Carter greets us at the entrance to the parlour, whisky in hand, looking every inch the villain he was born to be.

"Aiden," he greets coolly, his mouth barely twitching at the corners. "I trust you've been enjoying your time in London?"

I smile. Wide. Easy. Charming. "Oh, immensely. Alex has been an excellent tour guide. I even bought a magnet."

Alex *chokes* beside me. I feel her arm tense under mine.

Carter's lip twitches. "How quaint."

I lean in slightly, pressing a quick kiss to Alex's cheek, just to really sell it. Getting another whiff of that scent.

She goes rigid.

But she doesn't pull away.

"She's full of surprises," I say, still grinning. "You must be proud."

Carter's expression is unreadable. But his eyes? His eyes are calculating.

Assessing.

He lifts his whisky to his lips, never breaking eye contact. "Of course."

A beat of silence.

Then, suddenly, he steps aside, motioning into the parlour where the other guests have gathered.

"Come in," he says smoothly. "Let's introduce you to some of our... dear friends."

Alex exhales softly beside me.

I keep my arm firmly around her waist as we step into the lion's den.

The parlour is filled with the sounds of delicate laughter, clinking glasses, wealth. Endless chatter about investment portfolios, recent glitterati events attended. A world away from the kind of banter in the local pub. No mention of who could punch-out a goose here.
Waiters in crisp black suits weave between the guests, offering crystal flutes of champagne.
The good stuff.
I take one, because fuck it, and sip as I scan the room. It tastes different to a prosecco but if I'm honest, I prefer the prosecco. Less pretentious.
Men in expensive suits. Women draped in couture. The kind of people who invest in hedge funds, who own skyscrapers, who probably spend their summers on yachts in Monaco.
These aren't just rich people.
They're powerful people. The real top end of society. And they're all watching me.
I feel Alex tense beside me, but I don't let go.
*They want a show? Fine. Let's make it a damn good one.*
I keep her close, my hand resting just above the curve of her hip, guiding her through the sea of money and influence like I belong here. Like I own the place. And they don't know what to do with it. They don't expect it. They expect me to be intimidated. To falter. To stumble over my words, to trip over my own feet, to be out of my depth.

But I'm not.
Because these people might have money. They might have power.
But they don't scare me. They've not done the things I've done or seen the things I've seen. They've not stared down a bull in the back field. They've not delivered a struggling calf and brought it back to life. They've not had a real hard day's work in all their over-privileged lives.
I tug at the collar of my suit. Still too tight. Still too ridiculous.
Alex, ever poised, stands beside me, sipping her champagne with the kind of ease that only comes from growing up in places like this. She's in her element here, the sharp, polished ice queen, greeting guests with a perfectly curated smile. It's nothing like the real smile—the one I've seen when she's got a whiskey in her hand and my name on her lips.
And yet, despite her mastery of this world, despite her ability to walk through these halls without a crack in her armour, I can feel the tension in her shoulders. Because she knows we're being watched. Scrutinised.
I lean in, just close enough for only her to hear. "You know, Trouble, I think some of these people might actually like me here."
She snorts into her drink, but I see the way her lips twitch upward before she catches herself. "A shocking lack of good taste, apparently."
Before I can respond, I hear my name.
"Well, if it isn't Mr. Gage."

I turn, and there he is. Lord Everett.
The same Lord Everett who had barely cracked a smile at the Gala, until I'd somehow managed to make him laugh. More than once. A feat that, judging by the expressions of the other rich pricks in attendance that night, was about as rare as a solar eclipse.
Tonight, he actually smiles at me again.
"Well, Lord Everett," I say, shaking his hand. "It's good to see you again."
"I must admit, I was delighted to hear you'd be in attendance tonight. These things can be so stuffy. It's nice to have some new blood in our midst." Everett's voice is deep, the kind that commands a room without effort. He takes a sip of his whiskey, surveying me with the unreadable expression of a man who's seen empires rise and fall. "I assume you're still terrorising this fine establishment with your charm?"
I grin. "I do my best, my Lord."
Everett chuckles, and I hear a sharp inhale from somewhere behind me. A woman, watching. There are several, in fact.
They're hovering, champagne flutes poised delicately in their hands, eyes flickering over me like I'm a new and interesting specimen they've just discovered in the wild. The bit of rough who cleans up well.
I get it. I stand out here.
The others are all polished, groomed within an inch of their lives, and then there's me, a farmer in a

designer suit, looking every bit the lamb in the wolf's den.

And the women love it. This, I can play to my advantage.

A brunette in an emerald gown tilts her head, studying me with a slow, appreciative smile. "So, you're the one who tamed Alexis Whitehorn."

I arch a brow. "I think it's probably the other way around."

Lord Everett laughs outright at that, and now a few other men have turned to see what's so amusing. I glance at Alex, just briefly. She's watching me closely, her grip on her champagne glass just a little too firm.

The brunette takes a step closer, her lips curving playfully. "Tell me, Mr. Gage, what exactly is your secret?"

I smirk, eyes locked on Alex as I answer. "Sheer unadulterated persistence."

Alex takes a slow sip of her champagne, her expression unreadable. But her eyes are burning.

The brunette, oblivious to the silent war happening right next to her, trails a finger around the rim of her glass. "I can't imagine she makes it easy."

"Oh, you have no idea," I murmur, grinning as Alex digs her nails into her glass stem.

Before I can push it further, another guest, a distinguished older gentleman, steps forward, clapping me on the back with the kind of enthusiasm that nearly makes me spill my drink.

"I must say," he announces, his voice booming across the room, "your engagement is the talk of the town! Alexis, you've certainly found yourself an interesting one."

Alex smiles politely, but I can see it, the strain in her jaw, the way her fingers tighten slightly around her glass.

I take the opportunity to slide my hand to the small of her back, guiding her closer, pressing my fingers just a little too firmly against her spine.

"She didn't find me," I say, winking at the brunette woman, turning on the charm. "I found her. And I'm sure you can imagine how much she loves that."

A few polite laughs ripple through the group.

Alex, to her credit, doesn't react.

Not outwardly, anyway.

But when she finally turns to me, her voice is so sweet it's almost deadly.

"Careful, darling." She tilts her head. "Wouldn't want you to get too comfortable."

I grin, sliding my hand lower, just enough to make her breath catch.

"Who says I'm not already?"

She doesn't get a chance to fire back, because at that moment, a waiter appears, announcing that dinner is served.

And as we make our way inside, I feel it.

Her heartbeat, just a little faster than before.

And just like that, Carter's plan clicks into place.

Alex stiffens beside me.

I glance at the long, lavishly decorated table stretching out across the dining room. At the place settings. Where I am not seated beside Alex. Where I am seated across from her. Where, strategically, I

am wedged between a talkative investment banker, ludicrously named Horatio, and a stone-faced woman in her late fifties dripping in enough jewellery to single-handedly fund a small country.
While Miles Kensington, fucking Miles, is seated right beside Alex.
Carter's voice cuts through the room, smoothly directing people to their places.
I keep my expression neutral.
But inside?
Inside, I smile.
Because if Carter thinks I'm the type to fall for this bullshit, he's got another thing coming. I can play this game. And I can play it damn well.
I pull out Alex's chair for her, playing the doting fiancé perfectly, pressing a brief kiss to her temple before murmuring just for her, "Sit tight, Trouble. This is gonna be fun."
Her eyes flash.
And I know, this dinner is about to be a fucking game. But turns out I'm pretty good at chess.

# Chapter 33

Aiden

The cutlery glides over fine bone china, soft chatter ripples through the room like a well-rehearsed orchestra, and the scent of something rich, something French and complicated, wafts up from my plate.
It's all very elegant. Very poised. The kind of dinner where people discuss investments and art acquisitions between bites of filet mignon, sipping at wine that probably costs more than my entire farm.
And me?
I'm playing my part.
Engaging in polite conversation with the people beside me.
Horatio to my left is going on about something riveting, something about markets, returns, projections, I stopped listening after the third acronym. Jesus don't these people ever just let loose. *Get the fucking shots out already!*
Meanwhile, the woman on my right, a frostier sort, has yet to acknowledge my existence. She's eating with the precision of a surgeon, barely sparing me a glance as I attempt to engage.
But honestly?

Samantha Todd

I don't care.
Because my attention isn't here.
It's across the table.
Where Alex is doing her level-best to pretend that the absolute wanker beside her isn't running his mouth.
Miles fucking Kensington.
I already hate him. Not because he's done anything directly to me, but because of who he is. They say you shouldn't judge someone by his cover, and in this environment, I should know that more than anyone, but this idiot with his trust fund and slick-prick haircut can fuck right off.
The type of guy who thinks fake-charm is a substitute for a personality. The type of guy who always wins, because of who he is, not what he is. The type of guy who looks at a woman like she's a trophy, not a person.
And Alex?
Alex knows *it*.
She's doing that thing she does, sipping her wine, lips pursed, nodding occasionally while barely listening. Humouring him entirely while simultaneously maintaining a look of total indifference to his existence.
But, despite her practiced movements, I see the way she cuts her eyes toward me, looking for escape.
And then, his hand moves.
Casual. Too casual.
Sliding around the back of her chair.
Possessive. Entitled.

I see the moment she tenses, the way her fingers curl slightly around her fork, like she's about to stab him in eye with it.

And something in me snaps.

I set my wine glass down.

Loud enough to be heard.

And then, without looking away from my plate, I say, "So, Miles," I drawl, voice easy, calm. "Tell me something."

The conversation around us continues, but I see his head tilt slightly at my tone.

Alex glances up at me, her eyes widening slightly.

Hook.

Line.

Sinker.

"You and Alex," I continue, finally looking at him.

"You must have so many stories from school. I'd love to hear them."

Alex immediately stiffens.

Miles smirks. "Oh, we had our fun, didn't we, darling?"

Alex's smile is tight. "Define *fun*."

I chuckle, taking a sip of wine. "Define *darling*."

Horatio beside me snorts into his glass.

Miles' jaw ticks for just a second. "Well," he recovers smoothly, giving me a too-polished smile, "I suppose it's an inside joke."

"Ah," I hum. "I see. Inside jokes. The ones that make sense to some people, but not others." I smile back, pleasant. "Is you having your hand around my fiancés chair an inside joke too?"

The air between us shifts.

Samantha Todd

The conversation around us carries on, but there's a noticeable pause from Alex.
And then, Miles removes his hand. Slowly. Almost grudgingly. Alex exhales, her shoulder visibly relaxing.
I hold his gaze for a beat longer.
He inhales, a long draw of breath, designed to put you on edge, "Didn't have you pegged for the jealous, possessive type, Gage."
I grin. "Oh, see, that's where you're confused." I swirl my wine in my glass, taking my time. "Possessiveness is about ownership." I meet his eyes, smile widening. "And Alex isn't something to be owned."
Miles opens his mouth, but I lean in just slightly, lowering my voice.
"But see, that thing you just did? Sliding your hand behind her, leaning in like you had some sort of claim?" I click my tongue, shaking my head. "That's not inside jokes, Miles. That's insecurity."
His jaw clenches.
"Seems a little desperate to me," I add, shrugging lazily. "Reaching for something that doesn't belong to you."
Miles' lips press into a thin line.
I take a sip of my wine. "Then again, I've heard that you always were a grasping little prick."
There it is. That flash of irritation, that slight twitch in his jaw. That gobsmacked realisation that I actually went ahead and said it.
Alex is staring at me now, her expression unreadable.

Miles exhales through his nose, schooling his features. "Not everything's a competition, Gage."
I smirk. "That's the thing, *Kensington*. I don't need to compete. I already won."
And with that, I turn back to my meal, utterly uninterested in anything else he has to say.
Because, unlike him, I don't need to prove a damn thing.
I can feel Alex's eyes on me.
And then, so softly, so subtly, I see her lips move. Not out loud, just for me, as she mouths, "Thank you."
I fight a smirk and nod.
This dinner is just getting started and I'm enjoying myself far too much.
I feel the moment Carter sets his sights on me.
The hum of conversation softens, just slightly, like the air itself is bracing for impact.
"Tell me, Aiden," Carter begins, swirling his scotch, "remind me again what it is you do for a living."
There it is.
The question isn't casual, it's a calculated move, meant to put me under the microscope, to remind me that in this world, his world, I don't belong.
I set down my fork. Wipe my mouth with the linen napkin. Take my fucking time.
And then, with the easy confidence that I know gets under his skin, I lean back slightly and list it off.
"Well, let's see," I say, tapping my fingers against the table, "I work on my family's farm. Manage livestock, tend to crops, oversee operations. I get my hands

dirty, keep things running smoothly. You know, the simple life."
I hear a few polite hmms and murmurs from the guests around us, all intrigued by the novelty of an honest-to-God farmer sitting at their table.
Carter nods, expression unreadable. "And that... fulfils you?"
There's a slight lilt to the question, something condescending hiding just beneath the surface.
I don't flinch.
"It's a good life," I reply easily. "Hard work but rewarding. There's something about seeing the land change with the seasons, knowing that what you do matters. That you built something with your hands."
And then, almost as an afterthought, almost too casual, I add, "But my real passion is my furniture."
That gets their attention.
"Furniture?" one of the women pipes up, tilting her head slightly.
I nod. "Yeah. Woodwork, mostly. I design and build furniture in my free time; tables, chairs, cabinets, things like that."
Polite nods ripple through the table. This, they can accept. This, they understand; artistry, craftsmanship, something refined enough to take interest in.
Alex leans forward slightly, and with a voice so convincing it even makes me do a double take, she says, "I've seen them. They're wonderful. Aiden's a true artist."
I meet her eyes.
She's lying.

We both know it.
But it's a beautiful lie and she sells it so well that the whole table leans in with curiosity.

"An artist?" one of the men across from me muses, intrigued. "How fascinating. Do you sell your pieces?"

"Not yet," I admit with a grin, "but maybe Alex can be my agent."

A soft chuckle moves through the table.

Alex, ever the picture of poise, merely lifts her wine glass and smirks over the rim.

Carter, meanwhile, is watching. Calculating.

And then, smoothly, like he's been waiting for the moment all night, he says, "So, tell us, how did you do it?"

I blink. "Do what?"

His lips curve slightly. "Propose to my daughter, of course."

Shit.

I feel Alex still beside me.

We never rehearsed this part.

I scramble, just for a second, before slipping into the only thing I know how to do when I'm backed into a corner.

I ad-lib.

"Ah," I exhale, shifting in my seat, "it was... well, it had to be perfect, didn't it?"

I meet Alex's gaze briefly, just to make sure she's following my lead.

Her eyes flicker with intrigue.

"I spent weeks planning it," I continue, voice dipping into something low, something genuine. "I knew I

had to get it just right, something meaningful, something that she wouldn't expect."
The guests are leaning in now, listening intently.
Even Alex looks... a little taken aback.
I swirl the stem of my wine glass between my fingers, letting the tension build before I go in for the kill.
"It was at sunrise," I say softly, like I'm remembering it. "Out in the fields behind my family's farm. There's this one spot, this little hill overlooking the valley, where the sun hits just right as it rises."
The room is silent.
Alex's breath catches.
"I took her there," I go on, voice steady, smooth. "Just the two of us. I had a blanket laid out, a thermos of her favourite coffee, white, one sugar." My eyes flicker to hers, amused. "French press, of course."
A soft laugh ripples through the table.
Alex blinks rapidly, as if stunned by the detail.
"And then," I continue, voice dipping even lower, "just as the sun broke over the horizon, I told her that she was the best thing that ever happened to me. That I'd spend my whole life making sure she never had to question how loved she was. How I would support her through anything that life threw at her. And then," I spread my hands, "I asked her to be my wife."
I can feel the air shift.
The guests are looking at me like I just stepped out of a damn romance novel.
Even Alex looks momentarily... softened.
And for a brief second, I feel it too.

Because if this were real, if this were an actual moment, with an actual proposal, I think I would want it to be exactly like that.
I think I'd mean it.
Then, "But where's the ring?"
Carter's voice cuts through the spell like a whip.
And just like that, the tension snaps.
Shit.
We forgot about the damn ring.
The one bloody thing we're supposed to have to prove all of this is real. We can find out how we take our coffee, what bands we like and which side of the sodding bed we sleep on but the ring, the fucking engagement ring, we forget.
I glance at Alex.
She doesn't miss a beat.
"It's being resized," she says smoothly, as if she's been planning it all along. "It was a little loose. It's truly beautiful, though."
Carter raises an eyebrow. "I see."
There's something pointed in his expression, something that says he's filed this away for later.
But the rest of the table, eating it up.
Alex lifts her glass again, sips her wine. And beneath the table, as subtle as a whisper, she nudges my foot with hers.
I glance at her.
She mouths, *"Nice save."*
And I smirk.
I mouth back, *"Right back at you."*

Samantha Todd

I shake the last few hands, keep my expression polite, keep my answers smooth.

One of the men, a tall guy in a pinstripe suit and slicked-back hair, clasps my shoulder. "A pleasure, truly. I must say, Alexis has an eye for talent. Her praise isn't handed out lightly."

I nod, offering a firm handshake in return.

"Appreciate that. Maybe I'll send some pieces your way."

"Please do." He flashes a smile, then turns toward the door. "And best of luck with everything. We look forward to the wedding. "

The weight of everything lingers in the air long after the door closes.

The evening is wrapping up. The guests are filtering out. Soft music emanates from the drawing room and the heady scent of whiskey lingers in the air, But Alex is nowhere in sight.

I scan the room, just a few stragglers finishing their after-dinner drinks, but no Alex. I'd lost sight of her while discussing politics with Lord something-or-other.

Then I hear it.

A low, controlled voice, sharp as a blade, cutting through the air from the drawing room.

Carter.

And then, Alex.

I don't intend to eavesdrop, not at first. But something in the way he's speaking, like a predator circling its prey, like she's a goddamn child, makes my spine stiffen.

I step closer, just outside the doorway, keeping to the shadows.

"You've had your fun, Alexis."

Alex's voice follows, steady but simmering. "And what exactly does that mean?"

Carter exhales, a slow, indulgent breath. "You've made your point. Paraded your bit of rough around like a trophy. I'm sure you've both enjoyed the little charade, but let's be serious now. It's time to put an end to this."

My fingers curl into fists.

Bit of rough? Well, I guess I can't argue with that, not when surrounded by this kind of company.

Alex doesn't hesitate. "You don't know a damn thing about him."

Carter hums, like he's mildly amused by her defence. "I know enough." A pause. "He's quick on his feet, I'll give him that. The little engagement story, charming. But do you really think he can give you the life you're accustomed to?"

I grind my teeth so hard my jaw aches.

But then, Alex does something that knocks the breath right out of my lungs.

She defends *me*.

Without hesitation.

Without shame.

"Not that it's any of your business," she says coldly, "but Aiden is a good man. He's kind. He's brilliant. He doesn't pretend to be something he's not, which is more than can be said for more than half the people in this room tonight. And as a father, you should be happy for me. Instead, you're standing here trying to tear him down."

There's a pause.

I can picture Carter, watching her, his gaze cool, analytical.

"You're playing a dangerous game, Alexis."

"Am I?" she snaps. "Or are you just angry that for once in my life, I made a decision that you had no part in?"

His tone sharpens, like a knife pressed to a throat. "One day, I'll catch you. I'll catch whatever it is you're hiding. And when I do..."

"You'll what, Dad?" she hisses. "Disown me? Please. We both know you'd never risk that. I might be an inconvenience to you, but I'm still the Whitehorn heir."

A cold, clipped laugh. "Heir?" A sip of scotch. "Don't flatter yourself. You'll always just be a pawn in a much bigger game."

"And maybe I'm done with playing your fucking games."

I hear the movement before I see her, sharp, furious steps storming towards the door.

I don't even have time to move.

Alex rounds the corner at full force and collides straight into me.

The impact is immediate.

Her breath hitches, her hands gripping my jacket for balance.

My hands instinctively come up to steady her.

We freeze.

For a moment, we just stand there.

Her wide eyes lock onto mine, dark and stormy, still heated from the argument.

And for the first time since I met her, I see something raw, something unshielded flicker across her face. The weight of her father's words. The weight of everything. And it hits me. Tonight may have been a test for me, specifically orchestrated by Carter, but it was also a test for her. She left this world of glittering parties and obnoxious conversations a year ago. She's lived a quiet, humdrum life and she's also been thrown to the wolves. This isn't easy for her either.

Then, just as quickly as we slammed together, she pulls herself away.

Her fingers tighten briefly in my jacket before she lets go, stepping back, lifting her chin.

"It's time to leave."

Her voice is steady. Controlled.

But I don't miss the way her hands tremble slightly at her sides.

I glance toward the drawing room, where Carter Whitehorn is still inside, sipping his expensive scotch like he didn't just rip his daughter apart for sport.

Then I look back at Alex.

She won't meet my eyes now.

I exhale through my nose, steadying myself.

"Yeah," I murmur, voice quiet but sure. "Come on, let me get you out of here"

# Chapter 34

Alex

The car ride home is silent.
Not the comfortable kind. Not the kind where words aren't needed.
No, this silence is suffocating. Thick and swollen with the weight of my father's voice, his accusations, his dismissals.
I sit rigidly, staring out of the window at the city blurring past. The streetlights streaking like golden smudges against the glass.
I will not cry.
Not here. Not now.
Not in front of Aiden.
Aiden, who hasn't said a word since we left. Who is staring out the window as intently as I am. Only occasionally casting me quick glances. He must have heard every word my son-of-a-bitch father said about him. And despite his seemingly cool demeanour, his no-shits-given cavalier attitude, that must have stung. I hate that Aiden could have been hurt by father's words. I hate that I have put him in this position.
The car pulls up outside my building. The driver cuts the engine.
For a second, neither of us move.

Then he pushes open the door and step out, coming around to my side to open my door, like the gentleman he is before I have the chance to do myself. I step out, my heels clicking against the pavement and make my way inside. He follows a second later, closing the door with just a little too much force.

The lift ride up is just as silent.

*Still, I don't look at him.*

*Still, I will not cry.*

I unlock my apartment, push inside, and go straight to the kitchen. I drop my clutch onto the counter and brace my hands against the cool marble.

Deep breath in.

Deep breath out.

Steady. Controlled.

*Do not fall apart.*

I close my eyes, exhaling sharply through my nose. Then, before I know it, before I can even prepare myself, Aiden is behind me.

Close.

His presence is heat at my back. Solid. Unwavering. I feel, rather than see, his hand as it reaches forward and slowly turns me around.

I don't resist.

When I finally open my eyes, he's right there. His gaze locked onto mine.

He looks... different. Something softer, something deeper flickering behind the usual teasing smirk.

"I heard you," he says quietly.

I blink. "What?"

His jaw tightens slightly, like he's bracing himself. "I heard what you said to your father. About me. About... everything."

My stomach twists.

Aiden runs a hand through his hair, exhaling sharply. "I know you didn't mean it. I know it was just part of the charade. But..." He swallows. "Thank you. For saying it anyway."

I stare at him.

For a long moment, I don't say anything.

Then, "I did mean it."

The words slip out before I can stop them.

Aiden freezes.

His lips part slightly, his brows drawing together. "What?"

I swallow. My heart is hammering against my ribs, but I force myself to hold his gaze. "I meant every word."

Something shifts in his expression.

Something raw.

Something like understanding.

But instead of speaking, he steps closer.

He lifts a hand and gently tucks a loose strand of hair behind my ear. His fingers linger, brushing against my skin, his thumb running along my lower lip. Gently, teasing. My core heats and I feel that familiar throbbing between my legs. Because as much as I'd hate to admit it, Aiden Gage is affecting me. He looks so fucking good in his suit and the way he carried himself tonight was nothing short of remarkable. He just keeps on surprising me. Keeps on proving every assumption I've made about him to be entirely wrong.

The air between us thickens, charged with something neither of us want to name.

My breath catches.

His voice drops lower, a rough whisper. "When I said earlier... about how I'd proposed."

I nod, barely able to breathe.

His fingers trail down, skimming along my jaw. "That's how I'd do it."

My heart stutters.

And before I can second-guess myself, before I can think at all, I kiss him.

It's not tentative. It's not shy.

It's desperate.

A collision of lips and breath and heat.

Aiden makes a low sound in the back of his throat and immediately responds, his hands gripping my waist, pulling me flush against him.

His body is warm, solid, anchoring.

His hands? Everywhere. Exploring, searching, taking. His hands trail down to grab my arse and he lifts me, settling me onto the kitchen counter, and I wrap my legs around his waist, tugging him closer. Needing him closer. Needing to finally feel the heat of him between my legs, pressed against me, taking me.

The kiss deepens, becomes something hotter, something more.

His hands slide beneath my dress, fingers skimming along the bare skin of my thighs. My skin instantly turning to gooseflesh under his practiced caress.

I gasp, and he devours the sound, pressing harder, demanding more. My hands rise up his back, gripping his waist, pulling him towards me. The ache between my legs almost unbearable now, I want him to touch me, I want his hands on me. I want to feel him driving into me.
It's intoxicating. It's dizzying.
And I never want it to stop.
But then, suddenly, Aiden pulls back.
Panting, breathless, his forehead pressed to mine. His hands tighten on my waist like he's waging a war within himself.
Then, hoarsely, roughly, "Alex… I know why you're kissing me."
I blink, dazed. "What?"
He sighs, his breath warm against my skin. "You're trying to cover up what just happened with your father. You're upset. You're hurting. And as much as I want you… And Alex, I'll be honest, I really fucking want you right now, I won't be your distraction."
I open my mouth, but no words come out.
Because I am hurting.
Because he is right. Sort of.
He leans in just enough for his lips to brush the corner of my mouth. A whisper of a promise.
A cruel tease of what I could have had if not for this goddamn charade.
Then, low, steady, final
"When I kiss you again, Alex… And I will kiss you again…"
His grip on my waist tightens.
"I'm not going to stop."

And just like that, he steps back and walks away. Leaving me breathless and aching and wanting. And for the first time since this whole fake engagement began…
I fucking wish it wasn't fake.

"You kissed him?!"
I knew this was a mistake.
The moment I heard Aunt Edith's voice on the other end of the line, full of intrigue and far too much amusement, I knew I shouldn't have called her.
I pinch the bridge of my nose, sinking onto the plush armchair in my bedroom. "Yes, Edith. That is what I said."
A dramatic gasp. "Oh, darling, the cosmos must be singing right now! The stars have been aligning for weeks, and you finally did what was written in fate's great tapestry…"
I groan, tilting my head back against the chair. "For the love of—can we just leave the cosmos out of this for once?"
Edith tuts in that knowing way of hers. "Oh, darling." She sighs, almost pityingly. "You do realise this was inevitable, don't you?"
I scowl at the ceiling. "Nothing is inevitable."
"Oh, please. You think you don't believe in destiny, but I've seen the way you two orbit each other. The way you look at each other."
I swallow, shifting uncomfortably. "We don't look at each other in any particular way."

A delighted little laugh. "Oh, honey, you do. And it's not just me who's noticed. Anyone within a 100-mile radius can feel the sexual energy from you both!"
I rub my temples, heart pounding. "It doesn't matter. He stopped it. Said I was only doing it because I was trying to cover up that scene with my father."
Silence.
Then, softer, "Because he's a good man, Alex."
My breath hitches.
I know that.
I knew that the second his lips were on mine, the second his hands gripped my waist, the second he pulled away despite the fact that every inch of him, every inch of me, wanted him to stay.
Edith exhales gently, her voice warm and full of understanding. "He wouldn't want you to regret it in the morning, darling."
I hesitate, fingers curling against the armrest.
And then, so quietly, I barely hear my own words.
"But that's just it, I don't think I would have. Ever."
There's a long pause.
"Oh, Alex."
It's not mocking. Not teasing. It's sad. Like she knows something I don't.
I clear my throat, shaking off the strange knot forming in my chest. "It doesn't matter. We're almost done with this, anyway."
Edith hums, unconvinced.
I press forward. "Someone at dinner said that talks are already underway to arrange Miles Kensington's marriage to someone else."
"Oh?"

I nod, even though she can't see me. "Once that's finalised, Aiden and I can 'break up', make it public, move on with our lives."
The words taste bitter as they leave my mouth.
"Ah."
That's all she says.
Just ah.
Like she knows I'm lying to myself.
I press my lips together, staring at my reflection in the darkened window.
Then, after a moment, I let the words slip out, words that I shouldn't say.
Words that threaten to unravel the whole damn plan.
"I'm not sure I want that anymore."
Silence.
The kind of silence that weighs.
The kind that *sees* straight through me.
Then, after a long moment, "Well," Edith says, light and teasing, "I'll say one thing Alex dear, all I ever talk about is fate. And you called me of all people to tell me this. So perhaps there's a little part of you that does believe in it after all. Break up with him all you like, but if the engagement is fake, so is the breakup. You can't fight fate dear."
And she's absolutely right. We're not engaged. Not even dating, so breaking up means absolutely nothing. Nothing more than two, admittedly, very good actors, finishing a scene. But I don't even want to imagine acting this scene out, let alone actually do it.
Eventually we hang up.

Samantha Todd

And for the first time since this entire charade started...
I have no idea what the hell I'm going to do.

# Chapter 35

Aiden

It's been two days.
Two whole days of her avoiding me.
Two whole days of watching her slip out in the morning with some excuse about "business" in town, even though I know full well she's got nothing important to do.
Two whole fucking days of pretending nothing happened between us.
I lean against the counter in the kitchen, arms crossed, watching the door like a damn guard dog.
Because tonight? Tonight, she's not running.
The door clicks open, and in she walks, her heels tapping against the floor, moving through the apartment with practiced ease.
She doesn't even look at me.
I let her get about three steps in before I push off the counter and block her path.
"Are we gonna talk about it?"
Alex sighs, her eyes flickering up to me. Cool. Controlled. The exact same expression she's been wearing since the night at her father's house. Since she kissed me. Since she *ran from it*.
"Talk about what?" she asks, brushing past me.
I step in front of her again. "Try again, Trouble."

She exhales sharply, setting her bag down on the counter with a deliberate *thud*. "We don't need to do this."

"Yeah, Alex, we fucking do."

She crosses her arms. "We stick to the plan, Aiden."

Ah, there it is.

The safety net. The excuse.

The thing she's been clinging to like a lifeline.

I laugh dryly, shaking my head. "The plan. Right. Is that what you told yourself when you kissed me the other night? That it was all part of the fucking *plan*?"

Her expression tightens.

Bingo.

I take a step closer, lowering my voice. "Because unless I'm misremembering, you were the one who kissed me. Not the other way around."

She squares her shoulders. "I was upset. It didn't mean anything."

A muscle ticks in my jaw. I should be pissed. I should be fucking furious at that lie, but I can't bring myself to be, because I see the way her hands grip the edge of the counter. The way her throat bobs when she swallows.

She doesn't even believe it herself.

I step in again, closing the space between us. "Say it again," I murmur, reaching out, tracing my fingers along the sharp line of her jaw.

She stiffens but doesn't move away.

I tip her chin up, forcing her to look at me. "Say it again, Trouble. Tell me it didn't mean anything, while looking me in the eye this time."

Her lips part. But she doesn't say a word.

Instead, she glares at me, like sheer force of will is enough to make me drop this.

But it's not.

Not this time.

My thumb skims over her cheek, soft, coaxing. "You can lie like a pro to everyone else," I murmur, "but not to me."

Her breath hitches.

I can feel it, the way her body is caught between fight and surrender. She's always been stubborn. Always been too proud to admit what's right in front of her.

So, I give her an out.

I brush my lips against hers, slow, soft, barely a whisper of contact.

She doesn't move away.

She doesn't stop me.

But she doesn't kiss me back either.

Not yet.

So, I do what I promised her.

I pull back.

I drag my knuckles down her arm, watching the goosebumps follow in their wake. "I told you, the next time I kissed you, I wouldn't stop."

She lets out a shaky breath.

I lower my voice, the promise thick in the air between us. "So, tell me to stop."

Her hands curl into the fabric of my shirt. She's wrestling with this, caught between wanting to go forward and being terrified about what that means.

"Tell me to stop Alex" I repeat, each word a staccato.

I wait.

I fucking wait.

Samantha Todd

Her breathing becomes shaky, her forehead pressed against mine. She brings her hands up my sides, gripping me slightly, her brow furrowed. I brush my lips against hers, gently, softly, and again she doesn't pull away, she doesn't move
"Fuck it" she says, before pulling me to her, and kissing me. Hard.
I groan against her mouth, gripping her waist, dragging her flush against me.
She's not holding back anymore. Not hesitating. Not fighting herself.
And neither am I.
I lift her onto the counter, spreading her thighs, stepping between them, deepening the kiss until she's gasping into my mouth. Until there's no space left between us, no more pretending, no more lies.
She wants this.
She wants me.
And fuck if I haven't wanted her since the moment she walked into my life.
Her hands tangle in my hair, her nails scraping against my scalp, and I growl into her mouth, rolling my hips against her, letting her feel just how long I've wanted this. Just how hard I am for her.
"Aiden," she breathes against my lips.
I slide my hands up her creamy white thighs, she doesn't stop me. I brush my fingers over the soft fabric of her underwear, feeling how wet they are already, which only makes me harder. Then I pull the fabric and slide my fingers against her wet slit. Her back arches as she moans into my mouth, gripping my shirt tightly and tilting her hips to give me easier

access. I slide one finger, then two inside her, gently rubbing her clit with my thumb.

"Fuck" she says, breaking away from the kiss and leaning back on her hands as she lets me fuck her with my fingers.

I'm rock hard now, nothing, not an earthquake, not an argument, not her fucking sassy attitude is going to stop us. Two planets colliding with brutal force. Weeks of pent-up aggression, hatred, desire all spilling out of us in one fell swoop. She grapples with the button on my jeans, but I stop her.

"I want to taste you first" I say, my eyes locking with hers as I lower myself down, eye level with her eager, waiting pussy. I slide her underwear down, her lifting her hips to help me, and fling the flimsy pink (had to be pink) material over my shoulder before burying my head between her thighs. She cries out and god if it isn't the sweetest sound I've ever heard. Alex Whitehorn falling apart around me, as her thighs grip my head, her hands ruffling my hair as I go to work. My tongue flicking over her clit. She tastes so fucking sweet; I could happily eat her for every meal. I don't even want to be able to breathe.

Suddenly she pushes me away and brings me up so I'm eye level with her again, "Bedroom, now."

"Yes ma'am" I smirk and lift her off the countertop, her legs wrapped around me as we continue to kiss as I walk through the bedroom door. I lower her down on the bed gently, climbing on top her as she unbuttons my jeans which I shuck off with practiced ease. Her legs are spread wide around me, inviting me, begging me to enter her. My cock springs free of

my boxers as she pulls them down and pulls me towards her.
"Fuck me Aiden, please fuck me"
I push inside her, feeling her wetness slide over my dick, feeling her tightness, so fucking tight, wrap around me. And then I'm lost, lost to the rhythm of our bodies, each striving for a release we've been denying ourselves for weeks. Each needing the other pulled even closer. Our mouths crashing together, the kisses fierce and wild. I feel it building, the tightness in my balls, the aching for that moment when we explode together. Her breath is coming short and sharp as she chases her orgasm and my god, I'm going to make sure she gets there before me. I grind my hips into her, rubbing her clit against me, working the inside of her, pressing against all of the spots that make her whimper in response. And then, she shatters. Exploding around me, the feel of her inner walls convulsing under the power of her orgasm as it rips through her. I pull away slightly and fuck me, if she isn't the most beautiful thing I've ever seen. It sends me completely over the edge, a couple more thrusts and I'm joining her, falling off the edge of the cliff we've both been poised on, each one daring to jump first. I feel myself coming, hot and thick inside her before I collapse on top of her. For a moment, there's nothing but our breathing. Just the sound of two people completely lost to the moment that just happened. I kiss her neck, gently and she nudges her face into mine, taking my cheek in her hand and kissing me with an intensity I've only ever seen when she's throwing insults my way. I fall

into it, hopelessly and irrevocably gone. Never to come back.

"I told you I wouldn't stop." I say against her lips.

Alex laughs gently, "Well that's the thing about you Aiden Gage, you're certainly a man of your word."

I glance over my shoulder.

And immediately regret it.

Alex is leaning against the counter, my old Guns N' Roses T-shirt hanging off one shoulder, bare legs for miles. She's completely at ease, twirling a strand of auburn hair between her fingers, watching me with those unreadable, unreadable eyes.

And yeah. I'm a goner.

I clear my throat, turning back to the pot. Instant noodles. What a fucking way to celebrate mind-blowing sex.

"This isn't quite coffee at 8am," I say, lifting the wooden spoon, "but hey, at least you're finally in my T-shirt."

She lets out a small, amused breath through her nose.

"Are you ever going to come up with a new line?"

I smirk, tossing the spoon down. "Nope. Why mess with perfection?"

She rolls her eyes, but I see the way her lips twitch. That almost-smile she tries to suppress. That I won expression.

And it hits me then, I like her like this.

Relaxed. Unfiltered.

Mine.

Samantha Todd

A slow, almost lazy silence stretches between us, but it's not uncomfortable. It's charged as fuck.
I take a step toward her.
She doesn't move.
Another step.
Still doesn't move.
I place my hands on the counter on either side of her hips, caging her in. She tilts her chin up to look at me, eyes burning with something undeniable.
I drop my gaze to her mouth.
She notices.
A smirk tugs at the corner of her lips as she whispers, "Do you want to do it again?"
Her words hit me like a fucking freight train.
*Do you want to do it again?*
She might as well have set a match to every last shred of restraint I had left.
My hands tighten on the counter beside her hips. My heart pounds. My cock, already half-hard just from the sight of her in my shirt, goes fully hard.
I let the question hang between us for a moment, dragging it out. Letting the tension snap tighter, tighter.
Then I lower my head, my lips grazing the shell of her ear.
"Alex," I murmur, voice thick with heat. "That's a really fucking stupid question."
She gasps softly as my hands slide up her bare thighs, my thumbs teasing slow circles against the sensitive skin there.
I want to hear that sound again.

I want to make her ruin my name the way she did earlier.

She tilts her head, just slightly, inviting me in. Like she already knows she's lost this battle. Like she already knows I'm about to devour her.

I press my mouth to her jaw, trailing kisses down her neck, slow and purposeful. She shudders beneath my touch, her hands sliding up my bare chest, nails scraping lightly, sending shivers straight down my spine.

"Fuck," I whisper against her skin.

Then, before she can react, I lift her onto the counter, my hands spreading her legs so I can slot myself between them.

She gasps, gripping my shoulders for balance, her eyes dark and wild.

"You just can't resist picking me up, can you?" she breathes.

I smirk, dragging my fingers up the hem of my T-shirt on her body, exposing more of her bare skin.

"Nope." I brush my lips over hers, teasing, not quite giving her the kiss she's silently begging for. "And you? You just can't resist me."

She exhales sharply, glaring at me.

Then she grabs the back of my neck and pulls me down into a bruising kiss.

Fuck.

It's hungry. It's desperate. It's *her—us—*weeks of tension and unspoken words, pouring out of her mouth into mine.

I grip her hips, tugging her forward until there's not a sliver of space between us.

Samantha Todd

She's so fucking wet already, heat pressing into my stomach, and it's driving me insane.
I break away just enough to mumble, "You're not wearing any underwear, are you?"
She smiles, wicked and full of trouble.
I groan, my head dropping against her shoulder for half a second, before I drag my fingers through her slick folds, teasing her.
She moans, gripping the edge of the counter so tightly her knuckles turn white.
"You're a fucking menace. A menace that's all mine." I mutter, sliding two fingers inside her, curling them just right.
She gasps, her body jolting.
I grin against her neck.
"Say it," I command, thrusting deeper.
She barely manages a breathy, "I'm all yours."
"That's right," I say, pumping my fingers faster, feeling her muscles tighten around me. "And you're about to come for me again, aren't you?"
She grips my shoulders hard, her head tilting back, exposing that gorgeous throat.
I flick my thumb over her clit, and she shatters.
Her body trembles against mine, breathless, moaning, my name falling from her lips like a prayer.
I don't wait.
I don't hesitate.
I pull down my joggers and thrust inside her in one smooth stroke.
"Fuuuck," I hiss, gripping her hips, barely holding on.
Her legs wrap around my waist so tight, pulling me deeper.

I brace my hands on the counter, thrusting into her slow, hard, deep, watching the way her lips part, her eyes flutter.

"You feel so fucking good," I growl against her mouth. "Like you were made for me."

She grabs my face, kissing me like she's trying to ruin me.

And she is.

She really fucking is.

I can't stop.

I don't want to stop.

Her breath hitches, her nails drag down my back, her body tightening so perfectly around me.

I feel it building, both of us right on the edge, seconds away from falling over it together.

She gasps my name, begging for more, for all of me.

And then, the fucking stove timer goes off.

We freeze.

Alex is panting. Flushed. Wrecked.

I'm buried deep inside her, trying so fucking hard not to laugh at the sheer absurdity of the moment.

Then she mutters, "You are so lucky I don't give a fuck about noodles."

I lose it.

I'm laughing against her neck, breathless, forehead pressed to hers.

And then I kiss her again, slow, deep, and filled with every ounce of everything I feel for her.

Fuck the noodles.

We've got far better things to do.

It's fucking ridiculous how comfortable this feels.

Samantha Todd

Alex is sprawled on top of me, her leg draped over mine, her hand resting on my chest, fingers lightly tracing absent-minded patterns over my skin.
The TV flickers, casting dim light across the apartment, and the eerie, droning soundtrack of Paranormal Activity fills the silence.
Not that she's watching it.
I can feel the tension in her body, the way her fingers twitch every time something even remotely creepy happens.
She's trying so damn hard to act unbothered. But I know better.
I smirk, shifting slightly beneath her.
"You do realise," I murmur, lowering my voice to a near whisper, "that you chose to put on another horror movie."
She exhales sharply. "And?"
"And yet here you are, gripping my T-shirt like it's a life vest." I flick my gaze down, amused at how her fingers are clutching the fabric over my chest.
She snatches her hand back like she's been burned. "I was not gripping…"
A sudden, eerie creak from the TV makes her jolt, her fingers grabbing onto me again without thinking.
I grin.
She scowls up at me. "You're enjoying this, aren't you?"
"Immensely." I smirk, lacing my fingers through hers, locking her hand against my chest. "It's adorable, Trouble."
She groans, burying her face in my T-shirt. "I hate you."

"Nah." I press my lips to her hair, breathing her in.
"You love me."
Her body tenses.
Just for a second.
Then she exhales, shaking her head slightly.
"You're so annoying."
I chuckle, letting it go. For now.
The movie creeps toward its climax, and she burrows closer against me, like she thinks I won't notice.
Her breath is warm against my skin.
I tighten my arm around her waist, splaying my hand over the small of her back, fingers slipping just beneath the hem of my T-shirt she's still wearing.
She doesn't pull away.
Doesn't protest.
And fuck, if this isn't the best feeling in the world.
I like her like this. Soft. Tucked against me. Mine.
And it's not just the sex. It's this. All of this.
Being wrapped up in her. Holding her like she's meant to be here. Like she belongs here.
Like she's not still fighting it.
The credits finally roll, and Alex relaxes against me, her muscles uncoiling, her breathing evening out.
I press a lazy kiss to her hair.
"So... you're scared?" I murmur against her ear.
She shifts slightly, tilting her head up just enough to glare at me. "No."
I grin.
"Really?" I trace slow circles against her lower back, letting my voice drop lower. "Because from where

I'm sitting, you're cuddled up on top of me like you definitely need protection."
She exhales, rolling her eyes, but she doesn't move. Doesn't let me go.
And fuck if that doesn't say everything.
I trail my fingers slowly up her spine.
"Guess I'd better sleep in your bed tonight then," I say, completely casual, like it's the most obvious conclusion in the world.
Her body tenses again. I wait. She shifts slightly, and for a second, I think she's about to argue.
Then she exhales and mumbles, "Fine. But no snoring."
I grin, victorious.
"Oh, Trouble," I murmur, flipping her onto her back, pinning her beneath me, watching her eyes darken. "I can guarantee that my snoring is the least of your concerns tonight."
Her breath hitches.
Then she smirks. "That a promise, Gage?"
I lower my mouth to hers, "You can fucking bet on it."

# Chapter 36

Alex

The first thing I register is warmth.
The second is the heavy arm draped over my waist, the slow, steady rise and fall of someone else's breath behind me.
Aiden.
The memories from last night flood back instantly, his hands on me, his mouth, the way he felt inside me, the way he whispered my name like a promise.
I should move.
I should get up.
But I don't.
Because for the first time in a long time, I feel safe. Wrapped up in him, in his scent that lingers on my pillow, the warmth of his body against mine, the way his fingers lazily stroke my hip like he's still half-asleep but completely unwilling to let go.
I exhale slowly.
Just a few more minutes.
I let my eyes drift shut again, sinking into the quiet morning glow filtering through the windows.
Then, his voice rumbles against my skin. Sleepy, low, and far too smug.

"So, tell me," Aiden murmurs, his lips brushing the back of my neck, "how much do you regret it in the cold light of day?"

I smirk, but I keep my eyes closed.

"I don't."

There's a pause.

Then, his grip tightens on my waist, pulling me even closer. "Good answer."

I swallow, my heart betraying me with its ridiculous little leap.

"But," I add quickly, shifting to face him, "this is going to make things... complicated."

Aiden props himself up on one elbow, hair a total mess, sleep still clouding his green eyes, but he's smirking. "Trouble, everything about us has been complicated from the start. Why should it change now?"

I open my mouth to argue.

But he's not wrong.

Before I can come up with something witty my phone rings. We both groan at the same time.

I reach blindly for the nightstand, squinting at the screen.

Aunt Edith.

I sigh and answer. "Morning, Edith."

"You had sex!"

I choke.

Aiden, who's been propped on one elbow like a king surveying his kingdom, snorts so hard he shoves his face into my pillow, his body shaking with silent laughter.

"Jesus, Edith, keep your voice down!" I hiss, glancing at Aiden who is now fully crying with laughter into the sheets.

"Oh, please, darling. You think I wouldn't feel the cosmic shift? The stars realigned, the planets adjusted, the ether all but trembled."

I close my eyes and pinch the bridge of my nose. "Edith, I swear to…"

"Mercury is in retrograde, but your libido certainly isn't!"

I stare at the ceiling, praying for an earthquake to swallow me whole.

Aiden loses it completely, wheezing with laughter, his face still buried in my pillow.

I shove him, flushing red hot. "You're not helping!"

"I'm having the best morning of my life, actually." He grins, propping himself up, his voice still thick with amusement. "Put her on speaker."

I glare at him like I'm seriously considering smothering him with my pillow.

Edith gasps dramatically through the phone. "Oh, is he there? Oh, I bet he's there."

"Goodbye, Edith."

"Oh, pish-posh! You need my guidance now more than ever! When the universe orchestrates a union, you don't just…"

I hit the speakerphone button and toss the phone at Aiden before rolling out of bed and storming into the bathroom.

I hear him chuckling behind me, clearly enjoying my suffering. "So, Edith," he says far too casually,

"should we pick out star sign logos for the wedding invitations, or...?"
I slam the bathroom door.

I lean against the sink, exhaling.
My reflection stares back at me, hair a mess, lips slightly swollen, the glow of last night still evident on my face.
I look... happy. Genuinely happy. My stomach tightens. Because I already know what's coming. Tomorrow, we go back to Northwood Dale. Back to real life. And I have no fucking idea what happens next.

# Chapter 37

Alex

But reality hit far quicker than either of us anticipated.
I should have known.
I should have known the second I saw his name light up my phone later that day. The second he summoned us to his house. Something in his tone gave it away.
Carter Whitehorn is no fool.
I keep my hands folded tightly in my lap, my nails digging into my skin as I stare at the polished mahogany of his desk, my father perched behind it like a king surveying his subjects.
Aiden sits beside me, his shoulders squared, his expression blank but unreadable, his hands balled into tight fists on his thighs. I can feel the tension radiating off him, his whole body coiled like a spring, ready for a fight.
But this isn't a fight we can win.
Not against Carter.
Not against the meticulously built empire that is my father.
He leans back in his chair, completely at ease, the faintest curl of a smirk on his lips as he clasps his hands together.

Samantha Todd

"Did you really think I wouldn't find out?"
I force myself to meet his gaze. "I don't know what you're talking about."
Carter scoffs, shaking his head. Mocking. Smug. A predator toying with his prey.
"I had a rather interesting conversation with my lawyer this morning. With our lawyer, Alexis. It seems that he was ordered to make some assault charges against your *farmhand* here disappear. I'll admit, they were rather swiftly and conveniently dealt with. He's a very good lawyer."
I grit my teeth.
I feel Aiden shift beside me.
Carter turns his gaze to him, eyes cold and assessing. "I wonder... how exactly does a simple farmer get felony assault charges completely erased from his record?" He raises an eyebrow. "Unless, of course, he has the right kind of powerful connections."
Aiden doesn't speak. Doesn't move.
He's waiting.
Waiting for the real hammer to drop.
And it does.
"I've also made a few calls. Northwood Dale is a small town. People talk." He leans forward, placing his elbows on the desk. "It didn't take long to confirm my suspicions."
My throat closes up.
"The engagement," he continues, his tone laced with amusement, "is a farce."
Aiden lets out a short breath, his fingers tightening into fists. "That's not true."

Carter tilts his head. "Really?" He turns his gaze back to me. "Tell me, Alexis, did you enjoy spitting in my face with this little charade of yours?"

I lift my chin, trying to keep my voice steady. "I did what I had to do."

Carter exhales a sharp laugh, shaking his head like I'm a petulant child. "And now you're going to do what I tell you to do."

I clench my jaw. "And what might that be?"

His smirk fades, replaced by cold, merciless calculation. "You're going to marry Miles Kensington."

I balk.

"Absolutely not." The words rip from my throat before I even register saying them.

Aiden's head snaps toward me, his body going rigid beside mine. "No fucking way."

Carter doesn't even spare him a glance. His focus is entirely on me, his expression hard and unwavering. "Yes, you will. And if you don't…" He reaches into his desk drawer and pulls out a manila folder, sliding it across the desk.

I hesitate before picking it up.

Inside are documents. Legal ones. Financial records, letters, statements.

A sick feeling twists in my gut.

"What is this?" I ask, flipping through them.

Carter steeples his fingers. "The complete destruction of your dear Aunt Edith."

I freeze.

Aiden sits up straighter, his entire body tensing beside me. "What the fuck are you talking about?"

Samantha Todd

Carter sighs, leaning back in his chair, completely unbothered. "Edith's estate agency is… struggling, shall we say? A few strings pulled here, a few well-placed investments withdrawn there, and suddenly her business is drowning. Her house?" He gestures at the file. "repossession, should I will it." He shrugs. "Of course, I could choose to keep my hands off." His eyes pin me in place. "But only if you do what you're told."
My stomach drops.
"You wouldn't."
He gives me a slow, infuriatingly patient smile. "Oh, but I would. And I will."
I stare at him.
At the father I loathe. The man who has never cared for anyone but himself.
And he's willing to ruin Edith, the only family I have left, just to get what he wants.
Aiden speaks before I can. Low. Dangerous. "You're a real piece of shit, you know that?"
Carter barely glances at him. "And you are a speck of dirt beneath my shoe. You can go back to shovelling pig shit. You don't belong in this world. And you most certainly don't belong with my daughter."
Aiden moves like he's about to stand, but I grab his hand, gripping tight.
Not here.
Not now.
I shake my head once. Just once.
And he listens.
Carter watches the exchange with amusement, like we're pathetic little creatures beneath him.

"You have one week," he says, standing. "One week to make your decision before I start putting things into motion."
A cold wave of dread washes over me.
One week.
One week before I lose everything.
Before I lose Aiden.
Carter gives me a final glance, his voice soft but lethal.
"Enjoy your last taste of rebellion, Alexis." He rises to stand, gesturing towards the door, "And get the fuck out of my office."
Then he walks away.
Leaving everything crashing down behind him.

The apartment is too quiet.
Aiden stands by the window, his hands on his hips, his jaw ticking as he stares out over the glittering London skyline. He's breathing deeply, slowly, the way someone does when they're trying not to explode.
I sit on the edge of the couch, staring at the untouched cup of tea in my hands, feeling the heat seep into my palms, but it does nothing to warm me.
Because there's no warmth left here.
There's just this.
Aiden finally turns. His moss-green eyes are dark, stormy, dangerous.
"I don't accept this." His voice is low, gravelly.
I close my eyes. "You don't have a choice."
"Bullshit."

Samantha Todd

I hear the pound of his boots against the hardwood as he steps closer, radiating heat and frustration and something else. Something that makes my throat tighten.
"You're just going to give up?" His voice rises slightly, thick with disbelief. "You're just going to roll over and let that bastard win?"
I press my lips together. Swallow. Try to steady myself. "It's not about winning, Aiden. It's about reality."
"The reality is that your father is a complete prick, and you're letting him dictate your entire life!"
I stand abruptly, the chair scraping loudly against the floor. "I don't have a choice," I snap.
"Yes, you do!" He's pacing now, wild with frustration, dragging a hand through his already dishevelled hair. "For fuck's sake, Alex, you're the most stubborn, strong-willed person I've ever met, and you expect me to believe you're just going to…what? Lie down and accept this?"
I squeeze my hands into fists, feeling my nails bite into my palms. "You don't get it."
"Then make me get it!" He stops pacing, turning to me fully, his eyes blazing.
I inhale sharply. Steel myself.
And then I say the only thing that will make him stop fighting.
The only thing that will make him leave.
"This was never real, Aiden."
The words hang in the air like a loaded gun.
His face goes blank.
"Excuse me?"

I lift my chin, ignoring the sharp pain in my chest, the feeling of my own words slicing through me.

"You and I both knew what this was. A means to an end. And now it's over."

Something flickers in his expression, something pained, but then it's gone.

He shakes his head, his jaw tightening. "You don't mean that."

I cross my arms. "I do."

He lets out a humourless laugh, shaking his head. "Right. So, what? You're just going to marry Miles fucking Kensington and pretend none of this happened?"

I force a cold smile. "That was always the plan, wasn't it?"

Aiden's whole body stiffens, his hands curling into fists at his sides.

"You kissed me, Alex." His voice is lower now, darker. "Not the other way around."

Heat flares up my neck, my heart hammering against my ribs, but I don't let it show.

I just shrug.

"A mistake."

Aiden stares at me.

For a moment, it's dead silent.

Then, he laughs. It's not his usual boyish, teasing laugh. It's sharp. Rough. Undeniably angry.

"Wow," he exhales, shaking his head. "You really are your father's daughter, huh?"

I flinch.

I actually flinch.

But I don't let him see it.

Samantha Todd

I keep my face carefully blank, even as my stomach twists violently.
"Go home, Aiden."
His jaw clenches, his breath heavy.
"Say it." His voice is gritted.
I swallow. "Say what?"
"That you don't have feelings for me." His eyes burn into mine, daring me, begging me. "Say it, and I'll walk away. Right now."
My throat tightens.
I can't. I can't say it. Because it's not true. But I have to. Because if I don't, he'll never let this go. And I need him to let it go.
I take a breath. Look him straight in the eye. And I lie through my fucking teeth.
"I don't have feelings for you."
Aiden's expression doesn't change. Not for a second. Then, his jaw ticks. His hands clench and unclench at his sides. And that's it. That's the moment he gives up. His shoulders drop slightly, his eyes go flat, and he exhales sharply.
"Right."
He turns. Grabs his jacket. His bag.
I watch, my heart hammering, waiting for him to turn back. Praying that he'll turn back. But he doesn't.
He walks to the door.
Grips the handle.
And then, "You're a fucking coward, Alex."
The words hit like a gunshot. And then, he's gone.
The door slams shut, the sound echoing through the empty apartment.
I stand there for one second.

Then another.
Then another.
And then I break.
Tears blur my vision, my chest heaving as I let out a silent, choked sob, my hands gripping the side of the sofa for support. I force myself to breathe. Force myself to stop shaking.
Because this is what I wanted.
Right?
Then why does it feel like I just tore my own fucking heart out?

# Chapter 38

Aiden

The chisel bites into the wood with more force than necessary, sending splinters flying. I barely notice. My jaw is tight, my shoulders coiled, my whole body wired with frustration as I work on the solid oak surface of the table.

Each drag of the blade, each precise carving, is an outlet. A distraction.

But nothing fucking works.

Because no matter how hard I focus on the wood, all I can see is her.

Alex.

Naked. Under me. Around me.

Laughing at my dumb jokes. Giving me that look when she thought I wasn't paying attention.

The way she felt in my arms. The way she fit.

And then, "It was never real, Aiden."

I grit my teeth, carving another deep groove into the wood.

She's a fucking liar. She felt it. I know she felt it. But she chose to walk away. Chose to rip us apart before we even had the chance to begin. And for what?

For him?

For some slimy, coke-snorting, rich prick who treats women like accessories?

The thought of Miles Kensington's hands on her, of his lips on her, makes my blood fucking boil.

I drop the chisel and exhale hard, running a hand through my hair.

No.

I'm done thinking about this.

I'm done thinking about her.

Just as I grab for the sandpaper, I hear it.

The crunch of tyres on gravel.

I pause, frowning, brushing sawdust off my hands as I listen.

Then—

Footsteps. Coming up the workshop steps. I grab a cloth and wipe my hands, waiting. The door swings open.

And in walks Aunt Edith.

She's wearing layer upon layer of mismatched fabric, the colours clashing spectacularly; deep purples, burnt oranges, emerald greens. At least three scarves are wrapped around her neck, bracelets jingling as she moves.

Her wild grey curls are pinned up in what I can only assume is meant to be a bun, though most of her hair is still sticking out in every direction.

"Good evening, my sweet boy."

I sigh, tossing the cloth onto the workbench. "I don't suppose this is a social visit."

Edith smiles knowingly, strolling further into the shop, running a hand over one of my unfinished chairs.

"Lovely craftsmanship, Aiden. A chair that will last generations. Sturdy. Dependable. Unshakable." She hums, turning toward me. "If only all things in life were like that."

I cross my arms, raising a brow. "You drove all this way to talk to me in riddles?"

"Oh, don't be so grumpy." She waves a hand, jingling as she does. "You're always such a happy boy. You shouldn't let a little heartbreak change that."

My stomach tightens, but I keep my expression carefully neutral.

"I don't know what you're talking about."

Edith lets out a soft laugh, shaking her head. "You always were a terrible liar."

I grab a piece of sandpaper and start working on the table again. Ignore her.

She doesn't take the hint.

"Alex is a mess, you know."

I pause, just for a fraction of a second, before continuing to sand.

"Is that so?" My voice is even, unaffected.

Edith sighs, taking a seat on one of my half-finished stools.

"She's broken, Aiden."

I grit my teeth.

"She did that to herself."

Edith tilts her head, watching me closely. "Did she?"

I drop the sandpaper onto the table with a sharp slap and finally look at her. "She's the one who ended it. She's the one who told me it wasn't real. So, if she's miserable, that's on her."

Edith just smiles softly, like she sees right through me.

"She thought she was protecting you."

I let out a harsh laugh, shaking my head. "Yeah? Well, she's got a funny way of showing it."
Edith is silent for a moment, her gaze steady. Then she stands, adjusting one of her scarves.
"You're angry."
"No shit."
She smirks, but then her expression turns serious. "I know that Carter has something to do with this. Alex isn't telling me anything"
I don't even blink, of course she fucking isn't, because then she'd have to admit that she's making a shitty decision and allowing her fucking father to rule her life. Then she'd have to admit that behind everything, the bravado, the *I-don't-give-a-shit-about-anything-or-anyone* attitude, she's just a scared little girl doing whatever her daddy says.
I flinch at the thought, that was harsh, even for me.
Edith steps up closer to me, "You know Aiden, everyone has skeletons in their closet," she says softly.
I frown. "What the hell does that mean?"
She turns stepping towards the door. "Even men like Carter Whitehorn."
I stare at her, brow furrowed.
She reaches for the handle, then looks back at me over her shoulder, eyes twinkling.
"Sometimes, you just need to know where to look."
She smiles at me, something in it glimmering, a silent knowing. And then she's gone.
The door swings shut, leaving me standing there, staring after her, my mind racing.
Skeletons in the closet.

Samantha Todd

What the fuck is she trying to tell me?

The pub is warm and crowded, the scent of ale, good food, and wood polish thick in the air.
Laughter and the clatter of pint glasses fill the space, drowning out the noise in my own head, at least for now.
Dane, Tugsy, and Preach are already sat in our usual booth, each with a half-drunk pint in front of them.
I slide into the seat beside Preach, who claps me on the back. "About time, Gage. Thought you were off brooding somewhere."
I snort, shaking my head. "You sound like a nosy old grandmother."
"Wouldn't be the first time someone's said that," Dane mutters, taking a swig of his beer.
Tugsy leans in, voice low and conspiratorial. "Alright, mate, we've been talking, and we reckon we've figured out the real problem here."
I raise a brow, already regretting this. "Oh yeah?"
Dane smirks. "It's obvious, really. You need to get laid."
Preach groans, while Tugsy nods in agreement.
"No, no, listen," Tugsy insists, jabbing a finger in my direction. "The whole problem with your rich girl was that it was fake, right? A fake engagement, a fake relationship, fake feelings."
I grit my teeth, gripping my pint a little too hard. Fake. Right.
Tugsy continues, oblivious to the fact that less than a week ago I was having sex. Incredible sex with the

most incredible woman. "So, the solution is simple. You just need to shag someone who's actually real."

Preach rolls his eyes. "Yeah, because that always solves deep emotional trauma."

Dane smirks. "I mean, it can't hurt."

I shake my head, trying to summon the usual easy grin. The banter's there, but my heart's not in it. Not really.

Because no matter how much I want to forget, no matter how many drinks I down or jokes I crack, she's still in my fucking head.

Alex.

And then, as if summoned by my subconscious, the fucking door opens and there she is.

Every muscle in my body locks up.

She's standing in the doorway, still in her posh London clothes, her eyes searching the crowd until she finds me.

I don't even hesitate.

I stand, grab my empty pint glass, and walk straight toward the bar, straight past her.

Like she's no one.

Like she never meant a damn thing. Because fuck engaging in whatever game she's about to start playing. Fuck being another pawn on her chessboard. She ended this, not me.

Her hand catches my arm.

Her grip is small but firm and there's an underlying desperation to it.

"Are you just going to pretend I don't exist?"

Samantha Todd

I slowly turn my head, meeting her gaze. And despite all my bravado and *fuck-you*-Alex attitude, it nearly wrecks me.
She looks beautiful. Her auburn hair hangs loose around her shoulders and her cheeks are pink from the winter chill. But the dark circles under her eyes give away sleepless nights and her furrowed brow reveals her stress. I want to reach out to her, let her know it will all be ok, but I don't.
Because she's not mine.
Never was. Never will be.
I swallow down the ache, my voice cold, clipped, sharp as a blade.
"Where's your fiancé? Your real one."
She flinches.
And fuck, I hate myself for it.
Her mouth opens, then closes. Like she's trying to find the right words, the perfect way to fix this. But there is no fucking way.
Instead, she sighs, voice softer now.
"It doesn't have to be like this, Aiden. We can still be friends."
Friends.
Fucking friends.
I let out a sharp bitter laugh, shaking my head.
"Don't do me any favours, Alex."
Her lips part slightly, her brows draw together, and for a moment, just a moment, I swear I
see hurt flicker across her deep brown eyes.
But I can't let myself care.
I turn away, ordering another round for the lads, ignoring the tightness in my chest, the urge to turn

back, to grab her, to tell her that she can't just fucking walk into my life, destroy me, and expect me to be okay with it.

I feel her still standing there, lingering for a beat too long, like she's waiting for something.

But I don't look back. Despite everything within me screaming to do so, I don't turn back.

Eventually, she leaves.

And I exhale slowly, trying to ignore the fact that it feels like the final nail in the coffin. Like my stubbornness just well and truly ended this. Just shut the metaphorical door on the only girl I've ever actually felt something for. I've always been a stubborn bastard, but this, this is something different. My guts twist at the thought of this actually being over. Of not holding her again, not kissing her again, not touching her again. There's no way this can be over. I don't want this to be over.

I grab the beers, returning to the table, forcing a smirk as I slide into my seat.

Dane eyes me. "So, uh, that looked fun."

"Piss off."

They don't press, but I know they're all thinking the same thing.

That isn't the end. Not really. Because Aunt Edith's words are still rattling around my head.

*"Everyone has skeletons in their closet, Aiden. Even men like Carter Whitehorn. Sometimes you just need to know where to look."*

And if there's even the slightest chance that she's right?

Then this isn't over.

Samantha Todd

Not by a long fucking shot.

# Chapter 39

Aunt Edith

The chime above the estate agent's door rings, and I don't even need to look up to know who it is.
I can feel his energy before he even steps inside, restless, determined, carrying the weight of a war he's not even sure how to fight yet. Aiden Gage has always been a storm in human form, all windswept chaos wrapped in a charming smile. But right now? Right now, the storm is brewing into something much more dangerous.
And I know exactly why he's here. But I'm not about to tell him that outright, am I?
I glance up from my desk, casually adjusting the rings on my fingers. "Well, if it isn't Northwood Dale's most eligible bachelor," I muse, tilting my head. "Come to buy a cottage, love? I can offer you a good price."
Aiden doesn't smile. He steps inside, closing the door firmly behind him, shoving his hands into the pockets of that well-worn jacket of his.
"Cut the crap, Edith." His tone is light, but his eyes? Not so much. "What did you mean the other day? About Carter having skeletons in his closet?"
I arch a brow, keeping my expression perfectly neutral. "Oh, Aiden, everyone has skeletons. Yours

just happen to be frosty and five foot six feet tall with long auburn hair."

He doesn't take the bait.

He moves further into the shop, pacing slightly in front of my desk, like a caged animal working through his next move. "You didn't say it like it was just an expression," he continues. "You know something, don't you?"

I sigh, tapping my fingernails against my teacup. "Knowing something and being able to prove something are two very different things, my dear boy."

He narrows his eyes. "But you suspect."

I take a slow sip of my tea, letting the warmth settle me. "Carter Whitehorn is a man who doesn't take risks unless he knows he can control the outcome. And yet, over the years, he's made... let's say... calculated business moves that don't always add up."

Aiden watches me carefully. He's clever, very clever. People don't always give him enough credit for that, but I see it. He's putting the pieces together even as I give them to him in small, careful fragments.

"What kind of business moves?" he presses.

I sigh again, more theatrical this time, and set my teacup down with a soft *clink*. "Oh, the usual. Money being shuffled about, things appearing and disappearing. There were whispers once, years ago, that Carter got a little *too* lucky in the stock market. Right before some of his biggest acquisitions."

Aiden leans against the desk now, arms crossed. "You think he's into some dodgy financial shit?"

I chuckle. "Darling, I know he is. I just don't have the proof."

People just assume that I'm the crazy crystal-obsessed, batty old Aunt Edith. And to some extent that is an accurate portrait, but one thing I also do, is watch. And ever since my darling sister married that shark, I have certainly watched. I knew it could never be me to finally give Carter Whitehorn what he deserves. But this young man, with all his jokes and easy-going charm, he flies under the radar. No one suspects his abilities. But I see them. And the prince being brought down a peg or two by the lowly pauper is something I would relish the opportunity to witness.

His jaw ticks, his mind already working through possibilities.

"I take it Alex doesn't know about any of this?" he asks.

I tilt my head. "Do you think Carter Whitehorn raised his daughter to question him? No, Aiden. She was raised to be an extension of his empire, not a threat to it. But he underestimates her. And he has certainly underestimated you."

Aiden rubs a hand over his jaw, exhaling sharply. "But you don't have anything concrete? No records? No evidence?"

I shake my head. "Nothing that would hold up in court, my dear. But people like Carter, men who think they're untouchable, they always make mistakes. There's always a bread crumb to follow. The trick is knowing where to look."

Samantha Todd

Aiden is silent for a beat. Then he smirks, something sharp and knowing.
"Well," he says, pushing off the desk. "I've got a couple of people who might be good at looking."
I watch as he turns, heading toward the door, shoulders straighter, mind set on something bigger than just anger now.
"Make sure you be careful, love," I call after him. "You're playing in deep waters now. Make sure you have a life raft as backup"
He doesn't stop, just lifts a hand in a mock salute.
"Don't worry, Edith," he tosses back. "I'm a fucking good swimmer."
And with that, he's gone, off to dig up the skeletons I've always known were there, but never had the means to unearth myself.
A slow smile spreading across my face.
Because for the first time in a long time, I think Carter Whitehorn might just lose.
And who'd have thought that it would be Aiden Gage to do it.
How utterly delicious.

Alex pushes open the door to my estate agents about a half an hour later, the familiar chime ringing out as she steps inside.
My beautiful, headstrong niece, here to tie up loose ends. To say goodbye to the life she had started to build for herself. The one she now has to let go of.
Or does she?
Sitting at my desk I idly play with the assortment of rings stacked along my fingers. But I clearly could

never be a poker player, the glint in my eye, the smallest twitch at the corner of my mouth, it gives me away and of course, Alex notices.
Alex frowns. "What?"
I merely blinked innocently. "What do you mean, dear?"
Alex drops her bag onto the chair by the window, eyeing me with suspicion. "You're smirking."
I wave a dismissive hand, the bangles on my wrist jingling in protest. "I smirk all the time."
"No, you look like the cat that got the cream," Alex shoots back, narrowing her eyes. "What's going on?"
I shrug in a way that is anything but casual. "Oh, nothing of note. Just enjoying this fine morning."
Alex folds her arms. "Aunt Edith…"
"Would you like some tea?" I interrupt, standing up and making my way to the small kitchenette in the back. "Something calming, perhaps? You seem a little tense."
Alex's jaw clenches. She is tense. How could she not be? She's just spent the morning finalizing arrangements to leave Northwood Dale. To return to London. To fall in line like the dutiful daughter Carter Whitehorn expects her to be.
*Well not on my bloody watch.*
Aiden had left London over a week ago. He had walked away, and she had let him. What other choice did she have? She had tried to convince herself that it was for the best, but the hollowness in her chest made it hard to believe her own lies.
She runs a hand through her hair. "I don't have time for tea. I just came to grab the last of my things."

I still for just a fraction of a second before continuing with my tea-making charade. "Leaving so soon?"

"Tomorrow," Alex confirms, swallowing hard. "I move in with Miles next week."

I turn around, stirring the tea far longer than necessary, my expression unreadable. "Right. Miles."

Alex refuses to meet my eyes. And if I'm honest, I'm glad. She would see straight through me in an instant. "It's what's best."

"For who?" I ask, my voice soft.

Alex exhales sharply. "For everyone."

There's silence. A heavy, weighted silence that presses against my ribs like a vice. I finally set the tea down and walked toward her, placing a gentle hand on her arm.

"My dear girl," I murmur. "You and I both know that's not true."

Alex bites the inside of her cheek, forcing herself to hold it together. She picks up her bag, gripping it tight as if it could somehow ground her.

"I should go," she says, voice barely above a whisper.

I nod, stepping aside, but as Alex reaches the door, I call after her.

"Just remember, love," I say, my voice carrying a note of something that Alex is too occupied to place. "Not all cages have bars."

Alex hesitates, fingers curling around the doorknob. But she doesn't turn back.

I just smile.

My beautiful, headstrong niece. So blissfully unaware that the fight is far from over.

# Chapter 40

Aiden

"You know, for a bloke with a recently wiped criminal record, you have a seriously suspicious interest in illegal shit."

We're sitting in Preach's living room, him across from me at a desk lined with monitors, like something out of the damn Matrix, a half-finished bottle of beer in front of him. His fingers tap rhythmically against the table as he eyes me like a disappointed priest about to deliver a sermon. Which, considering his old man is the local vicar, is about right.

I lean back on the sofa, stretching my arms over my head. "I don't recall saying anything about illegal shit. Just some good, old-fashioned, morally questionable snooping."

Preach smirks, shaking his head. "Same thing, mate. Now, tell me again why I'm risking my WIFI privileges for the next decade?"

I exhale, my knee bouncing in anticipation. "Because Carter Whitehorn is a lying, manipulative bastard, and I need to find out exactly what skeletons he's been hiding before he forces Alex into a marriage she doesn't want."

Preach snorts. "Could've just said 'because I fancy the pants off her and want to save the day,' mate."

I glare at him. "Shut up and do your thing."

Preach grins, cracking his knuckles before spinning his chair round, "Alright then, if we're going after a Whitehorn, we need backup. And lucky for you, I know just the guy."

I roll my eyes. "You mean your brother? The 'financial genius' who single-handedly robbed your mum's Christmas fund to invest in Bitcoin?"

Preach scoffs. "First of all, that's an allegation. And second, that investment paid off, so let's not slander a man for being ahead of his time."

"Yeah, yeah. Just call him."

Preach taps a few keys, then props his phone against a pile of books to his right as the dial tone rings. A moment later, a deep, bored voice answers.

"Preach, if this is another attempt to get me to sort your taxes…"

"Rabbi, my darling brother," Preach says, in the kind of voice that suggests he wants something. "What a delight to hear your voice."

There's a long pause. "Jesus. What do you want?"

I stifle a laugh as Preach leans forward. "We need access to some financial records."

"Illegal."

"Not necessarily."

"And how do you figure that?"

"Come on, mate, it's for a good cause."

Rabbi sighs. "Fine. I'll bite. Who am I looking into?"

Preach glances at me. I nod. "Carter Whitehorn."

There's a beat of silence.

"*The* Carter Whitehorn?"

I frown. "Why do you sound like you already know him?"

Rabbi scoffs. "Because in the financial world, he's that guy. Ruthless, efficient, and always, always one step ahead. He doesn't just make money; he fucking manufactures it."

I lean forward, my fingers curling around my Coke can. "You ever hear anything about him being dirty?"

Rabbi chuckles. "Mate, every billionaire is dirty. The trick is catching them with their hands in the wrong cookie jar."

Preach grins. "Well, Aiden here is feeling particularly into cookies right now."

Rabbi exhales loudly. "Alright, fine. But if I get fired for this, you're explaining it to Mum."

Preach winks. "Appreciate you, bro."

Rabbi mutters something under his breath before the sound of furious typing fills the line.

I take a sip of my drink, my patience wearing thin. "What exactly are you looking for?"

"Any irregularities. Large transfers, offshore accounts, investments that don't make sense..." Rabbi trails off, humming in thought. "And if you're hoping to bring him down, you'll need something indisputable. A direct link to something illegal."

We wait as Rabbi's fingers click against the keyboard, scanning through what I assume is more money than I'll ever see in my lifetime.

We wait for what feels like an eternity, before, "Bingo."

Preach and I lean in. "What is it?"

Rabbi whistles low. "You weren't kidding about wanting dirt. Your boy Whitehorn has been funnelling money into a shell corporation for years. Millions shuffled between multiple accounts, all leading to one name."

I grip the edge of the table. "Who?"

"Whiteline Consulting."

I exchange a look with Preach. Edith's rumour, her cryptic warning, it's all clicking into place.

Rabbi continues. "The company looks like a front. It's listed as a consulting firm, but no actual business is being conducted. It's just an empty account receiving money every month. No expenses, no employees. That kind of setup usually means one thing, money laundering."

Preach lets out a low whistle. "Damn. Your future father-in-law's a major fucking criminal."

I snort. "Like I didn't already know that."

Rabbi clears his throat. "Right, well, as much as I enjoy playing financial Robin Hood, I'd like to keep my job. I'm sending you the documents now. They're encrypted, so don't go waving them around, yeah?"

I nod. "Understood. Thanks, mate."

Rabbi sighs. "Good luck. You'll need it."

With that, the call disconnects.

I turn to Preach, who's already skimming through the downloaded files.

"Well," he muses. "Looks like you've got your smoking gun." He stares at his laptop, fingers tapping against the edge of the table. "So, we've got money laundering, but let's see if we can get something even juicier."

I frown. "Money Laundering isn't juicy enough for you?"

Preach grins. "Come on, mate. This is Carter bloody Whitehorn we're talking about. A man like that? He's got his fingers in a dozen different pies. Let's see what else we can dig up."

I glance at the now-warm Coke in front of me on the coffee table, the weight of this whole thing settling on my shoulders. I need something bulletproof. If I'm going to take Carter down, I need evidence that will leave no room for negotiation.

Preach cracks his knuckles and gets to work, his eyes scanning the screens surrounding him as he navigates through layers of firewalls and security systems that I definitely don't want to ask how he's bypassing.

I lean in. "You do this kind of thing often?"

He smirks. "What, illegally accessing private emails? Nah, mate. I'm a law-abiding citizen."

I snort. "Sure you are."

Preach types faster, his eyes narrowing in concentration. "Alright, let's see what Daddy Whitehorn has been up to."

Preach scrolls through streams of encrypted emails, humming under his breath. "Okay, most of this is just boring business talk. Asset acquisitions, portfolio expansions, that sort of shit. But..." He pauses, squinting. "Oh, what do we have here?"

I lean over his shoulder. "What is it?"

Preach whistles low, clicking on a thread. "Looks like an email chain between Carter and someone called Philip Galloway."

Rabbi's voice comes through the speaker. "Philip Galloway? The Philip Galloway? The investment tycoon?"

Preach grins. "Ding, ding. Give the man a prize."

I rub the back of my neck. "And why is this significant?"

Preach opens the thread and tilts his screen so I can see it properly. "Because, my friend, this is an explicit conversation about insider trading."

My eyebrows shoot up. "Insider trading? As in… illegal, go-to-prison, financial fraud?"

Rabbi sighs. "Yep. And not just any insider trading, high-level, carefully orchestrated fraud."

Preach gestures to the screen. "See this? Carter was feeding Galloway information on government contract approvals before they were made public, allowing Galloway to invest just before the stocks soared."

Rabbi groans. "That's textbook market manipulation. Serious jail time if proven."

I exhale, my fingers tightening into a fist.

"How serious are we talking?"

Rabbi doesn't hesitate. "At least ten years. If the Financial Conduct Authority catches wind of this? It's game over."

I grin.

*Perfect.*

Preach clicks on another email. "And look at this, Carter wasn't just feeding Galloway info. He was benefitting from it too. Kickbacks, secret investment accounts… the whole damn operation was a well-oiled machine."

Rabbi huffs. "Christ. If these emails were leaked, he'd be finished. His reputation, his company, everything would go up in flames."

Preach leans back, cracking his neck. "Well, well, well. Looks like you've got two bullets in the chamber now, Gage."

I exhale, the pieces finally coming together in my mind.

One: Carter's been making regular, undisclosed payments to Whiteline Consulting, a probably fictional business used for money laundering.

Two: He's knee-deep in insider trading, feeding market-sensitive information to Philip Galloway for financial gain. Financial crime.

I glance at Preach. "Can you download all of this?"

He scoffs. "Please. Who do you think you're talking to? If you go public with this information, you better be damn sure it's the right move. Carter Whitehorn is powerful. He won't go down without a fight."

I run a hand through my hair, my brain whirring. "I don't need to go public. I just need enough leverage to force his hand."

Preach smirks. "Well, mate, you've got it. Now what?"

I grin, cracking my knuckles. "Now? Now I go free my girl."

# Chapter 41

Alex

The gravel crunches under my tires as I pull up outside the farmhouse. It's quiet. Too quiet. The kind of quiet that happens just before a storm breaks out or a tsunami hits. As if I haven't weathered enough already.

Aiden's truck isn't in its usual spot. A part of me is relieved. I don't know what I was hoping for by coming here. Maybe I just wanted to see him, maybe I wanted to talk. Or maybe, if I'm being brutally honest with myself, I just wanted one last excuse to be near him before I leave Northwood Dale for good. I know he basically blanked me at the bar, but he's angry. I can't blame him for that, I would be angry with me to. I am fucking angry with me. It's not like I have a choice though.

I slam the car door shut behind me, my breath clouding in the crisp autumn air. I tell myself I'll just turn around and go home. I should. But my feet betray me, leading me toward the workshop instead. The scent of sawdust and varnish greets me as I push open the heavy wooden door. Sunlight spills in through the high windows, dust motes dancing in the beams. And there, scattered around the space like pieces of him, are his creations.

Tables, chairs, bed frames, each one unique, each one handcrafted with such care and precision that it stops me in my tracks. I step further inside, running my fingers over the smooth wood of a dining table. It's beautiful. Sturdy yet elegant. Practical yet effortlessly stunning.

Just like Aiden.

I swallow hard. I never really understood before, not fully, just how talented he is. I always knew he was good with his hands (the thought makes my stomach clench in ways I don't have time to analyse), but this? This is artistry.

This is what he should be doing.

Not wasting away on a farm, shovelling mud and fixing fences. Not letting people assume he's just some charming, easy-going small-town boy with no real ambition. He could sell these pieces. Hell, people in London would pay thousands for this kind of craftsmanship.

I trail my fingers over a set of chairs, feeling the grooves in the wood, the way each curve has been shaped so purposefully. Aiden's work *feels* like him. Strong. Warm. Built to last.

And God, if that isn't a metaphor for the man himself.

"Didn't take you for a furniture enthusiast."

I spin around at the voice, my heart lurching into my throat.

Brynne, I presume from everything Aiden has told me.

She stands in the doorway, arms crossed, watching me with quiet scrutiny. She's even more striking than

Samantha Todd

I'd imagined, petite and poised, with warm brown eyes, the kind that don't miss a damn thing.

"I..." I clear my throat, dropping my hand from the chair like I've been caught doing something I shouldn't. "I was just..."

"Pining?" she supplies dryly, stepping inside.

I bristle. "I was looking."

She hums, her gaze flicking over the workshop before settling back on me. "Uh-huh."

I lift my chin. "Aiden's really talented."

"No shit."

I exhale sharply, crossing my arms over my chest. "Look, I get it, okay? You're his brother's fiancé, you're family. You don't like me..."

She cuts me off with a sigh, moving closer. "I don't know you, Alex. But I do know him."

Her words land heavy between us.

She walks past me, dragging her fingers along the edge of a beautifully crafted bench before turning back to face me. "And I know when he's hurting."

I swallow. My throat feels thick. "I..."

She shakes her head. "I'm not here to argue with you, or make you feel worse. But if you came here looking for some kind of absolution, you won't find it from me."

My chest tightens.

She watches me for a long moment before sighing, her voice softer when she speaks again. "I've known Aiden a long time. He's an annoying, stubborn, charming, oafish bastard, but he's also one of the best men I've ever met."

I stare at the floor. "I know."

"Do you?" She tilts her head. "Because if you did, you'd know that he doesn't just fall for people, Alex. He doesn't give his heart away easily."
My pulse stutters.
Brynne's voice is gentle but firm. "And unless I'm mistaken, he did give it away. To you."
A sharp ache settles in my chest.
She exhales, shaking her head. "I know how easily the Gage boys can get under your skin. Believe me, I know."
A small, dry laugh escapes me despite myself.
"But if you're going to walk away from him, then do it properly. Don't keep circling back like a moth to a flame. Let him go, or don't let him go." She pauses, pinning me with an unwavering look. "But don't half-arse it."
I feel like I've been seen in a way I wasn't prepared for. Like my carefully constructed layers have just been laid bare.
She steps back toward the door, her expression unreadable. "Just something to think about."
I nod, my throat too tight to speak.
And then, just as she reaches the door, she turns back, the corners of her mouth twitching. "And for what it's worth..." She tilts her head, eyeing me. "That looks like his t-shirt you're wearing. Strange thing to do if you're really set on letting him go..."
I look down at the Guns 'n' Roses T-shirt he left behind when he stormed out of my London apartment. I open my mouth to argue, but nothing comes out.
Brynne just smirks. "Thought so."

Samantha Todd

And with that, she leaves me standing there, alone in Aiden's world.
The phone buzzes in my pocket.
I don't want to answer it. Every single instinct in my body screams at me to let it go to voicemail; to pretend I never saw it, to throw the damn thing into the pig trough outside the barn and walk away forever.
But I can't.
Because if I ignore this call, if I so much as put a single foot out of place, Aunt Edith will lose everything. And I can't let that happen.
So, against every fibre of my being, I take a deep breath, steel myself, and press accept.
"Miles," I say, keeping my voice even, detached.
"Ah, my perfect fiancée," he purrs, dragging out the word like it's some inside joke. "Finally, you pick up. I was starting to think you'd developed cold feet."
I grip the phone tighter. "I've been busy."
"Yes, I imagine playing house with your little farmer has kept you occupied." His voice is all silk and arrogance, and I bite my tongue hard enough to taste blood. "Tell me, have you packed your bags yet? I do hope you're not planning on bringing
anything... provincial back with you. Your wardrobe, for example. It was already on the borderline before you ran away."
I close my eyes. Breathe in. Breathe out.
"Let's cut to the chase, Miles. What do you want?"
He lets out a low chuckle, like I've amused him. Like this is all a game.
"I want to talk about our wedding."

My stomach churns.

"Our wedding," he repeats, as if the word itself will make it real. "It's going to be quite the event, you know. My mother's already calling it the social season's most anticipated affair. Invitations will be very exclusive."

I press my palm into the nearest solid surface, Aiden's workbench, where rough-cut wood shavings scatter the surface. I trail my fingertips over them, grounding myself in something real, something steady, something not this.

He continues, utterly oblivious, or maybe just indifferent, to the fact that I'd rather rip my own heart out than marry him.

"You know, I was thinking," he muses, as if he's considering the colour of his next Aston Martin. "We should do a joint stag and hen party. Make it a whole weekend. Nothing tacky, of course, none of that Ibiza nonsense. I'm thinking Monte Carlo, or perhaps Santorini. Something tasteful."

I don't respond.

"Oh, don't tell me you've gone all shy, Alexis. I remember a time when you weren't so reserved."

I clench my jaw so hard it hurts.

Miles Kensington is exactly the kind of man I swore I would never allow myself to be tied to again. A man who sees women as accessories, as extensions of his own power and prestige. A man who cheats, lies, and always, fucking always gets away with it. Not because he's particularly clever or devious but because he's a Kensington and they can do no wrong.

Samantha Todd

And now, thanks to my father, I'm about to become his. Tied to him, shackled more like, for eternity. The thought of his hands on me, of kissing his puckered, disgusting lips makes me want to retch. A lifetime of being the dutiful little wifey, turning a blind eye to my husband's indiscretions (and there will be many of them), of dealing with his coke-addled rantings. The room starts to spin.

I stare down at the dusting of sawdust on my hands. Aiden's t-shirt had been covered in it the last time I saw him in the pub. His hands, the one's that had been all over my body, rough, calloused, strong had scuff marks from working with the chisel all day. God, I miss him.

I miss the way he looked at me. The way he argued with me. The way he touched me. I miss everything about him and if you'd told me a year ago that I would have missed Aiden Gage, I would have laughed in your face. But now...?

I shake my head, trying to literally eject the thoughts of him from my brain because I can't have him. And he can't have me. Not that probably would want me anymore. Now I don't have a choice.

I force my voice into something cold and distant. "If that's all, Miles..."

"Oh, don't be such a bore, darling." He sighs. "Look, we'll talk details when you're back in London. I just wanted to remind you that you'll be on my arm at the Mayfair Club on Saturday. It's a very exclusive guest list, and I'd rather not have to explain to people why my future wife is nowhere to be found."

I swallow down the bile rising in my throat.

"Of course," I manage. "I'll be there."

"Good girl."

The phone clicks off, and I let out a shaky breath, gripping the edge of the bench like it might keep me from collapsing entirely. I can't do this. I don't want to do this. But I have to.

For Edith.

For the only person in my life who has ever loved me unconditionally.

I shove my phone deep into my pocket and push away from the bench, straightening my spine.

One more week.

One more week of freedom before I move into Miles' overpriced and perfectly furnished house. One more week of being Alex before I have to become Alexis Whitehorn again. One more week.

Suddenly the door swings open.

I spin around so fast my hair whips over my shoulder.

Aiden.

He stops mid-step, boots scuffing against the wooden floor, his duffel bag slung over one shoulder. He looks rugged, a little windswept, like trouble, standing in the golden light of the doorway, watching me.

I take him in like it's the last time I'll ever get to. The way his t-shirt clings to his broad chest, the way his stubble frames his sharp jaw, the way his eyes, those deep, moss green eyes, lock onto mine like I'm something he just can't figure out.

And something inside me snaps.

I close the distance in three steps, grab his face, and kiss him.

Samantha Todd

There's no hesitation.
No teasing.
No back and forth.
Because there's nothing left to be said.
His duffel bag drops to the floor with a dull thud, his hands immediately finding my waist, yanking me against him, our bodies colliding in heat and desperation.
He groans into my mouth, his hands everywhere, gripping my hips, sliding up my spine, tangling in my hair.
I bite his lower lip, and it's like I've lit a match.
He growls, actually growls, and suddenly, I'm lifted off my feet, my back pressing against one of his unfinished pieces of furniture. Papers scatter, a chisel clatters to the floor, and I don't care.
None of it matters.
I need this. I need him.
Because this is the only thing that feels real. The only thing that feels like mine. And it might be the last time I get to feel like this.
Aiden kisses me like he's starving, like he's been waiting for this exact moment since the second he walked out of my apartment over a week ago. And maybe he has.
I gasp as his hands slide under my sweater, fingers dragging up my bare skin, rough callouses caressing my nipples and sending shivers down my spine.
"Alex," he breathes, mouth trailing down my neck. "You're gonna be the fucking death of me."
"Then die already," I whisper, raking my nails down his back.

His answering chuckle is dark and wrecked before he lifts my sweater over my head and tosses it somewhere behind him.

I reach for his belt, desperate, needy, pulling at the leather strap. He groans, letting me work his jeans open as his hands grip my thighs, spreading them, making space for him.

"I swear to God," he mutters, pressing his forehead against mine, "if this is goodbye, I'll lose my fucking mind."

I don't answer. I can't.

Instead, I draw my skirt up, pulling my underwear aside and arch into him, guiding his cock to my entrance, slick and so ready for him.

His lips part, eyes locked onto mine, searching, questioning.

Then I tilt my hips, and we both break.

The first thrust is brutal, sharp, filled with so much emotion it steals my breath.

I cry out, and Aiden buries his face in my neck, his hands gripping my hips, holding me still as he thrusts deep inside me.

The table creaks under our movements, papers fluttering to the floor. I claw at his back, dragging him closer, harder, more.

It's everything.

The weeks of tension, the stolen glances, the fights, the heated exchanges, the deal, the destruction, it all explodes between us in this moment, in this messy, desperate, all-consuming need.

I cling to him, arching against every movement, every snap of his hips, feeling him deep, deep, deep.

Samantha Todd

"I hate you," I whisper into his skin.
He bites my shoulder, smirking against me. "I hate you too, Trouble."
I fist my hands in his hair, dragging his mouth back to mine, kissing him with everything I have left.
Aiden presses a hand to my stomach, pressing me flat against the table as he slams into me, over and over, driving me toward the edge.
"Come for me, baby," he rasps, biting my jaw, my shoulder, my collarbone.
His fingers slip between us, rubbing tight, fast, perfect circles against my clit.
And then, I shatter.
A broken moan spills from my lips as I tumble over the edge, my body convulsing around him, clenching tight, gripping him as I spiral into pure,
blinding pleasure.
Aiden curses, his thrusts turning erratic, messy, and then he buries himself deep one last time and lets go.
I feel everything.
His pulse pounding against mine. His ragged breathing. The way his hands still shake against my waist.
We collapse, a tangled mess of limbs, chests rising and falling together.
For a long moment, we don't move.
I stare at the ceiling, catching my breath, my fingers absently tracing lazy circles against his back.
Aiden presses a lingering kiss to my temple, his breath still heavy, still warm against my skin.
Then, softly, too softly, he asks, "Stay?"

My throat closes.
I know what he's asking.
Not just tonight. Not just for another round of whatever the fuck this is. He's asking me to choose him.
To choose us.
To stay.
I turn my head, meeting his gaze. His green eyes are unreadable, guarded.
I open my mouth, and the truth comes before I can stop it.
"I can't."
His jaw tightens, but he nods. Just once.
And then, he lets me go.

# Chapter 42

Aiden

The workshop still smells like her.
I can feel her in every breath of sawdust, in every whisper of varnish clinging to the air. My hands rest against the table, the same table I just fucked her on, and I clench my fists, willing myself to hold onto this moment.
She's gone.
She left.
Again.
But this time, it's not fucking over.
Not even close.
I let out a long breath and push away from the table, running a hand through my hair, still damp from sweat, still laced with the scent of her.
No.
I won't let her do this.
I won't let her walk away, convinced she has to play the sacrificial lamb in Carter Whitehorn's chess game.
This isn't over.
Not until I say it is.
I grab my duffel from the floor, slinging it over my shoulder as I head for the house. My boots thud

heavily against the wooden floor, my pulse steady, sure, my mind made up.

I'm going to London.

I'm fixing this.

And I'm going to get my girl back.

I push the door open and barely make it two steps inside before I hear Ben's voice.

"You look like shit."

I huff a dry laugh, dropping my bag on the bench near the door. "Good to see you too, Dad."

He raises an eyebrow from where he leans against the counter, one arm crossed over his broad chest, the other scratching lazily at his slightly silvered beard. His usual steady, assessing expression is fixed on me, taking in the slight stubble I haven't bothered shaving, and no doubt the absolute fuckery written all over my face.

He doesn't say anything for a long moment.

Then, "She really did a number on you, huh?"

I exhale through my nose, shaking my head, because he has no idea.

He tilts his head slightly, studying me. "Look, I'm not gonna tell you what to do. You're a grown man, and you've always done whatever the hell you wanted anyway. But I've been watching you these past few weeks." He pauses. "And I like this version of you, Aiden."

I still.

He nods, like he knows exactly what I'm thinking. "This real version of you. The one who actually cares about something." His lips twitch. "Or someone."

I swallow hard, my jaw tightening.

Samantha Todd

Because he's right. I do care.
I care so fucking much it hurts.
I open my mouth to say something, but he beats me to it.
"When you love someone, you fight for them," Dad says simply, his voice level. "You don't just let them go because it's easier."
My heart slams against my ribs.
*Love*.
It's the first time anyone's said it out loud.
The first time I've really thought about it like that.
Like a truth I've always known but never had the guts to face.
And now, standing in the farmhouse kitchen, Ben watching me with quiet certainty, I know.
I love her.
It's as simple as that.
I love Alex Whitehorn.
I love the way she fights with me and matches my sarcasm, sometimes even surprising it. I love the way her eyes give her away every time she's nervous. That steely, practiced expression might fool some, but her eyes always betray her. I love that I'm the only one that can see that. I love that she adores horror movies but gets scared shitless from them. I love her need for fancy Italian food. I love the way she loves fiercely and unapologetically. I love the way she looks at me when she doesn't think I'm looking. The way she kisses me like I'm helping her to breathe. I love that she's doing this, putting herself in the most unimaginable situation for her Aunt

Edith. Fuck me, I even love her pink polka-dot pyjamas.

And when you love someone, you do anything for them. Even if it means taking down one of the most powerful businessmen in the country. Even if it means going head-to-head with a man who thinks he owns her. Even if it means forcing her to see that she doesn't have to do this alone.

My throat feels tight, but I swallow past it, straightening. I meet Ben's gaze, nodding once.

"It's gonna work out," I say, my voice steady. Totally resolved.

Dad watches me carefully before finally giving me a small, knowing smile. He knows that when I've made my mind up about something, nothing on earth will sway my resolve. "Then go." He says quietly.

I don't waste another second.

I grab my duffel, throw it over my shoulder, and head for the door.

London is waiting.

Alex is waiting.

And I'm not fucking letting her go without a fight.

I sit in the glass-walled meeting room, drumming my fingers against the sleek table, the London skyline sprawling behind me like some kind of ironic backdrop.

Carter Whitehorn walks in, his usual mask of smug superiority firmly in place. He takes his time, adjusts his cuffs, eyes me like I'm something he scraped off his shoe.

"Aiden," he greets coolly.

Samantha Todd

I don't rise, don't offer my hand. Just smirk and tilt my head. "Carter."

He steps forward, deliberately slow, the air of a man who believes he's already won. "I'll admit, I didn't expect to see you again, seems you're full of surprises. But then again, I suppose some men just don't know when they're beaten."

I huff out a short laugh. "That's funny, because I was just thinking the same thing about you."

His jaw ticks, but he schools his expression fast, taking the chair opposite me with a carefully measured breath. Running his hand over his immaculately coifed hair. "I assume this is about Alexis."

My smirk widens. "What gave it away?"

Carter leans back, crossing his arms. "She's already accepted her future. You should too. There's nothing left for you here. You don't belong in our world."

"Yeah, see, that's where you and I disagree." I pull a thick folder from my bag and place it in front of me on the pristine marble table. I run my hand over the smooth surface, I take my damn time. "You know I never liked marble. It's too perfect. Too polished. I prefer wood. It's cracked, it has a story. It's imperfect. Even when you sand it down and polish it to perfection. There's still knots and swirls, still something underneath."

"Does this materials-lesson have a purpose?" he says, almost sounding bored.

"Well see at first glance you look like you might be marble. You sit there in your perfectly tailored suit with your immaculately manicured nails and not a

hair out of place. But if you look closer, and Carter..."
I lean forward, "I've been looking very closely. You're just like the rest of us. You're wood. There are cracks. Men like you are too damn confident in your own invincibility to fully cover their tracks. And it got me thinking, what does Carter Whitehorn have to hide? What does a man who has seemingly everything at his fingertips have in between his cracks? And funnily enough, I did find something."
He eyes the folder, doesn't move to open it. "I hope for your sake, this isn't another one of your childish attempts to..."
"Oh, it's very real, Carter," I cut him off, sitting back with all the ease of a man who knows he's already won. "Insider trading, money laundering, offshore accounts. Want me to keep going?"
Carter finally picks up the folder, flipping through the pages.
And there it is.
The flicker of realisation.
Of panic.
His fingers tighten on the paper. "Where did you get this?"
I grin. "Looks like the lowly farm-boy might actually know a thing or two after all."
His nostrils flare, but he keeps his voice steady. "And you think this is enough to bring me down?"
I tilt my head. "Are you willing to risk it?"
Silence.
I lean forward, lowering my voice. "And that's not even the best part."
Carter's jaw tightens. "Oh, do enlighten me."

Samantha Todd

I pull out another file. This one thinner, but no less dangerous.
"Multiple monthly payments," I muse, tapping a finger against the paper. "All made out to one Kathryn Hastings."
His entire body stiffens.
Bullseye.
I chuckle. "Ten years, Carter. That's a long time to be sending a woman money if she's not your problem." I lower my voice. "So, what is she? An old affair? A mistress? Or something a little more... permanent?"
His hands curl into fists.
I let the words settle, watching him. "You know, I bet a lot of people would be very interested to know about the woman you've been paying off for the past decade." I grin. "Especially considering her father is one of your most lucrative business partners. And to think she's only 26 now... so that would have made her only 16... You are a naughty boy."
He breathes out through his nose, controlled, cold.
"You're playing a dangerous game, Gage."
I smirk. "And you're running out of moves."
Carter closes the file slowly, methodically. Then, he steeples his fingers, tilting his head at me.
"And what if," he says, voice soft, too soft, "you go tragically missing before this all comes to light?"
The air shifts.
The subtle, simmering threat settling between us like a coiled snake.
I let the words hang there for a beat, then exhale, shaking my head with a knowing smirk. "Yeah. See, I figured you might say something like that."

Carter's brow furrows.

I reach into my jacket pocket and pull out my phone, tapping the screen. A single link is displayed.

A countdown timer underneath it.

His eyes narrow. "What the hell is that?"

"Insurance." I lean forward, voice calm. "See, I have this little website. Completely untraceable. Completely encrypted. And if I don't enter a specific code by a certain time every day... well..." I shrug, feigning indifference. "That site goes live. And guess what's on it?"

His lips part, eyes flashing real fear for the first time.

"Oh yeah." I nod, grinning. "Everything. The bank records, the offshore accounts, the insider trading. Fucking all of it. Directly uploaded to every major news outlet, the FCA, HMRC." I tilt my head. "And your competitors."

Carter's entire body goes rigid.

"And here's the fun part," I continue, enjoying every second of this. "It's set up permanently. Even if I delete it, it's still there. If I don't enter the code by a certain time, ever again, it goes live." I smile, slow and deliberate. "So, whether it's today, next week, next year, fuck, let's go all out, 50 years from now. If anything happens to me, Alex or anyone I care about, or if you even think about going back on your word..." I tap the screen. "Game over."

Carter's nostrils flare, his fingers pressing into the table. "You think you can outmanoeuvre me?"

I sit back, stretching my arms behind my head. "Carter, I already have."

Silence.

Long, heavy silence.
Then, finally—
Carter exhales sharply.
His expression blank. His eyes furious.
"What do you want?" he spits out.
"Leave Alex alone, she is not to marry Miles Kensington, and you will not attempt to control her life ever again. Oh, and leave Aunt Edith the hell alone, forever."
He huffs out a defeated laugh, "You know if you weren't such a self-righteous little prick you would actually make a brilliant businessman." He chews the inside of his lip, "Fine," he bites out.
I grin, rising out of my chair and clapping my hands down on the desk, looming over him. "Pleasure doing business with you, mate. I wish I could say this will be the last you'll see of me, but that's unlikely to happen." I smile, "You see I'm in love with your daughter. So, we should probably start getting along. We should do golf sometime, or whatever it is you selfish, rich cunts like to do."
Then, without another word, I turn on my heel and walk out of Carter Whitehorn's glass palace.
*Check-fucking-mate.*

# Chapter 43

Alex

The bells above the estate agent door chime as I push it open, the familiar scent of lavender and old wood filling my senses. It's strange how comforting it is, how much this tiny office, cluttered with Edith's overflowing files and half-burned incense sticks, feels more like home than anywhere I've ever lived before.

And now I have to say goodbye to it.

Aunt Edith is at her desk, rearranging a chaotic stack of paperwork, though her expression is far too smug for it to be a simple morning of admin. She glances up at me over the rim of her enormous, jewel-encrusted glasses, eyes twinkling with something dangerous.

"Come to say your final farewell, then?" she muses, leaning back in her chair.

I exhale slowly, setting my bag down on the counter. "Yeah. I just… I wanted to see you before I head back to London."

She hums, the kind of knowing hum that makes my skin itch. "Mm-hmm. And is that what you really want, dear?"

I shoot her a look. "Not today, Edith."

Samantha Todd

She waves a hand, all bangles and rings clattering together like wind chimes. "Oh, alright, alright, I'll behave." But then she pauses, a small smile tugging at her lips. "But tell me something, darling. Do you really not believe in knights in shining armour?"
I frown. "What?"
And then I hear it.
The sound of a door opening behind me. A familiar presence. A voice I thought I wouldn't hear again.
"Because maybe you should," Aiden says.
I freeze.
For a second, I think I've imagined it. That my brain has finally snapped from the weight of all this shit and I'm hallucinating the man I haven't been able to stop thinking about since I left him standing in his workshop.
But then I turn.
And there he is.
Aiden Gage.
Standing in the doorway of the back office, hands shoved in his pockets, looking like he owns the room. Like he's always belonged here.
Like he belongs with me.
My heart is in my throat. "What...?"
He steps forward, closing the distance between us in three strides. "You don't have to marry Miles Kensington." His voice is calm, steady. "You don't have to go back to London. You don't have to do anything you don't want to do, because you, Alex Whitehorn, are finally fucking free."
I blink at him. "What do you mean?"

He smirks, tilting his head. "Exactly what I said. You're free. Miles is out of the picture. Your father has officially backed off. And Aunt Edith gets to keep her business, her house—her whole damn life." He lets that hang in the air before adding, "You don't owe them anything anymore, Trouble."

I can't breathe.

"You..." My voice is barely above a whisper. "You did this?"

His smirk falters, something softer taking its place. "Yeah. I did."

A storm of emotions swirls inside me. Relief, disbelief, overwhelming fucking gratitude.

And love.

God, so much love.

But before I can open my mouth, he keeps going.

"I didn't do it to win you back," he says, voice quieter now. "If that's not what you want, then fine. I didn't do it for me, Alex. I did it because you deserve better. You deserve to be able to call the shots in your own life. You deserve to be free. But..." He exhales a short laugh, rubbing the back of his neck. "If there's a chance that you do want me, if there's even the smallest hope that you could be mine, then I'm asking you to at least let me take you on a date. A real one this time. None of this fake engagement bullshit. Just me, you, and the best pub dinner Northwood Dale has to offer."

My chest tightens, the sheer weight of his words pressing into me. I don't think I've ever been speechless in my life, but right now? My mind is blank.

Samantha Todd

My heart isn't, though.
That organ is screaming, run to him.
And before I can talk myself out of it, I do.
I crash into him, my arms wrapping around his neck, my mouth pressing to his in a kiss that is every single unsaid thing between us.
Aiden stumbles back a step before groaning into my mouth, arms circling around me tight, pulling me in closer, like he's never letting me go again.
Behind us, Aunt Edith claps her hands. "Oh, finally! I was getting bloody sick of waiting."
I laugh against Aiden's lips, breathless, dizzy with him. With this moment.
And then I pause, my hands still tangled in his shirt. "Wait... how?"
Aiden leans back slightly, brows furrowing.
I swallow, trying to gather my thoughts. "How did you do this? How did you get my father to back off?"
His eyes flick over my face, assessing, deciding.
Then, to my utter surprise, he smirks.
"I promise I'll never keep any secrets from you ever again," he murmurs, voice low, teasing. "But just let me have this one."
I narrow my eyes. "You didn't punch anyone, did you?"
His smirk deepens. "Would I do a thing like that?"
I roll my eyes, pulling back slightly, but Aiden tightens his grip around my waist, not letting me go.
He lowers his head, his mouth brushing my ear.
"You're free, Trouble. That's all that matters."
I exhale, my entire body melting into his.
And then he pulls back, eyes glinting as he murmurs,

"And for what it's worth I'm pretty certain I'm in love with you."

I bite my lip, heart pounding. "Yeah?"

"Yeah," he breathes. "Fucking madly, actually."

I swallow, my entire soul alight. "I love you too, Aiden."

He smirks. "Yeah, yeah, tell me something I don't know."

And then he kisses me again.

And this time, I know for certain, I'm never letting him go.

# Chapter 44

Aiden

The workshop is quiet, save for the rhythmic scrape of sandpaper against wood and the faint hum of the old radio in the corner. It's playing some slow, bluesy tune, the kind that seeps into your bones.
I should be in bed.
Alex should be in bed.
But sleep wasn't happening, and when I turned over to find her side of the bed empty, I knew exactly where she'd gone.
Now she's here, leaning against my workbench in one of my old T-shirts, watching me with that soft, knowing smirk.
"I wondered where you snuck off to," she murmurs, crossing her arms over her chest.
I glance at her, then back at the rocking chair. "Didn't want to close my eyes."
She tilts her head. "Why not?"
I set down the chisel, rubbing a hand over my jaw. "Because if I did, I was worried I'd wake up and this would all be a dream. That I'd open my eyes, and you'd still be engaged to that prick, and I'd still be planning new and creative ways to commit murder."

Alex exhales a quiet laugh, stepping closer, her bare feet soundless against the workshop floor.

"You *do* have a flair for dramatics."

I smirk. "And you love me for it."

She hums noncommittally, but the curve of her lips betrays her.

I watch her run her fingers over the wood of the chair, tracing the grooves I've carved. She does this often—touches my work, moves through my world like she belongs in it.

Because she does.

"What are you working on?" she asks softly.

I lean a hip against the bench, watching her more than the chair. "A rocking chair."

She lifts a brow. "For who?"

I hesitate, then shrug. "Us."

Her fingers still.

I see her throat bob as she swallows, and when she glances up at me, something warm flickers in her eyes. She doesn't tease, doesn't deflect. Just nods. "Can I help?"

I exhale a quiet laugh. "You want to help *me* with woodwork?"

She lifts her chin. "I think I'd be rather good at it."

I grin, grabbing the sander and handing it to her. "Alright then, Trouble. Let's see what you've got."

She takes the sander with a confidence that's *so* very her, but when I see her fumble slightly with the grip, I shake my head and step behind her, wrapping my arms around her to guide her hands. She exhales sharply. I feel it more than I hear it.

Samantha Todd

My lips are right at her temple, my chest flush against her back, and when I cover her hands with mine, I swear I feel her pulse stutter.
"Hold it steady," I murmur.
She nods, and I don't miss the way her breath hitches.
"You have to let the wood breathe," I say, my voice dropping lower. "Work with it, not against it."
Alex's hands twitch under mine. "And what if I want to be the one in charge?"
I grin, pressing the button to power the sander. It hums to life in her grip, and she *jumps*, letting out a tiny yelp before glaring over her shoulder at me.
I laugh. "Relax, Trouble. You've handled worse things in your hands."
She scoffs, elbowing me lightly. "You *wish.*"
I chuckle, guiding her movements over the wood, feeling her muscles relax into mine. We work in silence for a while, the rhythm of it easy, natural. Then, after a few minutes, I lift the sander from her hands and set it down, keeping my arms caged around her.
She turns slightly, looking up at me. "Was I any good?"
I glance at the sanded wood, then back at her, grinning. "Could be better."
She gasps, swatting my chest. "You absolute—"
I catch her wrist before she can finish, spinning her to fully face me, pressing her back against the workbench. She lets out a sharp inhale, hands bracing against my chest.

We've always been good at this—at pushing, pulling, fighting.
But now, we're good at this too.
At letting go. At *giving in*.
I trail a finger along her arm, watching as goosebumps rise in its wake. "You like being here," I murmur.
Her chin tilts. "Your workshop?"
I nod, my hands sliding down to her waist. "My world."
She exhales slowly, and fuck if I don't love the way her breath catches every time I touch her.
"I like you," she says softly. "Which is... inconvenient."
I smirk. "You love me."
She rolls her eyes, but there's no real bite to it. "We really need to work on your arrogance."
I lean down, brushing my lips against hers, so lightly, just a whisper of a touch. "But you *do* love me."
She presses up on her toes, threading her fingers into my hair. "Unfortunately."
Then, she kisses me.
And just like that, nothing else matters.
I lift her onto the workbench, sliding between her legs, my hands pushing up the oversized T-shirt she's wearing, my shirt. My fingers trail along her thighs, gripping, kneading, as her lips move against mine.
Her hands roam too, slipping beneath my worn henley, running over my abs, my chest, nails scraping, teasing.

Samantha Todd

I groan, pulling her closer. "We're never gonna finish this chair."
She grins against my lips, breathless. "Who cares?"
And then, she kisses me again, and I'm lost to her.
Completely, hopelessly, forever lost to her.

# Chapter 45

Alex

The smell of fresh coffee fills Aiden's kitchen, mingling with the faint scent of sawdust and the crisp morning air drifting in through the open window. It's warm, homely, and undeniably his, just like the oversized t-shirt I'm currently wearing, the hem brushing the tops of my bare thighs.

Aiden leans against the counter, watching me over the rim of his coffee mug, a smug grin pulling at his lips.

"So," he muses, "look at that."

I arch a brow. "Look at what?"

He gestures vaguely at me, at the steaming cup of coffee in front of me, at the entire damn situation. "You. In my kitchen. At 8am. Wearing my t-shirt. Drinking coffee from my mug." He lets out a satisfied exhale, shaking his head. "God, I love being right."

I roll my eyes. "You say that like you knew this was going to happen."

Aiden smirks, setting his mug down. "Oh, I did."

I scoff. "You're insufferable."

"And yet, you love me anyway," he teases, stepping closer, his hands finding my waist.

I sigh dramatically, placing a hand against his chest. "It's a real burden, honestly."

Samantha Todd

He laughs, low and deep, before ducking his head and capturing my mouth with his.
And just like that, all the teasing, all the playful bickering, it melts away into something else entirely. Something warm and consuming.
Aiden's hands slide down to my thighs, fingers skimming over bare skin as he lifts me onto the kitchen counter. I gasp into his mouth, my legs wrapping instinctively around his waist.
*"Aiden..."*
"Mm," he murmurs, trailing kisses down my jaw, nipping at the sensitive skin beneath my ear. "God, I love you in my t-shirt."
His hands tighten on my thighs, his mouth brushing down my neck, and...
"Jesus fucking Christ, can you two not?!"
I yelp, jerking back as Aiden groans in frustration, his forehead dropping against my shoulder.
Ben stands in the doorway, arms crossed, looking equal parts amused and resigned.
"Keep it to your room, guys," he says flatly, grabbing a coffee mug from the cupboard. "Or literally anywhere that isn't the kitchen. Some of us actually eat in here."
I cover my face with my hands as Aiden leans back, rubbing a hand down his face. "Fucking hell, Dad."
Ben just shrugs. "What? It's bad enough we all had to endure Ethan and Brynne making heart eyes at each other for the last *year*, now you two are at it?" He gestures between us. "We get it. You're in love. Please, for the love of God, spare us the details."

I clear my throat, hopping off the counter, cheeks on fire. "Noted."
Ben grins, sipping his coffee. "So, what's the plan today? You two doing anything exciting?"
Aiden leans against the counter, arms crossed, that smirk playing at his lips again.
"Well," he says casually, "I actually have a meeting in London."
Ben and I both blink at him.
"A meeting?" I ask, tilting my head.
He nods. "Yeah. About my furniture business. A friend of Carter Whitehorn's wants to discuss some opportunities with me."
My jaw drops. "What?!"
Ben whistles lowly, clearly impressed. "Damn, Is my son finally growing up?"
Aiden shrugs like it's no big deal, but there's pride shining in his eyes. "I mean, I figured if Carter's people want to do business, who am I to say no?"
I stare at him, genuinely speechless.
This is huge.
Aiden, stubborn, doesn't-give-a-shit, happy-in-the-mud Aiden, is doing it. He's taking his talent and running with it. He's choosing this for himself.
I reach out, squeezing his hand. "Aiden, that's amazing."
He glances at me, something soft flickering behind his eyes before he smirks. "Yeah, well. Thought it was about time I started thinking about the future, y'know?"
Ben claps him on the back, beaming. "Proud of you, Aid."

Samantha Todd

Aiden grins, his fingers tightening around mine.
And as I look around the kitchen, this kitchen that I never thought I'd be standing in, this life that I never expected to love so much, I realise something.
This is the future.
Aiden and me.
Banter and bickering and bad horror movies.
Mornings in his t-shirt, drinking coffee in his kitchen.
This is what I want. This is living.
And for the first time in my life, I know—with absolute certainty—I've made the right choice.

# Chapter 46

Aiden

The late afternoon sun hangs low, stretching gold and amber across the farm. The air is thick with that lingering scent of earth and hay, warm and familiar. Ethan and I are perched on the wooden fence that runs along the edge of the pasture, beers in hand, boots kicked up on the bottom rail. The horses are lazily chewing in the distance, unfazed by the deep musings of two brothers solving all of life's problems.

Which, in this case, mainly consists of my useless girlfriend.

"She nearly killed me, Ethan." I take a long sip of my beer, shaking my head.

Ethan smirks. "Oh yeah?"

"Oh yeah," I nod grimly. "Do you know what happens when a city girl with zero farming experience tries to drive a quad bike?"

Ethan chuckles. "I'm assuming nothing good."

"Nothing good is a bloody understatement. First, she ran over my damn foot..."

Ethan chokes on his beer. "Wait, what?"

"...Then she overcorrected, panicked, and somehow managed to reverse into the chicken coop."

Ethan is full-on laughing now, shaking his head. "No."

"Oh, yes. Chickens everywhere. Feathers flying. The whole lot of them screeching like they'd just been sent to the afterlife."

Ethan wipes at his eyes, trying and failing to suppress his amusement. "Christ, Aiden, why'd you let her drive it in the first place?"

"I didn't! She stole it! One minute, I was fixing the fence, and the next, I hear an engine revving, she barrels across the field like she's trying to outrun the police, my foot's in tatters and the chicken coop is royally fucked."

Ethan is shaking with laughter now, wiping at his eyes. "That is so her."

"Oh, it gets better," I mutter darkly, taking another swig of beer. "After the whole chicken apocalypse, she gets off, brushes herself off, blames me, and then, *then*, has the audacity to look me dead in the eye and say: 'Well, that could've gone worse.'"

Ethan actually howls. "Could it, though?"

"No, Ethan. It could not."

We both sit there, laughing, sipping our beers as the sun inches lower behind the hills.

Ethan sighs, leaning back slightly, his voice turning softer. "You love her, though."

I glance over, smirking. "Unfortunately."

Ethan grins. "I get it."

And I know he does.

Because for all the teasing, for all the near-death farming experiences, I wouldn't trade a second of it. And neither would he.

"How's Brynne?" I ask, changing the subject.
Ethan immediately softens. "Excited. Wedding plans are coming along, though I swear to God if I have to listen to one more debate about table centrepieces, I might actually go insane."
I chuckle. "Didn't peg you as the floral arrangement type."
"Oh, I'm not. But apparently, I have opinions now. I made the mistake of saying I didn't care what colour the napkins were, and suddenly, I was unceremoniously informed that I do in fact care."
"That's marriage, mate."
He exhales a laugh, shaking his head. "You reckon you'll be ready for that one day?"
I pause for a second, letting the question settle.
Am I?
I glance down, picking at the label on the bottle.
I think about Alex. About her relentless sarcasm, her sharp wit, the way she still refuses to admit that she snores. I think about the way she argues just for the hell of it, the way she steals my T-shirts, the way she looks at me when she thinks I'm not watching.
And then I realise, I can see myself being married to her one day. Driving each other utterly crazy until we're old and in our rocking chairs.
I take another sip of beer, my lips tilting up. "Yeah," I say simply. "One day."
Ethan grins, nodding approvingly. "Good. Because you and Alex? You two are something else."
I huff a laugh. "Tell me something I don't know."
He chuckles, clinking his beer against mine.

Samantha Todd

For a few moments, we sit in easy silence, the kind that only exists between brothers.
Then Ethan exhales, staring out toward the fields. "You think Mum would've liked her?"
I don't answer right away.
The question catches me off guard. Not because I haven't thought about it before, I have. Many times. Adrienne Gage was the kind of woman who filled a room without even trying. Warm, clever, fiercely protective. She had this way of making you feel like the most important person in the world, even when you were covered in dirt and scrapes from climbing trees you weren't supposed to be climbing.
I let out a slow breath. "Yeah," I say finally. "I do."
Ethan nods, swirling his beer in his hand. "She would've told you to stop being a dick to her, though."
I smirk. "Oh, definitely. But she'd have loved Alex's fire. Would've seen right through the sarcasm and called her out on it immediately."
Ethan laughs. "Yeah. And Dad?"
I glance over, watching as Ethan's expression turns more thoughtful. "You think he'll ever..." He hesitates. "I mean, do you think he even wants to?"
I don't answer right away, because honestly? I don't know.
Ben Gage is a good man. A great man. He's been our rock for so damn long that I don't think any of us have ever stopped to really look at him, at what he's lost, at what he's still carrying.
"He deserves to be happy," Ethan says, almost to himself.

"Yeah," I murmur, staring down at my beer.

Ethan lets out a deep sigh and finishes off his beer. "Anyway, enough of the deep shit. Let's get back to your disaster of a girlfriend. She planning on causing more havoc on the farm, or do we need to buy a chicken insurance policy?"

I snort. "Oh, she thinks she's helping. She's fully convinced herself she's an asset to this farm."

Ethan laughs. "Brynne was like that at first, too."

"No, mate. Brynne actually learned. Alex is just collecting near-death experiences like they're fucking souvenirs."

Ethan chuckles, shaking his head. "Well, at least life won't ever be boring."

I smirk. "No. It definitely won't. Not with that girl around."

And as the sun dips below the hills, I think to myself, maybe that's the best part.

# Chapter 47

Ben

The pub is buzzing, laughter and conversation filling every corner of the room as I take a sip of my pint, leaning back in my chair. Ethan and Brynne are deep in discussion about their wedding plans, hands clasped on the table between them, their excitement practically radiating off them in waves. Aiden and Alex, on the other hand, are engaging in their usual brand of verbal warfare, thinly veiled as an argument but with so much heat between them it's enough to make a man choke on his beer.

"Christ, will you two ever just talk like normal people?" Ethan mutters, shooting them a look.

Aiden grins. "This is normal."

Alex rolls her eyes, but there's no real irritation there. "Your version of normal is being a persistent pain in the arse."

"And your version of normal," Aiden counters, draping an arm over her chair, "is pretending you don't love every second of it."

She opens her mouth, a sharp retort undoubtedly locked and loaded, but Brynne cuts in before she can fire.

"For the love of God, just kiss him and put us out of our misery."

Aiden waggles his eyebrows. "Careful, Brynne. I might start thinking you have a crush on me."

Ethan groans, pinching the bridge of his nose. "Why are you like this?"

Across from me, Aunt Edith chuckles, the many rings on her fingers clicking against her glass as she swirls her wine. There's a twinkle in her eye as she watches the whole scene unfold, like she's seeing something cosmic playing out right in front of her.

I like Edith. Always have. There's something calming about her, even when she's off on one of her fate-fuelled tangents about soul alignments and celestial energy. She reminds me of a softer time, a time when Adrienne was still with us.

I exhale, watching Ethan rub slow circles over Brynne's hand, Aiden throw another flirty quip at Alex, Edith watching the scene unfold with contentment.

"I wish Adrienne could see this," I murmur.

Edith turns to me, her soft gaze meeting mine. "She sees it," she says, voice gentle. "Somehow."

I nod, swallowing thickly.

It's not the same. It never will be. But sitting here, surrounded by my family, I know she'd be proud. Our two boys, all grown up and in love. Who would have thought it. And with two women that ignite the right sparks in each of them. Nothing could make me more proud.

Alex suddenly makes a small, high-pitched noise, sitting up straighter, her eyes wide. "Fuck me!"

Aiden smirks. "What here? Can you at least wait until we get home!"

She swats at him without even looking. "Aiden, shut up, she just walked in."
Ethan raises a brow. "Who?"
Alex's eyes are locked on the entrance, her fingers gripping Aiden's forearm so tight he winces. "Harlow West."
Brynne's mouth drops open. "What, THE Harlow West?"
"Yes!"
I frown, glancing between them. "Who the hell is Harlow West?"
Alex turns to me as if I've just personally insulted her. "Only the bestselling author. Absolute romance queen. Her mafia books own the charts."
Aiden snorts. "So, what you're saying is, she writes porn."
Alex glares at him. "It's spicy romance, Aiden. Learn the difference."
Brynne leans in, "I can't believe that Harlow West just randomly walked into our pub!"
Alex grips his wrist. "I need to talk to her."
"Do you need a minute?" Aiden teases.
Alex shoves him, making him laugh. But me? I'm suddenly frozen. Because as I glance toward the bar, my eyes lock on the woman in question.
And she's stunning.
Dark hair cascading in loose waves, piercing hazel eyes scanning the room with an effortless kind of confidence. A long, tailored coat draped over her shoulders, exuding class but with just the right amount of edge to make it intriguing.
But none of that is what makes my stomach drop.

No.
What does that, what stops my breath entirely, is the fact that I know her.
Not as Harlow West.
But as Rowan Sinclair.
The girl who got away.
My high school sweetheart.
The first girl I ever loved.
And just like that, after all these years, she's back.
"Benjamin Gage!"
Her voice, smooth, confident, with that teasing lilt I remember like it was yesterday, cuts through the noise of the pub like a damn arrow straight to my chest.
I stand so fast my chair nearly tips over, fumbling to set it right as I turn toward her.
And there she is.
Rowan Sinclair.
Or, as Alex and Brynne would put it, *Harlow-fucking-West*.
She hasn't changed much, not in the ways that matter. Her hazel eyes still burn with that same quiet fire, her dark hair still tumbling over her shoulders in loose waves, and the knowing smirk that used to drive me insane. Still very much intact.
But there's something else, something deeper beneath the confident stance and effortlessly tailored coat. Something I can't put my finger on.
I open my mouth, intending to say something, anything that doesn't make me sound like a fumbling idiot. But I don't even get the chance.

"Jesus," Aiden mutters beside me, smirking. "Didn't take much to break him."

Alex glares at him, then practically shoves me aside as she thrusts her hand toward Rowan. "Oh my God, I am such a huge fan."

Rowan chuckles, shaking her hand with a firm grip. "That's always nice to hear."

Alex's eyes practically sparkle. "You don't understand. Your books? The *best*. Your heroes? Incredible. The way you write tension? Unmatched."

Aiden leans in, faux-serious. "So, what you're saying is, she writes good porn."

Alex doesn't even hesitate; she slaps him hard on the arm.

"Ow," Aiden grumbles, rubbing the spot. "You need to stop abusing me in public."

Rowan raises a brow at me, clearly amused. "Your family's a bit... rowdy."

I clear my throat, still trying to regain my footing. "Yeah, well, they keep things interesting."

She hums in approval, then tilts her head. "So, Benny. No 'hello'? No 'it's been years, Rowan, how the hell are you'?"

Benny.

Christ. No one has called me that in years.

I scrub a hand down my face, trying to shake the fog in my brain. "Yeah, uh, sorry. It's just... you're here."

She grins. "Observant as ever."

I huff a laugh, shaking my head. "What are you doing in Northwood Dale?"

Her expression shifts slightly, the teasing edge softening. "Looking for a house. Looking to move back, actually. I'm staying with a friend for a while."

That throws me for a loop. Rowan Sinclair? The woman who left this town without looking back? The woman who built an entire empire under a pseudonym? Moving back here?

I don't get a chance to question it, though, because right then, Aunt Edith steps forward.

"Well, well," she says, her usual knowing smile firmly in place. "It just so happens I run the best estate agency in town."

Rowan turns to her, intrigued. "Is that so?"

Edith nods, the rings on her fingers clicking together as she folds her hands in front of her. "It is. And I'd be delighted to help you find what you're looking for."

Rowan smiles, but Edith's gaze flicks between the two of us, her sharp intuition missing nothing. I swear this woman is actually a witch of some sort. She sees it.

The crackling tension.

The way Rowan is standing just a little closer than necessary.

The way my hands keep clenching and unclenching, like they remember what it was like to hold her.

I swallow hard.

"Come sit with us," I say, the words slipping out before I even think them through.

Rowan arches a perfectly sculpted brow, like she's considering it. But then, with an easy grin, she slides into the empty seat beside me. "Don't mind if I do."

Samantha Todd

Alex, still practically vibrating with excitement, beams. "Oh my God, I can't believe you're here. Do you have any idea how much I love your books?"
Rowan smirks, sipping the whiskey she ordered. "I'm starting to get the idea."
Aiden, ever the shit-stirrer, leans in across the table. "So, these books of yours, on a scale from grandma's romance novels to straight-up porn, where do they fall?"
Alex glares at him. "They're romance."
"With smut," Aiden adds.
"With excellent smut," Alex corrects, completely unfazed.
Brynne, enthralled, rests her chin in her hands. "How do you even write that stuff? Do you just... make it up?"
Rowan laughs. "It's called an imagination, sweetheart."
Aiden tilts his head. "Or research."
Rowan just sips her drink, her smirk deepening. "I'll never tell."
I choke on my beer.
Rowan just pats my back like this is all perfectly normal. Like she hasn't just dropped into my life out of nowhere and turned my brain into a malfunctioning mess.
Aunt Edith, still watching with that all-knowing gleam in her eyes, leans forward. "Now, tell me, dear. What kind of home are you looking for? Or rather, what spirit are you seeking?"
Alex rolls her eyes, muttering under her breath, "Of course, she asks that."

But Rowan doesn't even blink. She rests her elbow on the table, thoughtful. "Something with history. A house that's lived, you know? With creaky floorboards and an old library no one's touched in years. The kind of place that smells like books and cinnamon. Big windows, too, ones that let the moonlight spill in at night, like something out of a gothic novel. And a garden, wild, overgrown, full of secrets. A place with character."

Edith beams, clasping her hands together. "Well, darling, you've come to the right woman."

Rowan grins. "I had a feeling."

Aiden whistles low. "Well, if that's not the most Aunt-Edith answer I've ever heard."

"I do love a woman with taste," Edith says, lifting her glass.

Rowan clinks her whiskey against Edith's tea, completely at ease.

I shake my head, chuckling. "You always were good at fitting in anywhere."

Rowan turns to me, head tilted. "You sound surprised."

I rub the back of my neck. "I mean, you left this place for good. Or so I thought."

She sips her drink, gaze steady. "Things change."

The words feel heavier than the moment calls for, but before I can press, Alex leans forward eagerly. "Wait, wait, wait, you two knew each other?"

Rowan laughs, nudging me with her shoulder. "You didn't tell them?"

"I didn't exactly get the chance."

Aiden crosses his arms. "Well, this just got interesting."

Rowan taps a finger against her glass. "Benjamin and me? We go way back. Like, reckless-teenage-years back."

Alex is practically vibrating with curiosity. "Tell me everything."

Rowan grins, glancing at me. "You want to tell them, or should I?"

I sigh, but I can't fight the smile tugging at my lips. "Fine. But let's just say... there may have been some fireworks involved."

Aiden perks up. "Literal or metaphorical?"

Rowan laughs. "Both."

And just like that, the stories start rolling.

We trade tales of sneaking onto rooftops to watch the stars, of midnight drives with music too loud, of bonfires on the outskirts of town, of Rowan convincing me to break into the school library just because we could.

Aiden snorts. "You got my Dad to break rules? *Benny Gage?*"

Rowan smirks. "What can I say? I'm persuasive."

I shake my head, taking another sip of my beer, and for the first time in a long time, I feel something I haven't in years.

Something dangerous.

Something thrilling.

Like my past has finally caught up with me.

Rowan stretches, setting down her now-empty whiskey glass with a satisfied sigh. "Alright, I'd better get going. I have an early morning, and I don't trust myself not to get roped into another round."

Aiden smirks. "Probably for the best. Wouldn't want to corrupt the innocent minds at this table."

Alex elbows him. "Oh, please. You're the one who's corrupted."

Rowan grins, sliding her chair back. "Edith, I'll drop by the estate agents tomorrow. Let's see if you can find me a place that doesn't come with a resident ghost."

Edith waves a hand, her bangles jingling. "Oh, darling, all the best ones do."

Rowan just laughs. "Fair enough."

Then, before I can process what's happening, she turns to me and steps right into my space, arms wrapping around me in a warm, firm hug.

I freeze.

I had forgotten how effortlessly confident she is, how unapologetic in everything she does. There's no hesitation in her movements, no second-guessing. Just pure, unfiltered Rowan Sinclair.

Her scent hits me first, something warm and familiar, like vanilla and cedarwood, wrapped up in the faintest trace of whiskey. Her body presses against mine, and for a moment, I'm seventeen again, sitting on my old bed, listening to her rant about how she was meant for bigger things than this town.

I force myself to react, lifting my arms and hugging her back, but it feels like my whole system is short-circuiting.

She pulls back, a teasing smile playing at her lips. "You still make that face when you're overthinking, you know."

I blink, shaking my head. "I'm not..."

She laughs, poking me in the chest. "Oh, you absolutely are."

Aiden coughs into his drink, fully enjoying my suffering.

Rowan just smirks and steps back, adjusting the strap of her bag. "Alright, Gage. I demand coffee soon. You owe me a proper catch-up."

I nod, feeling like my brain is running on delay. "Yeah. Coffee. Sounds good."

She gives me one last knowing look, then with a casual wave to the table, she strides toward the door.

Alex is still grinning like an idiot. Aiden is openly amused. Brynne looks like she's already planning out our wedding in her head.

But I?

I'm absolutely reeling.

Conversation continues around me, but it's distant, like I'm hearing it through water. My thoughts are still stuck on the way Rowan smelled, the way she felt pressed against me, the way she looked at me like I was still that boy she knew, even after all these years.

My fingers drum against the table, restless.

Aunt Edith, of course, notices. She eyes me, tilting her head slightly, and then, because she's Edith, she hums and says, "Your aura is all off-kilter, Benjamin."

I huff out a laugh, shaking my head. "Know-it-all witch."

Edith just grins, eyes twinkling like she knows something I don't.

And hell, maybe she does.

# Chapter 48

### Aiden

The room is bathed in the warm glow of the bedside lamp, casting golden light over Alex's skin as she straddles me. My hands grip her thighs, my fingers digging into soft, warm flesh as she rolls her hips, dragging a groan from deep in my chest.

"Fuck, Trouble," I rasp, eyes locked on hers. She's breathtaking like this, lips parted, cheeks flushed, auburn hair spilling around her face like a wild halo. Mine.

Her hands press against my chest, nails skimming over my skin, igniting every nerve ending. "You like watching, don't you?" she teases, her voice laced with wickedness as she moves, taking me deeper, making my head fall back against the pillow.

I chuckle, low and dark, dragging my fingers up her sides, gripping her hips and pulling her down to meet every thrust. "Damn right I do." My thumb traces the line of her waist before I slide my palm up to cup her breast, my other hand tangled in the mess of sheets at my side. "But I like touching even more."

She shivers at that, her breath catching, and I grin, rolling my hips up into her, watching as she tilts her head back and moans my name.

I sit up suddenly, wrapping an arm around her waist and pulling her against me, chest to chest, skin to skin. I kiss along her collarbone, nipping at her throat as she whimpers. "You're so fucking beautiful," I murmur against her skin, unable to stop the words from slipping out.

She grips my jaw, forcing me to look at her, and something passes between us, something heavier than just lust, something that settles deep in my chest and refuses to leave. She kisses me then, soft at first, then desperate, as if she knows exactly what I'm thinking but isn't ready to say it out loud yet.

Her pace quickens, hands tangled in my hair, body pressing so close I don't know where I end and she begins.

"Let go for me, baby," I whisper against her lips, guiding her through it, my own body chasing after hers.

And then she falls apart, gasping my name, her fingers gripping my arms so tightly I know I'll find her marks there in the morning. The thought alone pushes me over the edge, pleasure crashing over me like a tidal wave as I groan into her mouth, my body locking up against hers before we both collapse back into the sheets, spent, tangled, utterly wrecked.

For a long moment, there's nothing but the sound of our heavy breathing, the warmth of her body against mine, her hair tickling my jaw as she curls into my chest.

Samantha Todd

I press a kiss to the top of her head, my hand lazily tracing circles on her back. "I should've told you to stop fighting me months ago."
She snorts against my skin. "I should've known you'd find a way to win anyway."
I grin, fingers brushing through her hair. "I always win, Trouble."
She hums, pressing a lazy kiss to my shoulder. The room is still heavy with the scent of her skin, of sex, of something I don't want to name yet but can feel pressing against my ribs like a fucking vice. Alex is still stretched out across my chest, her bare leg draped over mine, her fingers idly tracing patterns over my stomach.
I should probably say something. But I don't. I just take her in, the warmth of her, the way her auburn hair spills over my skin, the way her breathing syncs with mine like it's always meant to.
She turns her head slightly, resting her chin on me, looking up at me with those big, sharp-as-hell eyes. "So?"
I raise a brow. "So?"
"Tell me." She pokes my side. "You said you had something to show me."
Right. That.
I reach over to the nightstand, grabbing my phone. I pull up the branding designs and hold the screen in front of her face.
She squints, eyes adjusting to the light, and then, then she freezes.
Alexis Gage Designs.

Her brows shoot up. "You think I'm taking your name?"

I smirk, dragging a hand down the smooth length of her back, watching the way her breath stutters.

"Trouble, you've taken every other part of me, why fight me on that?"

She rolls her eyes, but she doesn't move away. She doesn't tell me to shut up. She doesn't even argue. She just stares at the name on the screen like she's feeling it. Like she's taking it in.

And then she shakes her head, a small smirk curling at the corner of her lips. "You're insufferable."

I grin. "And you love it."

She doesn't answer.

She just pulls the phone from my hand, tosses it on the nightstand, and straddles me again.

We can discuss business later.

Right now, I've got better things to focus on.

Samantha Todd

# Epilogue

Alex

The exhibition hall hums with the energy of the furniture showcase, the air thick with the scent of polished wood, leather, and freshly brewed coffee. Aiden is in his element.

I watch from the sidelines, arms folded, lips quirking as he leans casually against one of his handcrafted dining tables, chatting animatedly with a group of high-profile buyers. He's wearing that easy, self-assured grin, the one that once made me want to throttle him.

Now?

Now, it makes my heart skip a beat.

The transformation in him is staggering. The cocky, insufferable farmer who waltzed into my life two years ago is now standing here, commanding a room of designers, investors, and collectors with the kind of quiet confidence that makes people listen. He's not just another name in the industry, he's a force.

Alexis Gage Designs has soared, and so has Aiden. His custom furniture is in high demand, every piece imbued with his signature craftsmanship. His name, our names, are gaining recognition in places neither of us ever imagined.

And he deserves every bit of it.

Aiden catches my eye from across the stand, his gaze flicking to me as he smirks. Smug.
Still cocky.
Some things never change.
I roll my eyes, but the warmth in my chest is undeniable. You're so proud of him, my heart whispers.
And I am.
I think back to the man who first strolled up to me in the pub that night in Northwood Dale, all rough edges and lazy charm, utterly insufferable. If you had told me then that we'd be here, partners in life, in business, in everything, I would have laughed in your face.
But here we are.
Life is Good.
Ethan and Brynne's wedding is coming up in a few months. Ethan has never looked happier, and Brynne is in full wedding-planning mode, dragging all of us into the madness. Even Aunt Edith, with all her cosmic energy, is taking part, insisting that the "alignment of their auras" is essential to the wedding day running smoothly.
Aunt Edith, by the way, is thriving. Her business is booming, her name more respected than ever.
Rowan Sinclair, the Rowan Sinclair, best-selling author of Mafia romances, has settled into her farmhouse, bringing a whole new level of chaotic, fascinating energy into the town.
And then there's Ben and Rowan.
It's slow, it's subtle, but something is definitely happening there.

Samantha Todd

I smirk just thinking about it.
Life is peaceful.
Aiden and I are moving in together next month, finally taking the next step that somehow feels both inevitable and terrifyingly real. A lovely three-bedroom house, bought with the proceeds of the sale of my London apartment. We plan to do it up, to make it ours. I plan on having a library full of my smut books (as Aiden calls them) and much to his utter dismay.
We're building something, something solid, something we fought for.
And my father?
Remarkably quiet.
Carter has barely made a ripple in my life over the last year, and I know that's because of Aiden. Whatever he has over him, whatever blackmail material he's sitting on, I respect his stance not to tell me. I don't need to know the ins and outs. I not certain I even want to know.
All I know is that my father is behaving himself, and that's good enough for me.
Aiden finishes up his conversation and walks over, hands in his pockets, looking ridiculously pleased with himself.
"Still checking me out, Trouble?"
I scoff, tilting my chin up. "Please. I was actually wondering how much longer I have to endure this before we can get a drink."
He grins, leaning down, voice dropping just enough to send a delicious shiver down my spine. "You

weren't complaining when you were 'enduring' me last night."

I shove him lightly, laughing despite myself. "You are impossible."

He just watches me, eyes gleaming, and my breath catches for a moment.

Because this is it.

This infuriating, exasperating, stupidly handsome man is my life now.

And I wouldn't change a damn thing.

He wraps an arm around my waist, pulling me close. "Come on, let's go celebrate. I just closed another deal."

I arch a brow. "Really? Who's the buyer?"

His grin turns wicked. "One of your father's business friends."

I blink. Then I burst out laughing. "Slipping into the 'old money' scene effortlessly I see."

"Yeah, turns out I'm quite loveable."

I roll my eyes, "That's debateable Aiden Gage."

"Well, you love me."

I don't argue. I just kiss him.

Because he's right.

I do love him.

And after everything, he's still my greatest risk. The man who I should never have fallen for.

But he turned out to be my greatest reward.

In the game of chess that I've been playing forever, Aiden Gage officially called checkmate on my life.

Samantha Todd

Stick around for Ben's story.
"Breaking the Gage' coming soon!

# Acknowledgements

Writing a second book has been just as much about the people in my life as it has been about the words on the page. The unwavering support, the critiques that push me to be better, the late-night brainstorming sessions, and the constant encouragement, this book exists because of a lot of people.

It took me a long time to have faith in my writing. To believe that the stories in my head were worth telling. But the people in my life, the ones who build me up, who challenge me, who remind me why I love this, they are the reason I keep going. Their faith in me is unshakeable, even when my own wavers, and I will never be able to thank them enough.

The Gage boys have taken up permanent residence in my heart. I almost didn't want to leave Alex and Aiden behind, writing them was too much fun. Their endless jibes, their tension, the way they got under each other's skin and into each other's hearts... They were a joy to bring to life, and don't worry, this won't be the last you see of them.

To my husband, your patience is unmatched, your support is relentless, and your ability to listen to me talk (for hours) about character arcs, plot twists, and book ideas that I absolutely must write next is a superpower in itself. I couldn't do this without you.

Samantha Todd

To my friends, who bought the first book, even if romance isn't your thing, even if you don't usually read, you have no idea what that means to me. Your belief in me is everything.

And to every reader who picked up this book, who fell in love with these characters, who sent me a message or left a review, thank you. I see you, I appreciate you, and I hope you know how much your support means.

If I could spend my life doing nothing but bringing you stories, I would. Maybe one day I can.

Until next time...

Sam x

Printed in Dunstable, United Kingdom